Lovecraft Alive!

Lovecraft Alive!

A Collection of
Lovecraftian Stories

John Shirley

Hippocampus Press

New York

Published by Hippocampus Press
P.O. Box 641, New York, NY 10156.
http://www.hippocampuspress.com

Cover art © 2016 by Harry O. Morris.
Cover design by Barbara Briggs Silbert.
Hippocampus Press logo designed by Anastasia Damianakos.

First Edition
1 3 5 7 9 8 6 4 2

ISBN 978-1-61498-178-7

Dedicated to the memory of
Howard Phillips Lovecraft . . .

SPECIAL THANKS
to Paula Guran, Micky Shirley and S. T. Joshi
. . . for archival and editorial complicity.

CONTENTS

PREFACE

I was a mere stripling, an adolescent lad, when I discovered Howard Phillips Lovecraft in a library. He was there, at his desk, in a dark corner of a horror anthology.

Certain qualities drew me to him immediately: the atmospherics, the bravely flowing prolixity, and his ability to evoke *something* in the shadows, some half-formed locus of horror that seemed to conform itself to whatever particular fear the reader held dear. In due course I became the typical young H. P. Lovecraft cultist. I found Arkham House advertised in a fanzine, or perhaps it was the back of *Fantastic* magazine, and soon ordered its catalog. I remember being very excited by the prospect of reading Lovecraft's poetry offered in Arkham House's edition of *Collected Poems* (which included *Fungi from Yuggoth* and other poems), and bugged my mother for money to order it. I was quite into Poe's verse at the time.

I wrote a snarling, probably semi-literate letter to Arkham House after six weeks passed and the book didn't come; they wrote back counseling patience . . . and eventually the thin but handsome volume appeared. The thirty-six-sonnet cycle of *Fungi from Yuggoth* itself was the delectable cosmic horror I had hoped for, and I reread it numerous times; in my boyish state of mind I was a bit put off by the other poetry filling out the book—for example, poems extolling the old neighborhoods of Providence—and I thought Lovecraft rather a stiff-necked old geezer after that, though I continued to read his fiction.

Stiff-necked old geezer? He was one, in some ways—and proud of it. In other ways he was rather progressive. Still, he was racially biased, to varying degrees of fulmination, for much of his life. (L. Sprague de Camp seems to think HPL let go of his racism at the end.) He often scowled upon immigrants and spoke longingly of having been born too late for an "ideal" time, which he placed, as I recall, somewhere in the colonial American eighteenth century. In time the Great Depression showed him that workers needed to be able to unionize when necessary and that social safety nets are part of a civilized society; he forthrightly declared for them. He was dismissive of religion and endorsed scientific skepticism. It's a pity he didn't apply that skepticism to his racial assumptions.

In bygone days my favorite works by Lovecraft were *At the Mountains of Madness*—a place I revisit in my short story "The Witness in Darkness"—and *The Dream-Quest of Unknown Kadath*. The phantasmic fringiness of *Dream-Quest* caught my attention; the whole concept of a dream-quest enticed me. As tales like *The Dream-Quest of Unknown Kadath*, *At the Mountains of Madness*, and "The Shadow out of Time" demonstrate, Lovecraft's fiction was conceptually bold. And that kind of boldness is something I have always admired.

Eventually, as a young man, I went on from Lovecraft to more modern writers. But inevitably I returned to him, as one does. It happened when I was first asked to write for a Lovecraftian anthology. I returned to the fount for inspiration, rediscovered HPL, and found that his best qualities were as powerful as ever. I appreciated him anew, and in new ways. I reread his whole canon, and this led me, quite agreeably, back to many of his contemporaries, like Clark Ashton Smith and Robert E. Howard. The exotic perfume of the *Weird Tales* writers drew me back, helpless and fated, into their otherworldly gardens. As Clark Ashton Smith said in "The Garden of Adompha," "the growths of that garden were such as no terrestrial sun could have fostered."

I have revised these stories since their publication, but they are essentially the same as my original narratives. I cleave to my own notions of writing Lovecraftian horror. I diverge from Lovecraft, of course: some of these stories are from a woman's point of view; some are in a very modern, street-inflected voice.

But in other stories I have tried to write as if I were trying to sell to *Weird Tales*. In my own weird tales I did not try to mimic Lovecraft's voice, his writing style itself, but I *did* try to compose in a way that would not have been out of place in that musty venue. And I wrote those particular stories in a way that would make them dovetail with the stories that inspired them. "The Witness in Darkness" is set in the world, the very location, of *At the Mountains of Madness*. But—and I think this is unique to my story—it is written chiefly from the point of view of one of the alien creatures, the apparent horrors, of the Lovecraft tale.

"Those Who Come to Dagon" was certainly written in a *Weird Tales* manner, as best I could evoke it, and it is almost entirely composed of ingredients from Lovecraft's literary recipes . . . yet I must admit there is one aspect that might have troubled him: it is a kind of anti-racist tale, in a horrific sort of way.

"The Rime of the Cosmic Mariner" is composed as if scrivened by the famed poet Samuel Taylor Coleridge, author of *The Rime of the Ancient Mariner*. (Coleridge spelled it "rime" as opposed to rhyme, hence my own use of that spelling.) My Coleridgean venture is in the form of a letter written by Coleridge to Thomas De Quincey. As much like one of Coleridge's letters as I could make it while still telling the story in a brisk way, "The Rime of the Cosmic Mariner" would have fitted fairly well into *Weird Tales*. It is very much a Lovecraftian tale, about an encounter I imagined for Coleridge with the diabolical entity Nyarlathotep.

The plot of "The Holy Grace of Cthulhu" could have fit fairly well into *Astounding Stories*: alien invaders versus an ancient leviathan.

But other tales in the book are "postmodern" Lovecraft. "When Death Wakes Me to Myself" is a hybrid of modern and old-school, for reasons that will become clear when it is read. Since Lovecraft himself is a character in this tale of transmigration and cosmic horror—and since my take on the man pervades it—I thought the story an apt opening for the book.

"How Deep the Taste of Love," "Buried in the Sky," "Windows Underwater," and "At Home with Azathoth" are all endeavors at fusing the Lovecraftian with the contemporary world or the world of the near future. I'll just add that "Buried in the Sky," as it goes on, reflects my own preoccupation with making the surreal and the real as indistinguishable as possible. And speaking of *Weird Tales,* it was first published in the modern version of that publication.

Putting this book together, I wondered what Lovecraft would have thought of it, and I found myself imagining Lovecraft traveling in time and reading my stories. Though HPL might need a cultural "translator" for these stories, since they're all twenty-first-century fare, I think he would at least recognize them as refractions of his work.

I have tried to organize the stories in what would be chronological order in the sense of the chronology of their narratives. Except . . . the very first story is set in our time, and also in Lovecraft's time, and outside of time. Hence "When Death Wakes Me to Myself" is in its own chronological category. The concluding tale, "Broken on the Wheel of Time," written specifically and freshly for this book, is set alternately in 1878, in our own time and "above" time—this follows logically, since the story works with ideas, references, and even characters found in Lovecraft's "The Shadow out of Time," a work that makes time travel a mercurially metaphysical process. (I did not make up the Superfast Laser Pump, by the way; and I described some of its basic possibilities authentically.)

Time inexorably passes; it ruthlessly deconstructs and reconstructs and reimagines reality.

If Lovecraft somehow takes a temporal expedition into the twenty-first century to inspect Lovecraftian fiction, he might be a bit shocked by one or two of these tales. Possibly he might not approve. It might be best if H. P. Lovecraft does not engage in time travel after all.

WHEN DEATH WAKES ME TO MYSELF

"Someone's broken into the house, doctor."

Fyodor saw no fear in Leah's gray eyes. But he'd never seen her afraid, and she'd worked closely with him for almost eight years, since he'd finished his internship.

She brushed auburn hair from her pale forehead, adjusted her glasses, and went on: "The window latch in your office is broken—and I think I heard someone moving around down in the basement."

"Did you call the police?" Fyodor asked, glancing toward the basement door. His mouth felt dry.

They stood in the front hallway of the old house, by the open arch to the waiting room. "I did. I was about to call you when you walked in."

They didn't speak for a long moment, both of them listening for the burglar. Wintry morning light angled through the bay windows of the waiting room, casting intricate shadows from the lace curtains across the braided rug. A dog barked down the street; a foghorn hooted. Just the sounds of Providence, Rhode Island . . .

Then a peal of happy laughter rippled up through the hardwood floorboards. It cut short so abruptly he wondered if he'd really understood the sound. "That sound like laughter to you?"

"Yes." She glanced at the window. "The police are in no hurry . . ."

"You should wait out front, Leah." He was thinking he should try to see to it that whoever this was, they weren't setting a fire, vandalizing, doing serious damage to the house. He was negotiating to buy it, planning to expand it into a suite of offices

15

with various health services—especially bad timing for vandalism. It was a big house, built in 1825, most of it not in use at the moment. The ground-floor den was ideal for receiving patients; the front living room had been converted into a waiting room.

Fyodor took a step through the archway, into the hall—and then the basement door burst open. A slender young man stood there, a few paces away, holding a bottle in his hand, toothy grin fading. "Oh! I seem to have lost all track of time--and I have intruded on you and the lady." He wore a neat dark suit with a rather antiquated blazer, thin blue tie, starched white shirt, silver cufflinks, polished black shoes. His fingernails were immaculately manicured, his straight black hair neatly combed back. Fyodor noted all this with a professional detachment, but also a little surprise—he'd expected the burglar to be scruffier, more like the sullen young men he sometimes counseled at Juvenile Detention. The young man's dark brown eyes met his; the gaze was frank, the smile seemed genuine. Still, the strict neatness might place him in a recognizable spectrum of personality disorders.

"You seem lost," Fyodor said—gesturing, with his hand at his side, for Leah to go outside. Foolish protective instinct—she was athletic, would be more formidable in a fight than he was. "In fact, young man, you seem to have lost your way right through one of our windows."

"Ah, yes." His mouth twitched. "But look what I found for you, Dr. Cheski!" He raised the dusty bottle in his hand. It was an old, unlabeled wine bottle. "I never used to drink. I wanted to take it up, starting with something old and fine. I want a new life. I desire to do things differently. Really *live!* I would just bet you didn't know there was any wine down there."

Fyodor blinked. "Um . . . in fact . . ." In fact he didn't think there *was* any wine in the basement.

A siren wailed, grew louder—and cut short. Radio voices echoed, heavy boot-steps came up the walk, and the young man, sighing, put the bottle on the floor and walked past Fyodor to open the front door. He waved genially at the policemen.

"Gentlemen," said the young man, "I believe you are here for me. I'm told that my name is Roman C. Boxer."

*

Carrying the dusty wine bottle, Fyodor descended the basement steps, wondering if this Roman C. Boxer could have been a patient, someone he'd consulted on, at some point. The face wasn't familiar, but perhaps he'd been disheveled and heavily acned before. *I'm told that my name is Roman C. Boxer.* Interesting way to put it.

The basement was a box-shaped room of cracked concrete, smelling of mildew; a little water had leaked into a farther corner. A naked light bulb glowed in the cobwebbed ceiling, bright enough to throw stark shadows from what looked like rodent droppings, off to his left. To the right were his crates of old files, recently stored here—they seemed undisturbed. He saw no wine bottles. He could smell dirt and damp concrete. A few scuffs marked the dust coating the floor.

Fyodor started to turn back—it was not a pleasant place to be—but he decided to look more closely at the files. There was confidential patient information in those crates. If this kid had gotten into them . . .

He crossed to the files, confirmed they seemed undisturbed—then saw the hole in the floor, in the farther corner. A small shiny crowbar, the price sticker still on it, lay close beside the hole. His view of it had been blocked by the crates.

He crouched by the hole—almost two feet square—and saw that a trapdoor of concrete and wood had been removed to lean against the wall. He could make out a number of dark bottles down inside it, in wooden slots. Wine bottles.

One slot was empty. The bottle he'd brought down with him fit precisely in that slot.

*

A week later.

"Deal's done," Fyodor said, with some excitement, as he came into the waiting room. He took off his damp coat, hanging it up, sniffling, his nose stinging from the cold, wet wind. "I own the building! The bank and I do, anyway."

"That's great!" Leah said, glancing at him, the corners of her eyes crinkling with a prim smile. She was hanging a print of a Turner seascape: vague, harmless proto-Impressionism in gold and umber and subtle blues; a choice that suggested sophistication, soothing to psychiatric patients. Still, some patients were capable of feeling threatened by anything.

Leah stepped back from the painting, and nodded.

Fyodor thought it was hanging just slightly crooked, but he knew it would irritate her if he straightened it—though she'd only show the irritation as a faint flicker around her mouth. Surprising how well he'd gotten to know her and, at the same time, how impersonal their relationship was. A professional distance was appropriate. But it didn't feel appropriate somehow, with Leah . . .

"That police detective called," she said, straightening the painting herself. "Asking if we're going to come to the arraignment for that burglar."

"I'm not inclined to press charges."

"Really? They've let him out on bail, you know. He might come back."

"I don't want to start my new practice here by prosecuting the first mentally ill person I run into." He went to the bay windows and looked out at the wet streets, the barren tree limbs of the gnarled, blackened elm in the front yard. Leafless tree limbs always made him think of nerve endings.

"He hasn't actually been diagnosed."

"He was confused enough to climb in through a window, ignore everything of value, go down to the basement, and dig about."

"Did you have that wine looked at? The stuff he found downstairs?"

Fyodor nodded. "Hal checked it out. Italian wine, from the early twentieth century, shipped direct from some vineyard—and not improved with age. Gone quite vinegary, he told me."

How had Roman Boxer known the wine was there? It seemed to have been sealed up for decades.

Something else bothered him about the incident, something he couldn't quite define, a feeling there was something he should recognize about Roman Boxer . . . something just out of reach.

"Oh—you got approval for limited testing of SEQ10. The letter's on your desk. There are some regulatory hoops, but . . ."

SEQ10. They'd been waiting almost a year. Things were coming together.

He turned to face Leah, feeling a sudden rush of warmth for her. It was good to have her on his team. She was always a bit prim, reserved, her wit dry, her feelings controlled. Still . . .

"And," she said a little reluctantly, going to the waiting room desk, "your mom called."

She passed him the message. *Please call. The Psycho Psych Tech is at it again.*

His mother: the fly in the ointment, ranting about the psychiatric technician she imagined was persecuting her in the state hospital. But then she was the reason he'd gotten into psychiatry . . . her mania, her fits of inexplicable amnesia. His own analyst had suggested she was also some of the reason he tended to be rather reserved, wound tight—compensating for his mother's flamboyance. She was flamboyant on the upswings, almost catatonic on the downswings. Firm self-control helped him deal with either extreme.

And her intervals of amnesia had prompted his interest in SEQ10.

The doorbell rang, and he went to his office to await the first patient of the day. But his first patient wasn't the first person to arrive. Instead, Leah ushered in a small middle-aged woman with penciled eyebrows, dark red lipstick, and a little too much rouge, her black hair very tightly caught up in a bun. She wore a pink slicker, her rose-colored umbrella dripping on the carpet as she said, "I know I shouldn't come without an appointment, Doctor Cheski . . ." Her cadences tripped rapidly, her voice was chirpy, the movements of her head, as she looked back and forth between Fyodor and Leah, seemed birdlike. "But he was so insistent—my son Roman. He said I had to see him *here* or not at all, and then he hung up on me. God knows he's been a lot of trouble to you already. Has he gotten here yet?"

"Today?" Fyodor looked at Leah. She shrugged and shook her head.

"He said he'd be upstairs . . ."

There was a thump from the ceiling. Squeaking footsteps; brisk pacing, back and forth.

Leah put a hand to her mouth and laughed nervously. Quite uncharacteristic of her. "Oh my gosh, he's broken into the house again."

Roman's mother looked back and forth between them. "Not again! I thought he'd made an appointment! He said he didn't trust anyone else . . . He barely knows *me,* you see . . ." Her lips trembled.

Leah's brows knit. "He barely knows you?"

Another thump came from above. They all looked at the ceiling. Mrs. Boxer nodded slowly. "He . . . claims he *doesn't remember* growing up with us. With his own family! I show him photographs—he says they're 'sort of familiar.' But he says it's like it didn't happen to *him*. I don't really understand what he means." She sighed and went quickly on: "He just keeps wandering around Providence—*looking* for something . But he won't say what."

Fyodor knew he should call the police. But when Leah went to the phone, he said, "Wait, Leah." *Claims he doesn't remember growing up with us. With his own family.*

SEQ10 was a hypnotic drug for treating, among other things, hysterical amnesia.

Fyodor looked at Mrs. Boxer. She had some very high-quality jewelry; new pumps, sensible but elegant. A rather showy diamond bulked on her wedding ring. She had money, after all. She could pay for therapy. Insurance wouldn't cover SEQ10. And there was something about Roman that aroused Fyodor's curiosity.

Fyodor took a deep breath and, wiping his clammy palms on his trousers, went up the stairs.

He found Roman Boxer in the guest room right over the office. Roman was sitting on the edge of the four-poster bed, nervously turning a glass of wine in both hands, around and around—he'd put the wine in a water tumbler from the upstairs bathroom.

"Brought your own wine this time, I see," Fyodor said.

"Yes. A California Merlot. Still trying to learn how to drink." Roman smiled apologetically. He wore the same suit as last time. Neat as a pin. "Strange sensation, alcohol." After a moment he added, "Sorry about the door. No one was here when I came. I needed to get in."

Fyodor grunted. He planned to rent the room out as an office, and now this guy was damaging it—the door to the outside stairs stood open, the wood about the lock splintered. There was a large screwdriver on the bedside table. He would see that Mrs. Boxer paid to have the door fixed.

"Why?" Fyodor asked. "I mean—why the urgency about getting in? Why not make an appointment?"

Roman swirled his wine. "I'm . . . looking for something here. I just—couldn't wait. I don't know why. I'm sorry about the door--and the intrusion."

*

It was an evening session, after Fyodor would normally have gone home. Roman's mother had already had the broken door replaced and paid a large advance on the therapy. And Roman was more interesting than most of Fyodor's patients.

Leaning back on the leather easy chair in Fyodor's office, Roman seemed bemused. Occasionally he smoothed the lines of his jacket.

"Your mother gave me some background on you," Fyodor said. "Maybe you can tell me what seems true or untrue to you."

He read aloud from his notes.

Roman was twenty-one. An only child, he'd had night terrors until he was nine, with intermittent bedwetting. Father passed on when he was thirteen. They weren't close. Roman had difficulty keeping friends but was likable, and elderly people loved him. He loved cats, but his mother made him stop adopting them after he accumulated four. One died, and he gave it an elaborate burial ritual.

Good student in high school at first, friends mostly with girls—but no girlfriends. Not terribly interested in sex.

Bad last year in high school when some sort of Internet bullying took a more personal form. Reluctant to talk about it. Refused to attend the school thereafter. Finished with home schooling, GED. Two years of college, attendance quite patchy. Autodidact for the most part.

Tendency to have unusual difficulty with cold weather.

No close friends "except in books."

"All that sound right to you, Roman?" Fyodor asked, getting his laptop into word processing mode.

Roman looked vaguely about him. "Not very flattering, is it? Sounds like someone I *knew*—but it doesn't feel like it happened to me personally. *Apparently* it's me."

Fyodor typed in his laptop, *Possible dissociation due to unacceptable self-image.*

"But since last year—your memories seem like . . . you?"

"Yes—since last year. All that seems real. I can't remember anything before that unless somebody reminds me, and then it's

. . . like remembering an old television episode. Except I can't really remember those either."

Roman's eyes kept wandering to the Victorian fixture hanging from the ceiling. "That fixture's been here a hundred years."

"I would have thought it's older than that, really, as this house was built in the early nineteenth century," Fyodor said absently, adjusting his laptop to make sure Roman couldn't see what he was typing.

"No," Roman said firmly. "Installed early twentieth century. But it was made in the nineteenth."

Fyodor made a note: *Possible grandiosity? Faux expertise syndrome?* "Your mother says you feel your name is not Roman, although she showed you a birth certificate. Do you feel the birth certificate is—"

"Is faked, unreal—part of a conspiracy?" Roman chuckled. "Not at all! What I said was, I *feel* my name is not Roman. I answer to it for simplicity's sake. And as for what my name really is—I truly don't know. Roman Boxer is correct—and incorrect. But don't waste your time asking why that is, I don't have an answer for you."

"And this started when you took a walk on a beach . . ."

"Yes. Last September. We went to Sandy Point. Myself and . . . well . . . *Mother*. She has a little place at Sandy Point . . . so I have learned. My real memories start—really, as soon as I *arrived* on the beach that day. Before that I don't remember much. She's prompted a few memories, but . . ." He cleared his throat. "Well, I was feeling odd from the moment I stepped onto the sand." He smiled dourly. "Not 'feeling myself.' And then—it'll take some telling . . ."

"Tell me the story."

Roman brightened. "Now *that* I enjoy. I've got half a dozen notebooks filled with my stories. But this one is true. Very well: It was a fine Indian summer afternoon." He cleared his throat and went on. "I was in the mood to be alone—this woman who insists she's my mother brings that out in me, and did even then—so I went out to Napatree Point. Big sandy spit of land, you know. The sea looked blue, fluffy clouds scudding in the sky, a real postcard picture. Just me and the gulls. Now, I don't much care for walks on the beach. Rather dislike looking at the unidentifiable things that wash up there. And the smell of the sea—like the smell of some giant animal. I'd rather go to the library. But I keep hearing people talk about how *inspirational* the sea is. I keep looking to *connect* with that Big Something out there. So I was walking on the beach, trying to shake the odd feeling of inner dislocation—I *did* manage to appreciate the way the light comes through the top of the waves and makes them look like blue glass. I shaded my eyes and gazed way out to sea, trying to see all the way to the horizon—and I got this strange feeling that something was *looking back* at me from out there."

Fyodor repressed a smile, and typed, *Enjoys dramatization.*

"All of a sudden I felt like a giddy little kid. Then I had a strange impulse—it just charged up out of my depths. I felt it go right up my spine and into my head, and I was yelling, 'Hey out there!'" Roman cupped his hands to either side of his mouth, mimicking it. "'Hey! I'm here!' I don't know, I guess I was just being spontaneous, but I felt truly very impish . . ."

Fyodor typed: *Odd diction, archaic vocabulary at times. It comes and goes. Possibly clinically labile? Showing agitation as he tells the story.*

". . . and I yelled 'I'm here, come back!' and it's funny how my own voice was echoing in my ears and a response just came into my head from nowhere: They tolled—but from the sunless tides that pour . . . And I yelled that phrase out loud! I'm not sure why. But I'll never forget it."

Auditory hallucination, Fyodor typed. *Feelings of compulsion.*

Roman squirmed in his chair, licked his lips, went on. "It was a curious phrase to come to me—like an unfinished line of poetry, right?"

Use of antiquated expressions comes and goes: e.g., curious *an adjective. An affectation or intrinsic personal style?*

"And as soon as I said it I heard gigantic bells ringing, like the biggest church bells you ever heard—and it sounded as if they were coming from under the sea! A little muffled and watery, but still powerful. It got louder and louder—the sound was so loud it hurt my head, as if I were getting slapped with each clang of the bell, and each time it rang it was as if the sea, the stretch of the sea in front of me, got a little darker, and pretty soon it *just went black*—the whole sea had turned black . . ."

Hallucinogenic episodes, possible seizure—drug use?—

". . . and no, I don't use drugs, doctor! I can see you thinking it!" He smiled nervously, straightening his tie. "Never have got into drugs! Oh fine, a few puffs on a bong once or twice—barely felt it."

Fyodor cleared his throat—strangely congested, it was difficult to speak at first—and asked, "This vision of the sea turning black—did you fall down during it? Lose control of your limbs?"

"No! Well . . . I didn't *fall*." Roman licked his lips and sat up straight, animated with excitement. "It was as if I were *paralyzed* by what I was seeing. The blackness sucking up the ocean was holding me fast, you see. But it was really not so much that the sea was turning black—it was that the sea was *gone,* and it was replaced by a—a night sky! A dark sky full of stars! I was looking down into the sea, but in some other way I was gazing *up* into this night sky! My stomach flip-flopped, I can tell you! I saw constellations you never heard of, twinkling in the sea—galaxies in the sea!—and one big yellow star caught my eye. It seemed to grow bigger and bigger, and it got closer—till it filled up my vision. Then, silhouetted on it was this black ball . . . a planet! I rushed closer to it—I could see down into its atmosphere. I saw warped buildings—you could hardly believe they were able to stand up, they seemed so crooked, and cracked domes, and pale things without faces flying over them—and I thought, that is the world called . . ." He shook his head, lips twisted. "Something like . . . *Yegget?* Only not that. I can't remember the name precisely." Roman shrugged, spread his hands, and then laughed. "I know how it sounds. Anyway—I was gazing at this planet from above and I heard a *sizzling* sound. Then there was a flash of light—and I was back on the beach. I felt a little dizzy, sat down for a while, kept trying to remember how I'd gotten to that beach. Could not remember, not then. The memory of what I'd seen in the sea, the black sky—*that* was vivid. And what was before that? Arriving at the beach. Notions of escaping from some bothersome person."

"Nothing before then?"

"An image. I saw myself lying in a small bed, in a white room, with this sweet little nurse holding my hand. Remembering it, I had a yearning, a *longing* for that bed, that nurse—that white room. For the comfort of it. I could almost hear her speak.

"Then, back on the beach, I felt this scary buzzing in my pocket! I thought I had a snake in there, and I was clawing at it, and then . . . something fell out. This shiny, silvery, little machine fell onto the ground. It was buzzing and shaking in the sand as if it were furious with me. I could see it was some kind of instrument—a device. It seemed strange and familiar, both at the same time, right? So I had to think about how to make it work and I opened it and I heard this tiny voice saying, 'Roman, Roman, are you there?' It was the . . . it was my mother." He stared into the distance. His voice trailed off. "My mother."

"But you didn't recognize the thing as a cell phone?"

"After she spoke, I remembered—but it was like something from a science-fiction movie I'd seen. Some *Star Trek* film. I couldn't recall buying the thing."

Fyodor made a few notes and nodded. "And since then—the persistent long-term memory issues, your own name seeming unfamiliar. And you had feelings of restlessness?"

"Restlessness. An inner . . . goading." Roman settled back in the chair, staring up at the antique light fixture. "I would have trouble sleeping. I'd go out before dawn for these long rambles . . . in the old section of Providence—with its mellow, ancient life, the skyline of old roofs, Georgian steeples . . ."

Archaic affectation cropping up more frequently as patient reminisces.

"You said you felt like you were looking for something—?"

"Correct. And I didn't know what. Just this feeling of 'It's right around the next corner, or maybe around the next one' and so on. Till one day—I was there! I was standing in front of this house, looking at your sign. No one answered at your door. I took a cab to a Target store, just opening for the day. I bought a little crowbar. Went back to the house—the rest is history. I still don't know exactly what it is about this house. You just bought the place, right? How'd you find it, doc?"

"Oh, my mother suggested it to me, actually. She was in real estate before she . . ." Fyodor broke off. Not good to talk about personal matters with a patient. "So—anything else? We're about out of time."

"Your mother! She was *committed*, right?" Roman grinned mischievously. "The inspiration for your career! And you an only child, too, like me—imagine that!"

Fyodor felt a chill. "Uh—exactly how—"

"Don't get spooked, doc," Roman chuckled. "It's the Internet. I Googled you! The paper you wrote for the Rhode Island Psychiatric Association—it's online. Tough childhood with sick mother led you to want to understand mental illness . . ."

Fyodor kept his expression blank. It annoyed him when a patient tried to turn the tables on him. "Okay. Well. Let's digest all this." He saved his notes and closed his laptop.

"No therapeutic advice for me, Doctor Cheski?"

"Yes. Something behavioral. Don't commit any more burglaries."

Roman came out with a harsh laugh at that.

*

Roman Boxer went home with the woman he doubted was his mother. Fyodor watched through a window as they got into her shiny sky-blue Lincoln.

An unstable young man. Perhaps a dangerous young man— researching his doctor's background, breaking into his office . . . twice. He should not be seen here.

But in the pre-therapy interview, when Fyodor had met with Mrs. Boxer and her son, Roman had made himself quite clear. *"I won't take those horrible psychiatric meds. I don't wish to be a zombie. I'll just run off, end up back here again. This is the place. It took me a long time, wandering around Providence, to find this house. I know, Mom says I never lived here. But I was happy here once. I have to get help right here . . ."*

Roman and his mother were both amenable to the use of SEQ10 to search out the core trauma, since it was something the patient only took on a temporary basis, with the doctor in the room. There were forms to be filled out, approval from the APA. Fyodor went to his office, feeling restless himself. He wished he'd tucked a bottle of brandy away in the house. But he was trying to keep his drinking down to a dull roar. Too bad the wine in the basement was off. Be crazy to drink the stuff anyway.

*

Fyodor puttered at his desk, organizing his computer files, sending out emails to colleagues who might want to rent office space. Making the occasional note on Roman Boxer. The late November wind hissed outside; the windows rattled, the furnace vents rumbled and oozed warm air. He wished he'd asked Leah to work late. The big old house felt so empty it seemed to mutter to itself every time the wind hit it.

About 9:30, Fyodor's cell phone vibrated in his pants pocket, making him jump.

Fyodor reached into his jacket and fumbled the phone out—his hands seemed clumsy tonight. "Hello?"

"You forgot me . . ." It was Fyodor's mother, her unmistakable smoky voice recognizable even through the poor connection; static crackled; other voices were heard unintelligibly in the background.

"Mom, what do you mean I forgot you?" Then it struck him. "Oh. It's that night?" His night for an evening visit. "Sorry. Caught up in work."

"You bought the house?"

"Yes—thanks for the tip. I sent you a note about it. You've got a good memory—it was so long ago you were selling houses. I'm hoping if I can rent out the other rooms as offices, it'll more than pay for the mortgage. You still there? This connection . . ."

"I was born . . ." Her voice was lost in the crackle. ". . . 1935."

"Right, I know you were born in 1935—"

"In that same house. I was Catholic. Lived there till I got married. Your father was Russian Orthodox. Father Dunn did not approve. Father Dunn died that year . . ." Her voice sounded flat. It was difficult to make out at all.

He frowned. "Wait—you were born in *this* house? I'm sure you showed me a house you were born in, when I was a kid—it was in Providence, but . . . it was an old wreck of a place."

"It was . . . restored."

"Oh yes." Could this really be that house?

". . . *through sunken valleys on the sea's dead floor,*" she said . . . her voice sounding suddenly younger . . . as the wind howled at the window.

"What?"

The phone on his desk rang. He jumped a little in his seat and said, "Wait, Mom . . ."

He put the cell phone down, answered the desk phone. "Dr. Cheski."

"Fyodor? You weren't at home . . ." She coughed. "But here you are!" It was his mother. Coming in quite clearly. On this line, this quite different line. "You need to talk to that psycho Psych Tech, he's following me around the ward."

Sleet rattled the window glass. "Mom . . . you playing games with their phones there? You get hold of a cell phone? You're not supposed to have one."

On impulse he picked up the cell phone and put it to his other ear. "Hello?"

"They tolled but from sunless tides . . ." The rest was lost in static—but it did sound like his mother's voice, in a kind of dead monotone. *Click.*

Monotone—and now a dial tone. She'd hung up.

He put the cell phone slowly down, picked up the other line. "What, Mom, have you got a phone pressed to each ear or what?"

"You sound more like a patient than a psychiatrist, Fyodor. I'm trying to tell you that the 'Psycho' Tech who claims he works here is—What?" She was speaking to someone in the room with her now. "The doctor said I could call my son . . . I did call earlier; he wasn't at home . . ." A male voice in the background.

Then a man came on the line, a deep voice. "Is that Dr. Cheski? I'm sorry, Doctor, she's not supposed to use the phone after eight. I could ask the night nurse—"

"No, no, that's all right—does she have a cell phone too? It seemed like she was calling me on two lines."

"What? No, she shouldn't have one. . . . Oh, there she goes, I have to deal with this, Doctor. But don't worry, it's no big problem, just her evening rant, yelling at Norman . . ."

"Sure, go ahead."

He hung up. After a moment's hesitation he picked up the cell phone and put it to his ear.

Nothing there. He checked to see what number had called him last.

The only cell phone call he'd gotten was from Leah, two days before.

*

Next morning, a cold but sunny winter day, Fyodor dropped by the ward at the facility across town. A bored supervisory nurse waved him right in. "She's in the activities room."

His mom wore an old Hawaiian-pattern shift and red plastic sandals, her thin white hair up in blue curlers. Her spotted hands trembled, but they always did, and she seemed happy enough, playing cards with an elderly black woman. Someone on a television soap opera muttered vague threats in the background.

"Mother, that house you suggested to Aunt Vera for me— did you say you were born there?"

Mom barely looked up when he spoke to her. "Born there? I was. I didn't say so, but I was. Don't cheat, Maisy. You *know* you cheat, girl. I never do."

"Did you call me twice last night, Mom? Talk to me twice, I mean?"

"Twice? No, I—But there was something funny with the phone, I remember. Like it was echoing what I said, getting it all mixed up. Hearts, Maisy!"

"You remember reciting poetry on the phone? Something about tides?"

"I haven't recited poetry since that time at Jimmy Dolan's. Your dad got mad at me because I climbed up on the bar and recited Anaïs Nin. . . . What are you laughing at, Maisy, you never got up on a bar? I bet you did too. Just deal the cards."

He asked how things were going. She shrugged. For once she didn't complain about Norman the Psych Tech. She seemed annoyed he'd interrupted her card game.

He patted her shoulder and left, thinking he must have misheard something on the cell phone. Perhaps some kind of sales recording.

Or his imagination. The lonely house, the odd story from Roman.

Auditory hallucination?

It wasn't likely he'd be bipolar like his mother—he was thirty-five, he'd have had symptoms long before now. He was fairly normal. Yes, he had a little phobia of cats, nothing serious . . .

Fyodor got back to the office a few minutes late for his first patient. He had six patients scheduled that day: four neurotics, one depressive, and a compulsive finger biter who sometimes needed bandages. He listened and advised and prescribed.

A few days later, Fyodor was sitting beside Roman's bed, in the guest room, with its repaired lock, waiting for the drug to take hold of his patient. Roman had signed several waivers, and SEQ10 was used fairly often in a clinical setting, but Fyodor was still nervous about trying the therapeutic drug on his patient.

Roman was lying on the coverlet, eyes closed, though he was awake. He looked quite relaxed. He wore a T-shirt and creased trousers, his blazer and tie and Arrow shirt folded neatly over a chair nearby, the shiny black shoes squared under it. His arms were crossed over his chest; his mother had provided the warm slippers on his feet. There was a small bandage on his right arm, where he'd been injected. The furnace was working full-bore, at Roman's request, and the room was too warm for Fyodor's liking.

On a cart to one side was the tape recorder for the session, a used syringe, and the little tray with the prepared syringes for adverse reactions. Superfluous caution.

Leah entered softly, caught Fyodor's eye, and nodded toward downstairs, silently mouthing, "His mother?"

Fyodor shook his head decisively. No monitoring mothers. Roman was of age.

"I do feel a pleasant . . . oddness," Roman murmured, his eyes fluttering as Leah left the room.

"Good," Fyodor said. "Just relax into that. Let it wash over you." He switched on the tape recorder, aimed the microphone.

"I feel . . . sort of thirsty." His eyes closed; his hands dropped loose, occasionally twitching, at his sides.

"That will pass. . . . Roman, let's go back to that experience by the ocean, a little over a year ago. You said after that, you were remembering a white room, with a nurse. Could we talk about that again?"

"I . . ." His eyes flicked under his closed eyelids.

"Take your time."

"My wife . . . divorced me . . . there's only the nurse. Who holds my hand. That's what I remember about the nurse. The soft pressure of her hand. Trouble breathing—a pressure, a pushing inside me, crowding my lungs. And then—*my very last breath!* I remember thinking, *Is this indeed my last breath?* Gods, the pain in my belly is returning, the morphine is wearing off. . . . They say it's intestinal cancer, but I wonder. Perhaps I should try to tell the nurse about the heightened pain. She's sweet, she won't think me a whiner. The others here are more formal, but she calls me Howard. In this moment I feel closer to her than I ever did to Sonia . . . my own little Jewish wife, ha ha, to think I married a Jewess. My closest friend, for a time, before he got the religion bug, was Dear Old Dunn, a Mick. . . . I want to raise the nurse's hand to my lips, to thank her for staying with me. But I can't feel her hand anymore. I'm detached. No more pain. I see the nurse—I'm floating over her! There's a voice, an inhuman guttural voice, calling me from above the ceiling—no, from above the roof. Above the sky! *I must ignore it.* I must not listen. I must go away from there, to find something, something to anchor me safely in this world. . . . I want to tell my friends I am all right. . . . And now I drift and drift, find myself in front of Dunn's house. . . . There is a cat, heavy with pregnancy, curled up under the big elm tree. I love cats, have always had the feline affinity. I feel drawn to her. That calling comes again, from the deep end of the sky. I need an anchor. *The cat.* I reach for her—and then fall . . . fall into her. Warm crowded darkness

. . . I am born, pressed into the world with the rest of my litter . . . then sounds, the scent of her milk and her soft belly . . . light! . . . and I remember exploring. I was exploring the yard . . . the big tree, overshadowing me, days pass, and I grow . . . the sweet mice scurrying to escape me . . ."

Fyodor had to lean close to hear him.

"Oh! The mice taste sweeter when they almost escape me! And the birds—they seem happy to die under my claws. Their eyes, like gems . . . the light goes out . . . the gems fall into eternity . . . mingle with stars. . . . I can scarcely think—but my body is my thought as I patrol the night. I pour myself through the shadows. The other cats—I avoid them most of the time. If I feel the urge to mate, I go into the house . . . this house! . . . through the back door . . . the girl lets me in . . . I know what a girl is, what people are, I remember that much. I know there is food and comfort there. I rub against the girl's legs, climb onto her lap. I will let my embers smolder here. She admires my golden eyes. The girl tells her mother, and Father Dunn, who has come to visit, that the cat understands everything she says. When she says follow, the cat follows. She tells them, 'I think it understands me right now! It is not like other cats . . . '"

Fyodor shook his head. This was not going as planned. Roman should be incapable of fantasizing under the influence of this drug; the formula was related to sodium pentothal, but more definitive; it had a tendency to expose onion-layers of memories, real memories . . . but a memory of being a cat? Was Roman remembering a childhood incident in which he'd imagined being a cat?

"How . . ." Fascinated, Fyodor cleared his throat, aware his heart was thudding. "How far back do you remember . . . before the white room—and before the cat?"

Roman moaned softly. "How far . . . how deep . . . the night-gaunts! Oh, but I have only come to this house to see Dunn. Of all my friends in the Providence Amateur Press Club, he was the one I trusted the most. Curious, my trusting a Mick—I sometimes sneer at the Irish in the North End, but even so, I love to work with dear old Dunn on his little printing press, in the basement of that magnificently musty old house. I am even tempted to take him up on the wine his father kept in that hidey-hole down there. But I never do. Dunn loves to cadge a little wine from his father's bottles. Makes up the difference in grape juice. The old Irish rogue conceals the bottles from his wife, she doesn't like him drinking . . . wine from Italy, a local Italian priest got it for him, ha ha! Dear old Dunn! I even ghostwrote a little speech he made . . . ghostwriter, wondrous and most whimsical to think of that term, considering how long I wandered, here, from house to house in Providence, afraid of the Great Deep that yawned above me when I breathed my last. Gone. Did anyone notice?" He made a soft rasping moan. "What will people remember of me? If anything they'll remember the intellectual sins of my youth. But why *should* people remember me? I'm sure they won't. . . . If I could tell them what I saw that day, on my trip to Florida!"

"And—what did you see?"

"I hadn't yet reached Florida. Getting out of the bus on the South Carolina coast, an interval in the bus trip . . . my last real journey of note, in 1935 it was. Driver told us the bus would be delayed more than an hour . . . there's time to visit the lighthouse on the point near the station. Determined to get to know the ocean. Wanting to go against my own grain. But you can't grow the same tree twice. Yet I writhe about, trying to change the pattern. I will go to the lighthouse upon the sea, until I make peace with its restless depths. Despite what I told Wandrei—or because of it. I'll show them I'm more than the polysyllabic phobic they think me. Found the lighthouse—tumbledown old structure, seems to have been fenced off . . . a broken spire . . . what a shame . . . there's been a storm, I can see the wrack from the sea mingled with its ruins . . . the breakers have shattered the

seaward wall of the lighthouse . . . There, is that a hollow beneath it, in the circular ruin of the old lighthouse?

"I clamber over fence, over slimed stones, drawn by the mystery, the possibility of revealed antiquity. Perhaps the lighthouse
was built on some old colonial structure. It may well be so, for
look here, a hollow, a cobwebbed chamber, and within it a sullen pool of black water—its opacity broken by a coruscation of
yellow. What could be giving off that glow, that lambent sulfurous yellow within a pool hidden beneath a lighthouse? It's as if
the lighthouse had one light atop and a diabolic inverse sequestered beneath. There, I stare into it and I see . . . something I've
glimpsed only in dreams! The tortured spires, the cracked domes,
the flying faceless ones. . . . I'm teetering into the pool! I'm falling—swallowing saltwater. Something writhes in the water as I
swallow it. An eel? An eel without a physical body. Yet it nestles
within me, biding, whispering . . . Darkness. Walking . . ."

"Then?"

"Then back on the bus, in my seat looking fuzzily about me.
How did I make my way back to the bus at all? Cannot remember. The driver solicitous, asking, 'You sure you're all right, mister? You're wet clear through.' I insist I'm well enough. I take a
few minutes to change my clothes in the station restroom. The
other passengers are exasperated with me, I'm delaying them
even further. I feel quite odd as I return to the bus. Must have
struck my head, exploring that old lighthouse. Had a dream, a
nightmare—can't quite remember what it was . . . dream of
something crawling into my mouth, worming through my
stomach, down to my intestines . . . something without a body
as we know them. . . . I'm quite exhausted now. I fall asleep in
my seat and when I wake, we're in northern Florida."

Fyodor glanced at the tape recorder to make sure it was going. Had he administered the drug wrongly? This could not be a
memory—Roman could not possibly remember 1935. He had
not been born yet. Still, it was surely a doorway into Roman's

unconscious mind. A powerful mind—a writer's mind, perhaps. A narrative within a narrative, not always linear; a nautilus shell recession of narrative . . .

Eyes shut, lids jittering, Roman licked his lips and went hoarsely on. ". . . trip to Cuba canceled but still—Florida! Saw alligators in the sluggish green river—seemed to glimpse a slitted green eye and within that eye a sulfurous light shining from some black sky. . . . A great many letters to write on the bus back, handwriting can scarcely be legible . . . oh, the pain. In the midst of my midst, how it chews away. Cursed as always with ill health. Getting my strength in recent years, discovering the healing power of the sun, and then this—the old flaw chews at me from within now. I fear seeing the doctor. Nor can I afford him. Little but tea and crackers to eat today . . . can't bear much more anyway, the pain in my gut . . . I seem to be losing weight . . . Bob Howard is dead! Strange to think of 'Two-Gun Bob' taking his own life that way. He should have been a swordsman, striking the life from the faceless flying ones when they struck at him in some dire temple—not muttering about his Texas neighbors, not stabbed through the soul by his mother's passing. We should not be what we are—we were all intended to be something better. But we were planted in tainted soil, Bob and I, tainted souls blemished by the color out of space. I wrote from my heart, but my heart was sheathed in dark yellow glass, and its light was sulfurous. So much more I wanted to write! A great novel of generations of Providence families, their struggles and glories, their dark secrets and heroics! I can be with them, perhaps, when I die—I will become one with the old houses of Providence, wandering, searching for its secrets. . . . And I refuse to leave Providence, will remain when I gasp my last. . . .

"The sweet little nurse takes my hand, more tenderly than ever Sonia did. But God bless Sonia, and her infinite patience. If only . . . but it's too late to think of that now. The nurse is speaking to me, *Howard, can you hear me? . . . I believe we've lost*

him, doctor. Pity—such a gentlemanly fellow, and scarcely older than
. . . I can't hear the rest: I'm floating above them, amazed at how
emaciated my lifeless body is; my lips skinned back, my great
jutting jaw, my pallid fingers. I'm glad to be free of that body.
There's no pain here! But something calls me from the darkness
above. Is the light of Heaven up above? I know better. I know
about the opaque gulfs; the *deep end* of the sky. The Hungry
Deep. *I will not go!* I will go to see Dunn! Yes, dear old Dunn.
Something so comforting about the company of my fellow amateur pressmen. I'll find my way to Dunn's house . . . Here, and
here . . . I flit from house to house . . . Is it years that pass? It
is—and it doesn't matter. I drift like a fallen leaf along the stream
of time, waft through the streets of Providence. How the seasons
wheel by! The yellowing leaves, the drifting snow, the thaw, the
tulips . . . I see other ghosts. Some try to speak, but I hear them
not . . . There—Dunn's house! I'll see if he's still within. But no.
Father Dunn has moved on. There is the little Irish girl, adopted
by the Dunns. And her cat, fairly bursting with kittens. Oh, to
be a cat. And why not? The mice . . . sweeter when they run.

"I speak to the girl . . . she shouts in fear hearing a cat speak
human words, however blurred—and she throws something at
me! She chases me from the house!

"What's that? One of the great metal hurtlers in the street!
Truck's wheel strikes me, wrings me out like a wet rag . . . Agony sears . . . I float above the truck, seeing my body quivering in
death: the body of the cat.

"But I am at peace once more, drifting through Providence.
Let me wander, as I did once before . . . let me wander and wait.
Perhaps next time I'll find something more suitable. Someone. A
pair of hands that can fashion dreams . . .

"The Great Deep calls to me, over and over. I won't go! My
ancient soul has strength, more strength than my body ever had.
It resists. I remember, now, what I saw in the ruins of that old
lighthouse—under its foundations: the secret pool, the shamanic

pool of the Narragansett Indians. A fragment of a great translucent yellow stone was hidden there—a piece of a larger stone lost now beneath the waves, once the centerpiece of a temple in the land some called Atlantis.

"The cat-eye stone struck from Yuggoth by the crash of a comet—whirling to our world, where it spoke to the minds of the first true men; gave the ancients a sickening knowledge of their minuteness, the vast darkness of the universe.

"It has been whispering to me since I was a child—my mother heard it, she glimpsed its evocations: the faceless things that crawled from it just around the corner of the house. She'd tell me all about them, my dear half-mad mother Sarah. She had visited that place, and heard its whispering. And that seemed to plant the seed in me—which grew into the twisted tree of my tales . . .

"I drift above the elm-hugged street, refusing to depart my beloved Providence. But the call of the Great Deep is so strong. Insistent. I hear it especially loudly when I visit Swan Point Cemetery. No longer summoning—now it is demanding.

"There is only one way free this time—I must hide within someone . . . I must find a place to nestle, as I did with the cat. . . . Here's a woman. Mrs. Boxer is with child. I feel the heartbeat, pattering rapidly within her—calling to me . . . I go to sleep within her, united with him, the *tabula rasa* . . .

"I wake on the beach, full-grown. I cannot quite speak. I cannot control my body. It moves frantically about, speaking into a little invention, from which issues a voice. 'Why, what do you mean?' says the voice. 'This is your mother, for heaven's sake! Whatever are you about, Roman?' If only I could speak and tell her my real name . . . A voice comes from my mouth—but it is not my voice, not truly. I want to tell her my name. I cannot . . . My name . . ."

Fyodor leaned closer yet. The next words were whispered, hardly audible. " . . . is Howard. Yes. Howard Phillips. Howard Phillips Lovecraft . . ."

Then, Roman was asleep. That was the natural course of the drug's effects. There was no safely waking him now to ask questions.

Stunned, Fyodor sat beside Roman, staring at the peacefully sleeping young man. Seeing his eyelids flickering with REM sleep. What was he dreaming of?

*

Fyodor had grown up in Providence. Everyone here had heard Lovecraft's name. Young Fyodor Cheski once had his own Lovecraft period. But his mother had found the books—he was only thirteen—and she'd taken them away, very sternly, and threatened that he would lose every privilege he could even imagine if he read them again. She *knew* about this Lovecraft, she said. "Things whispered to that man—things people shouldn't listen to."

It was one of his mother's fits of paranoia, of course, but after that, Fyodor was taken with a more modern set of writers, Bradbury and then Salinger—and a veer into Robertson Davies. Never gave Lovecraft another thought. Not a conscious thought, anyway.

His mother, in her manic periods, would babble about a cat she'd had as a small girl, a cat that used to talk to her; she'd look into its eyes, and she'd hear it speaking in her mind, hissing of other worlds—dark worlds. And one day she could bear it no more, and she'd driven the cat away, chased into the street, where it was hit by a passing truck. She feared its soul had haunted her, ever since; and she feared it would haunt Fyodor.

A chill went through Fyodor as he realized he had fallen entirely under the spell of Roman's convoluted narrative. He had almost believed that this man was the reincarnation of the writer who'd died in 1937. Perhaps he did have a little of his mother's . . . susceptibility.

He shuddered. God, he needed a drink.

He thought of the wine in the basement. It was still there. Hal said it was vinegar, but he hadn't tested the other bottles. Fyodor had a powerful impulse to try one out. Perhaps he'd see something down there that would spark some insight into Roman.

His patient was sleeping peacefully. Why not?

Fyodor went downstairs, to find that Roman's mother, anxious, had gone to see her sister. Leah was yawning at her desk.

He looked at her, thinking he really should take Leah out, once, see what happened. She's not dating anyone, as far as he knew.

He almost asked her then and there. But he simply nodded and said, "I'll take care of things here. He's sleeping . . . he'll stay the night. You can go home."

He watched Leah leave, and then turned to the basement door, remembering the agent had mentioned the house had belonged to the Dunn family for generations. Doubtless Roman had found out about the house's background, somehow, woven it into his fantasies. Probably he was a Lovecraft fan.

Fyodor found the switch at the top of the steps, switched on the light and descended to the basement. Really, that bulb was too bright for the basement space. It hurt his eyes. Ugly yellow light bulb.

He crossed to the corner where he'd replaced the cap over the hole in the floor. The crowbar was still there. He pried up the cover of cement and wood—took more effort than he'd supposed.

But there were the bottles. How was he to open them?

Why not be a little daring, opening the bottle as they did in stories? He pulled a bottle out and struck the neck on the wall; it broke neatly off. Wine splashed red as blood against the gray concrete.

He sniffed at the bottle. The smell wasn't vinegary, anyway. The aroma—the wine's bouquet—was almost a perfume.

The bottle neck had broken evenly. No risk in having a quick swig. He sat on one of the crates, put the bottle to his lips, and tasted, expecting to gag and spit out the small sip . . .

But it was delicious. Apparently this one had been sealed better than the one his friend Hal had looked at. Strange to think it had been here undisturbed all those years—even when his mother had lived here. Only once had she mentioned the name of the people who'd adopted her. The Dunn family.

Fyodor wanted badly to sit here awhile and drink the wine. Quite out of character—he was more the kind to have a little carefully selected Pinot in an upscale wine bar. But here he was . . .

Strange to be down here, drinking from a broken wine bottle, in the concrete and dust. It's not like me. It's as if I'm still under the spell, the influence, of Roman's ramblings. It's as if something brought me here. Something is urging me to lift the bottle to my lips . . . to drink deeply . . .

Why not? One drink more. If he was going to ask Leah out he'd need to be more spontaneous. He could call her up, tell her the wine was better than they'd supposed. Might be worth something. Ask her to come and try some . . .

He licked his lips—and drank. The wine was delicious; a deep taste, and unusual. Like a tragic song. He laughed to himself. He drank again. What was it Roman had said?

I never used to drink. I wanted to take it up, starting with something old and fine. I want a new life. I desire to do things differently. Live!

Fyodor drank again . . . and looked up at the light bulb. He blinked in its fierce sulfurous glare, its assaultive perihelion. It seemed almost part of an eye, a glowing yellow eye, looking at him from some farther place . . .

He stood up suddenly, shaking himself, his twitching hands dropping the bottle—it shattered on the concrete with a gigantic sound that seemed to resound on and on, echoing . . . and in the echo was a voice. His mother's voice . . . the part of her mind that had spoken to him through the sea of static. This time it said something else: *We need souls. We have few left in our world. Come to us, across the Great Deeps. Restore our world. Become one with us.*

The room, which should be dull gray, seemed to quiver in ugly colors. He turned and staggered to the stairs. His head buzzed. Then he looked up to see . . .

Roman Boxer was standing at the head of the stairs. "Doctor? Are you well? You *are* Doctor Cheski, are you not? I believe that was the name . . ."

Fyodor started wobblingly up the stairs. Alcohol level must have gotten very high in the wine. Seeing things. Unable to climb damn basement stairs very well . . .

He got to the third step from the top—and Roman put out his hand to him. "Here—take my hand. You look a trifle unsteady."

But Fyodor held back, afraid to touch Roman and not sure why. "You . . . should be asleep."

"Yes, well—I simply woke up. And everything was fine! Whatever you gave me helped me enormously. The pain in my stomach is gone! I was surprised to be no longer in the hospital . . . Yes. Thought I was a goner. Kind of you to bring me home—if that's what this place is. That nurse—is she here?"

"The nurse? What . . ." Fyodor licked his lips. "What is your name?"

"You really *have* overindulged, my friend. I am your patient, Howard Lovecraft . . ." Roman smiled widely and once more reached for him. Fyodor jerked back, irrationally afraid of that hand. *The hand of a dead man*.

And Fyodor tipped backwards, flailed, tumbled down the stairs. He heard a sickening crunch . . .

Darkness entered through the crack in his skull. It swept him up, carried him away . . . He drifted through the darkness— orbiting a far world. Beginning to sink toward that cloud-clotted planet . . .

No. He refused to go.

"In time, you will come. We traded him for you . . ."

Fyodor struggled, psychically writhing, to get back. A long

ways back, and an endless time somehow folded within a few minutes . . . Then he was crawling across the basement floor.

Someone was helping him up. Roman . . . was that his name?

The young man, quite solicitous, helped him up the stairs to the front hall—and then Leah stepped in the door. "Oh, my God! Fyodor! Roman, what happened! Have you hurt him? He's got blood on his head! I knew something was wrong! I was sure of it! Never mind, just sit down, Fyodor, I'll call an ambulance . . . and the police."

*

How the seasons *do* wheel by. Spring, summer, fall, winter; spring, summer, fall; a year and another . . . And then an early summer day . . . the roses were pretty, quite new, not yet chewed by the fungus. . . .

Mom drooped in her chair across from him, eyes completely hidden in sunglasses. She would want to play cards when she woke up. He preferred the puzzle.

"Fyodor?" It was Leah, speaking from the back door. Smiling. Dressed up rather formally. "We're going out. To the book signing."

"Hm?" Fyodor looked up from his Old Providence jigsaw puzzle.

Mother had been grumpily helping him put the puzzle together on the card table, in the late summer sunshine; the rose garden behind the Dunn house. But Mom had gone to sleep, a jigsaw piece in her hand, slumped in her chair. She looked contented, snoring away there.

Roman was so good to take care of her—to care for them both here.

"I said, we're going to Roman's signing—for his book? You sure you won't come? The man from the *New York Times* is going to interview him."

"Is he? That's good. Big crowd?"

"Oh, yes. It looks to be a bestseller. I know you don't like crowds."

"No. Crowds and cats . . ."

He had heard Roman's agent, a pretty blond lady, chattering away over breakfast.

"They're framing it as *Roman Theobald, the man Lovecraft might have become* . . ." Then she'd turned to him. "How are you this morning, Fyodor? Would you like some more orange juice?"

Very kind of her. Everyone was very kind to him, since the accident. Since the damage to his head.

Leah had married "Roman Theobald"—that was his pen name. Roman Boxer was his real name. Anyway—the name on his birth certificate. Sometimes, in the house, she used a funny little affectionate name for him. "Howard." Odd choice. Anyway, she was Mrs. Roman Boxer now. She was almost ten years too old for Roman, but Mrs. Boxer had approved. She'd bought the Dunn house as a wedding gift for them. Mrs. Boxer had died, soon after the wedding, of cancer. Buried at Swan Point Cemetery.

Fyodor felt good, thinking about it. Maybe it was the Prozac. But still—it was true, everyone *was* very kind. Roman, Leah, the doctors—all very kind to him. And Leah made sure he took his pills in the evening. He really couldn't sleep without them. Particularly the pills against nightmares. He was quite sure that if he dreamed of that place again—the place the bells in the sea spoke of—he would not wake up the next morning. He might never wake up again. And Mother, then, poor old Mumsy, would be all alone.

Until they came for her too.

THOSE WHO COME TO DAGON

The Journal of Caleb Ward

June 21 (?), 1806

Leseur, the bosun of a lost ship, declares me foolish to expend strength dashing off these lines, for all of us in the launch of the late *H.M.S. Feveringale* feel the weakness of eleven days without food. And for two days running, little more than a mouthful of fresh water. I hope that though we perish in the launch, my papers might be preserved and found with my body. How I could wish for a rainstorm to bestow drinking water on us, if the storm did not blow overhard; one such gale, rendering but little rainwater, took our launch's only mast. The equatorial heat is relentless, and I feel my throat chafe against itself and burn with salt. Sometimes Tantalus has his way with us, when we scent the greenness of the West African coast and espy a bit of palm or liana floating in the sea, but the current never carries us close enough to bring hope of landfall.

The Reverend Mothe, though his voice sounds like a rusty pump o'er a waterless well, continues to spout of Providence, to be of good cheer, for God will not forget us. I have not succumbed to the temptation to ask him why God should remember us and not the scores of men (and the cook's wife) who died in the fire or who drowned in the consequent sinking of the *Feveringale*. I have long been one of "The Lord's Stray Lambs": my regard for His creation was blackened by the knowledge of my inherited fate, even before we few survivors of the catastrophe were cast adrift, for as a young man I watched as my father died of a cancer; his going was slow and terrible. He had not seen forty summers. I know that my grandfather, and his father too, died in the selfsame way. The disease is in our blood, and I fancy I feel it working its malignity upon me already. So it was that at close to the age my father was when he was stricken, I gave off clerking at the bank and took to poetry and the penning of Observations for the Weekly Journals, reckoning that at least I might live out my greatest hopes for myself, for a few months. . . . And then this! Cast adrift in an open boat! Yet it may be that this death by drowning or thirst is preferable to death by the slow inner consuming of cancer. It may be that this is a mercy after all. I could only wish I had died quickly on the *Feveringale.*

Any who chance to find this hasty journal will remark that the edges of the paper are scorched, and the lettering murky. I did manage to snatch a few necessaries from my trunk, even as the flames that engulfed the ship seared the trunk's right side—I burnt my fingers lightly doing so—and to one whose hope is to write for the *Boston Gazette,* quill, ink, and paper are more necessary than the dueling pistol and compass I snatched up as an afterthought. (I do hope my handwriting is legible, there being more than enough swell and pitch and salty spray to make writing difficult. I fear my vanishing ink may dry out entirely and sometimes I am tempted to drink it.)

Our sound ship should have carried us easily to the Canary Islands; but the voyage has been blighted with bad luck all along. We had survived an encounter with privateers, Captain O'Brian having outrun them when they lost a mizzen; we had triumphed over a breached gun-room which flooded because a drunken sailor forgot to close a port—we weathered these vicissitudes only to have the ship burn down around us for the misplacing of a candle! Dr. Bessemen insists it was not he who left the candle too close to a case of spirits; however, the fire commenced in his quarters. His loblolly boy, not having survived the fire, cannot protest his innocence. In truth, so far as we know, only those of us in the launch survive—dour old Bessemen, Gaddle the squint-eyed first mate, sallow, glowering Leseur (whose presence has always made me uneasy), the sailors Brackin and Milford, Sergeant Sparks of the Marines, and myself.

We are all quite burnt and bearded now, looking like folk any one of us would have avoided on the street in London—or perhaps Boston, respecting myself, for I am the only American, and though our nations are now at peace, I have been more than once the object of an unjustified suspicion. Would I be so absurd as to sabotage a ship in which I too am sailing?

My hand stiffens. I must close for now. There is a strange smell in the air, a foul reek carried on the rising breeze from the south: a dead whale nearby, perhaps. O and this is cruel, the ink is quite drying out. It does not mix well with seawater but I shall att

June 25, 1806

I was unable to finish my sentence at the conclusion of the previous entry, for want of serviceable ink, but I recommence my journal aboard the ship which has picked us up, for here ink is plentiful, thanks to the generosity of Captain Hoek, the stout, bluff Dutchman who is the chief Argonaut of the *Burdened Pelican:* a brig of two masts, a ship neither prodigious nor small. Only the peeling paint on the bow declares the ship's true name; her captain and crew call her "the dratted ol' *Pelican.*"

Three days I've been on this leaky old vessel, recovering strength, as the ship works its way north to Holland. Yet it makes scarcely any headway; "'tis all leeway," says the bushy-browed captain—he speaks always around the ancient curved pipe clutched in his teeth, a pipe usually turned upside down and empty of tobacco. "The winds, the winds rush agin' us and agin' all natural blowin', for they should northerin' this time of year, do ye hear? But they blow southwest and we must tack, and beat and tack again and more, and scarcely any progress do we make. We must find an island to stop for water and meat, soon, if the wind do not change . . ."

And so the time wears away, with little progress in our journey—but at least we are rescued! The other survivors of the *Feveringale,* perhaps surfeited with the sight of one another on the launch, have largely kept to themselves. I have a cabin to myself, once belonging to an officer now lost at sea. The officer was lost along with the ship's doctor and several other men during an "unnatural blow," as Hoek has it, not long before we were picked up. (They were pleased to have a new doctor in our Bessemen, but when they discover his drunkenness and absence of real parts, they will be less sanguine.) Yet the first mate, Van Murnk, a heavy-cheeked man with hair so blond it is almost white and a face so sunburned he sometimes resembles a Red Indian—a man, indeed, perpetually sodden with drink—claims that those who went missing, including, says he, "Even Monsieur Galange . . . took it on their own to hie to the sea, and have not yet left us, *mein herr,* but follow in our wake." He would say no more and I had no wish to pursue his meaning and encourage the fallacies and fancies so common to sailors.

Van Murnk is not alone in his oddity; it must be said that it is, withal, a strange ship. The crew seem sullen and fearful except for spare occasions when they are caught up in an inexplicable and outlandish glee, their eyes feverish, their mien giddy; they have a proclivity for gathering in groups far aft, whereupon they take up tittering and whispering . . .

Today is Sunday. Captain Hoek rigged church this morning and read from Proverbs, a certain desperation in his voice; but most of the crew remained well apart from the ceremony, staring with hollow eyes in the dull light of the overcast morning, with a cast of face both unreceptive and obscurely ashamed.

June 26, 1806

It called for some persuading—they were strangely disinclined—but I have just taken a meal with Dr. Bessemen, Rufe Gaddle, and Reverend Mothe. The doctor and Gaddle seemed to share an unvoiced mutual understanding—something dire, judging by their expressions and by the dark glances they exchanged; their strangely resonant silences. The pastor seems to be at odds with them over some matter he does not wish to evince in my presence.

"Have you not heard a sort of *droning* from below decks and aft?" I prompted, as if making light of it, as we enjoyed our watered-down after-dinner porto. "And other sounds I could not identify—a kind of squawking, a squeaking sound that almost seemed to form words?" They did not reply, but I went on, "I ventured to investigate and found the way blocked by Leseur! He turned me back and refused to explain! The fellow was more forbidding than ever, Captain—the only one of us not to avail himself of the ship's razors since our rescue. A bit of beard is quite natural, but he is as shaggy as an old bear. And the look in his eyes! Like a bear indeed—but a bear with a toothache!" Thus I tried to disarm them with levity, to ease the taut atmosphere and perhaps provoke confidences. But my attempts at humor at Leseur's expense were met with sullen stares from Gaddle and the doctor—who was quite noddingly drunk—and a long sigh from the Reverend. At last the Reverend said, "Indeed I have heard the noises of which you speak." He gave the other two a vinegary look of accusation. "Perhaps someone else might share their knowledge of these . . . sounds."

"Why," said the doctor, after a pull at his porto, "they are but sea chantys. And you heard a cat mewling, the ship's cat. How they do like to tease the poor brute."

Sea chantys? I most certainly had heard nothing of the sort!

But I did not dispute him, and could draw them out no further. After some grudging speculation about the weather and hope for a landfall, we adjourned.

I then went to the deck for some air, and met a man I must describe. I find myself bemused by this most peculiar individual, a man the hue of coal. He has only just emerged after several days in his cabin, and now strides the deck as freely as any of the whites: one Louis Nukanga, an "associate in business" of the captain.

Nukanga wears a fine suit of clothing, and his head is shaved bald. His only departure from European dress is the copper on his wrists, bracelets that one only sees when he lifts his arms to some task or gesture, and the sleeves fall back. I found myself staring at them as he approached the rail close by me and raised a spyglass to scan the western horizon, just at sunset.

"The island, I feel its loom," he said (to himself, though I stood close beside him at the rail). "The island . . . I feel her . . ." So he muttered as he peered through the spyglass. He said something more in his own language—I know not what, precisely, but it had the sound of frustrated longing. It was then that I saw the bracelets and made out the figures carved upon them. On the underside of the wide bracelet clasping his left wrist was a graven image of a creature I at first supposed some cephalopod of the deep, until I beheld its lower body that was almost like a man's; the other bracelet showed the image of a thing like a great scaled worm, with the face of a man, and tentacles bristling here and there—rude spirits of the African continent, I'm sure. I seemed to see both images too easily, as if they drifted from their metal hosts and floated upon the air. Under each image was writing in a script I could not read; I have seen samples of ancient Sumerian, and while it was not Sumerian perhaps it was not so different. Strange, for that land was far, far north of the equatorial Africa from whence Nukanga sprang.

I pressed Nukanga for an account of his provenance. He shrugged and informed me that he hails from the jungles two days' march inland of the Gulf of Guinea, a place "not so far south of the Niger River," where he had struck a deal with a Frenchman named Galange who was in partnership with Captain Hoek.

His accent was strong but his English was otherwise quite good. A freed slave, educated by his Master in England, Nukanga had returned to a place called, "to freely translate, sir, the Uneasy Mountain." Here was the home of his youth. But he found the entire village in bondage to M. Galange, who was searching for treasure, commanding a small but well-armed cadre of Dutch and French brigands to force labor upon the natives. At gunpoint, Nukanga's people dug shafts into the mountain, fruitlessly searching for rumored wealth. "The search was wont to kill my people," said Nukanga grinning, "So I showed Galange where he and Hoek could obtain their heart's desire, in exchange for a special arrangement for myself. Of course, I have promised them another treasure, in another place, on their return. If I did not, they would have cut my throat as I slept, so that I would not trouble them for my share. . . . However, Monsieur Galange will do no more harm—he has gone from the ship . . . in a sense."

I registered his words but distantly; it was his grin that transfixed my attention. His teeth were covered in copper, and each one, I saw in the ruddy gleam of the setting sun, was inscribed with one of the unknown letters of the sort etched into his bracelet. What did his grin spell out?

"You try to read my teeth, eh?" he said, chuckling, lowering his spyglass. "These names you cannot read; their alphabet you are not likely to know. They are names you may yet wish to call out! You may wish to call them . . . and implore, yes, *implore* for their mercy!" His eyes were glittering with a contained, cruel mirth as he spoke.

Stung by his contemptuous tone, which he hardly troubled to conceal, I felt constrained to reply somehow. "I call on no deities, sir, neither yours nor those of my own land," I declared. "I am a man of the new era, a man who values Reason, and such men, the hope of the world, deny all superstitions—meaning no disrespect to your beliefs."

"Superstitions? If you meet a god, will you then believe?"

"Yes, if I recognize his godliness! But there are those who claim to bear gods within them—I have heard of such things in the West Indies, a practice called voudoun—and to meet this 'god' is to meet a man deluded!"

"I do not speak of such," he said, snorting dismissively, collapsing the spyglass with a sharp report of metal on metal. "I speak of—But perhaps you shall know, soon enough . . . soon enough . . ." And with that he turned away, muttering in quite another language, and went below. So ended my interlocution with Mr. Nukanga!

Only a few heartbeats later I was joined by the captain, who had been drinking with Dr. Bessemen. "Your Bessemen," snorted the captain, "cannot hold his liquor—one bottle, or mebbe it was two, and he babbles without sense, and then falls to snoring!" He clutched the rail and in his drunkenness seemed to sway in exact counterpoise to the swaying of the westering ship, his upright body like the inverted working of a pendulum. "My friend," he said, breathing a gust of spirits upon me, the unlit pipe wagging in a corner of his mouth, "what think ye of Nukanga?"

"He seems a strange mix of the learned and the superstitious! And he spoke obscurely of an island . . ."

"An island? Did he now?" He turned and peered into the gathering gloom, sniffing the air. "I believe I can smell it. Land." He removed the pipe and called up to the lookout in the crow's nest. "Ho! You there! Do you see land to the west? An island?"

"I do not, Captain!" came the reply.

"Well, watch close! We need the water, damn you!"

He then addressed me, while swaying in place and packing the pipe with tobacco he kept loose in a weskit pocket. "I do not trust Nukanga—he is a Jonah! Since he came on board the winds blow us always west, no matter how we beat and tack, tack and beat. Always west and even south! And our route is north and east!"

"For my part, I am glad the wind has taken you out of your way, for I'd have perished on the sea otherwise. But perhaps you are concerned to protect your cargo, Captain. We are driven into the sea-lanes of privateers by these winds . . ."

"My cargo?" He looked at me suspiciously. "What do ye know of that?"

"Nukanga says he helped you find a treasure, but he did not say what treasure—"

"Aye, if he said so much, it can't matter if ye know—and you seem an honest man. I would trust you, for I have need of someone to tell my mind. There are few enough—perhaps there is no one—I can trust. Come!"

He staggered away and I followed. We made our way below decks, the captain swearing when he nearly fell going down the ladder. The captain catching up a lantern along the way, we wended a narrow, malodorous corridor, descended two more ladders, each deck's passageway more noisome than the last, until we came to a locked room. Here a sailor leaning on the bulkhead nodded in sleep, musket clutched against him, keeping some sort of watch. "Idiot pig!" the captain bellowed, snatching the musket and slapping the hapless fellow so that he stumbled sputtering away. "Ye sleep when I pay you to guard my cargo? I should hang you!"

Some time a-fumbling later, the captain found his key and unlocked the heavy padlock and bade me follow him within. Within the low-ceilinged hold were a row of five goodly chests. "In the other hold below, there is crude tin, copper, and other ores, but here is the real treasure! Now let your eyes feast, Mr. Caleb Ward!"

He unlocked the nearest of the chests and flung its lid back. At first I thought it filled with rough rocks of quartz, but when he lifted the lantern over the chest I saw the blue glimmerings, as if from a multiplicity of eyes, shining back from the pure hearts of the gems. "Diamonds!" I cried.

"Quiet! Never so loud, ye hear?" he hissed. "Rough they are, but diamonds right enough. Five chests full! All mine, and Nukanga's—Galange has gone missing from the ship and I do not like to guess at how it happened. Still, he will not share the diamonds—so sad! And Nukanga offers four times as many in another place—but only when he is paid, he says, in Amsterdam! It was in Galange's mind, before we left the village, to make Nukanga tell of this other place—to use ropes and fire to make him tell. But I have no belly for torture, and who knows what friends the man might have in civilized places! So I bear Nukanga, though he sneers and speaks in the lower deck to the men, speaks things . . . such things . . ." He shook his head. "Things . . . I don't know."

He tried to light his pipe on the lantern, and repeatedly failed. In the end I held the lantern for him while he puffed the pipe alight—I was fearful of fire on the wooden ship, after what had happened to the *Feveringale*. Another kind of fire, a blue fire, glimmered in the chest of rough gems. The diamonds, I confess, made my heart pound. So many! And I was so poor! But I had been raised austerely and was unable to think of larceny, but for a fitful moment.

"Captain," I said, "I am indeed awed. You will be a rich man! But surely there are yet mysteries on this ship—there is the curious murmuring of numerous voices, something like a chant, heard from the deep aft in the night watches. . . . Seeing this treasure, perhaps the mystery is solved. Could not the sounds I heard be a crew in conspiratorial colloquy? Could they not be thinking of making this treasure their own?"

"Eh?" He turned and looked at the door, then hastened to close the chest. "Ye think I would trust them? They don't know what is here! They think it's all tin and copper ore! Ye have seen, and Nukanga, and none other! For these are not the men we took with us to the interior. *Those* men wait for us at the village of the Uneasy Mountain."

"What then, is the trouble with the crew, Captain? Is it but my imagination?"

"As to that ye have heard—they do something aft, and below, in the orlop! O, aye, there is a sickness on this ship, a slow, infectious madness, like a man crying out in fever . . . while there is no fever! And something has taken our own doctor, and four of my best hands!"

"But with respect, Captain Hoek, are you not master of your ship? Surely you can penetrate this mystery by demanding an explanation; by entering the orlop where these rites are held, and seeing for yourself!"

"Had I the heart, the courage . . . Something about the business affrighted me, so I sent the doctor—the ship's own doctor, before you came aboard. I sent him that night, as the storm rose . . . and where is he now? It was that very night he went missing, with them others! The crew say those five was swept o'erboard. Myself, I think it were something . . . *other*."

"What other, Captain?"

"Ach, my head hurts, I speak strange things when the drink begins to wear off. Have ye not noticed how many of the crew are hiding below, saying they are sick? How few remain to work the ship? I have almost no one left to turn to—and I say this: if you would find out what goes on below, you would find me grateful."

He would say no more. But I determined to do as he requested. I shall write a great story for the newspaper—I sense it coming.

*

I wrote out the previous entry two hours ago. It seems an age.

After I spoke to the captain, I went on deck to stand brooding by the aft rail. A strong wind blew from the east, filling the sails, driving us west, ever west, at about seven knots. I had heard one of the hands say that it seemed if the captain tried to tack, the wind shifted, continuing pushing the vessel west, as if actively, deliberately frustrating his efforts!

The wind in my face, I watched as the failing light seemed to soak into the glimmering white tips of waves, to re-emerge in the luminescence of the *Pelican*'s wake. Like diamonds!

I beheld something, then, disporting in the seam the ship cut in the sea. Dolphins? Seals? Sometimes I thought so, other times I thought they were more disturbing shapes; I thought I saw a buckle upon one, a strip of cloth trailing from another. There were at least three of them; sometimes I thought there were more. Whenever I supposed I had distinguished their shape, it would seem to change, skirl, and wash in the dark sea, and I was again unsure of the creature's form. The thought came that they might be sharks, with bits of human victims trailing from their jaws. . . .

Then a hatch opened on the stern of the ship below me. Lamplight shone out upon the water, and I looked eagerly to try to see what creatures followed in our wake. But as if aware of my scrutiny, they dropped back into shadow.

I thought I saw something before they went—a human face, staring up at me from the water. Perhaps a dead man, caught in some old fishing line. . . .

I thought to tell the captain—but then the chanting began, the sound coming from that same square of light, the anomalous hatch on the stern. I could not make out what was said. Sometimes I thought I heard, repeated amidst the gibberish, *"Dae-gon . . . eck k'lool-hew . . . dae-gon . . . eck k'lool-hew . . ."*

And the inchoate shapes in the wake of the ship seem to hiss and thrash in response. I heard a sibilant squeaking from them— like a dolphin trying to form words, and failing.

An icy tingle spread out from the back of my head, to seep corrosively down my spine, seeming to drain all firmness from it, and I clutched the rail that I might remain standing.

Come, this is foolishness! I told myself. *Go now and see what is below and do not let your imagination play upon you! You wish a story to tell—here is one waiting to be found out!*

So I made myself go below, in search of the orlop—the lowest deck on the ship, where chains and rope are coiled and ballast stored. But I did not neglect to stop momentarily at my cabin for my dueling pistol. Once in my cabin, I once more had to summon strength of will to continue my investigation, for I had a sudden pervasive desire to lock the door and sit on my hammock with that pistol in my hand, my eyes fixed on the cabin door, the gun at ready . . .

No, sir, I told myself. *You will not hide from adventure. It is what you came to sea to find!*

Thereupon I set out, making my way, lantern in hand, down two ladders and along the passage toward the stern. Just a few paces outside the door to the orlop I found my way blocked by Leseur, who huddled into the dim shadows of the narrow passage like a tunnel spider in its den. The light from my lantern appeared to shy from him; to quail just short of him. I was determined, this time, that he would not deter me—and indeed a feverish curiosity was beginning to replace the fear that had crawled from that primeval cranny at the back of my brain, an inquisitiveness tugged by the droning chant from beyond the closed oaken door.

"Leseur—move aside, if you please!" I said, trying to keep the quavering in my hands from reaching my voice. "I have this night entered into Captain Hoek's service and he has sent me to make certain enquiries in the orlop."

When Leseur spoke, the sound seemed to come, muffled, from the base of his throat, and a sickly reek came with it, something more alien than a man's foul breath—and it was a smell I thought I recognized. I had caught it once before . . .

"You may not pass unless Nukanga says aye."

"Move aside, I say! Look you on this pistol and know I will make use of it if I must!"

He turned and put a hand on the door—and there seemed a splaying in the spread of his fingers, as if each was melting into the next. I felt a shivering ring out from his contact with that door; it resonated through the damp timbers of the old ship, so that its seams worked in response, oozing seawater. I was obscurely aware that water was pooling, very slowly, at my feet.

Then the door opened; a glutinous yellow light silhouetted Nukanga from behind: he was a dark figure but for his teeth shining copper-red in the feebler light of my lantern. I leaned to peer around him, but could scarcely make out the room beyond. I glimpsed a great coil of heavy cable, the outlines of a group of men seated on it, their backs to me, facing that anomalous hatch in the stern. The hatch looked hastily built, and recent. And there through it came the smell of compressed seawater and decayed fish and living muck, that distinctive reek from the bottom-most trench of the sea . . .

I knew then where I had smelled it before—that day in the launch, just before we were sighted by the *Pelican*.

"So—you have come to us? I thought you would," said Nukanga. "Come a little closer and look, Caleb Ward . . ."

Leseur grudgingly pressed aside—there was just enough room to squeeze past him, an inexpressibly disgusting process, to slip into the orlop after Nukanga. I scrutinized the semicircle of crew. There were Brackin and Sparks and Gaddle and Milford and Van Murnk and two other crewmen I had seen when I first came . . . and Bessemen.

But Bessemen was lying upon the deck, curled on his side, within the circle of rope on which the others sat, and he was not alone. He was clutched against a being not quite twice his bulk, a thing green-black and wetly slick; a creature with the proportions of a human woman, but at its throat were gills, and in place of human eyes were round yellow orbs on the two sides of its oblate head; in place of hair on its head were tresses of slender fins; its mouth . . .

O, it's hard to write it; for that means I must again invoke the picture; I must once more see that lamprey mouth, that great round fibrous, membranous sucker clapped over Bessemen's eyes and forehead, sucking, and pulsing; taking and replacing . . . and Bessemen squirmed in the thing's grip, struggled to escape, his hands clawing, his bare feet scrabbling at the deck, finding no purchase, no escape. He was like a feeble child trying hopelessly to wrest free even as it was strangled by a brutish overpowering mother.

I stared and choked and turned away, covering my eyes, even as the men seated on the coil of rope persisted in their chant, gurgling and squeaking syllables no human mouth was made to express, invocations interspersed with the litany, *"K'lool-hew eck dae-gon, k'lool hew eck dae-gon!"*

"Ho ho, my little friend," chortled Nukanga as I tried to claw my way from the orlop. "What is the matter? Hm? Do you suppose this man is the victim of a bestial predation?" He locked powerful hands on my shoulders and held me back with little apparent effort. "Not at all! He *begged* for this! He is but in the throes of transfiguration! And my friend—" He spun me about and looked me in the eye. "He will never die!"

The words struck to the aching quick of me. *He will never die!*

I wanted to run—but it was as if those words spiked me to the spot. "What?" I rasped. "What do you mean?"

"All men crave immortality—but immortality in this world comes with a price! Wait—what is this I see? I am a magus of my people, and I see a man's fate written in his eyes . . ."

He took the wrist of my left hand and drew it close between us so that the lantern which I still held shone into my eyes. I blinked and tried to turn away. But with his other hand he took my chin in his big hand and turned my face to him. "Some gaze into a crystal ball to see a man's living fate, but I would look into these soft orbs and see—your *death!* I see you lying on a hammock of a ship, and I see blood streaming from your mouth! You clutch at your chest and you groan, but there is no doctor to attend you! You die the death of your father and his father and his father before him! A cancer eats at you and will take you before this year is worn away! Look—see for yourself!"

And then he struck my forehead with the heel of his hand, and it was as if his vision of my death was carried in the blow, from his hand into my skin and skull and into my brain where it rippled mockingly before my mind's eye.

I saw it clearly, more clearly than I see the paper on which I now scribble this account. I saw myself dying in a hammock, in a small, mould-splashed room; dying as my father had—all the signs of his death upon me. And I saw that it would be soon. And I knew the truth of this vision, as I would know the face of my own father, were I to behold him again. It was the truth of recognition. This was my death.

"But wait!" Nukanga said, as the image dissolved into his coppery grin, his exultant eyes. "That is your death *as a man!* And there is no escaping your death as a man! But if you were to become *other* than a man—then the curse of your destiny is lifted, and you will not die that death, *you will not die at all* . . . not if you become as those who come to Dagon!"

"No . . ." My heart shriveled with in me as I began to comprehend.

"Choose! Only choose! Dagon has seen you from the wake of the ship! Dagon has looked into you from the depths of the sea and Dagon desires you! You are choice, something quite choice to Dagon! Come to Dagon, and live forever . . . or die alone, spitting blood in that damp, forgotten room . . . with no one to attend you, no one to pity you, no one to care!"

Then he let go of my shoulders and I staggered away, past Leseur, who was emitting a high-pitched bark and a terrible stench—the sound and the smell of his laughter.

June 27, 1806

It is morning and yet it is not morning.

Somewhere in this ashen mist, the sun has arisen. An etiolated light has diffused the ash-thick fog. But it is scarcely like real day. We stalk the deck, looking to the west. Our eyes are burning and we can scarce see through the murk, but we sense the loom of the land; we smell stone and beach and fire and jungle.

"This is a volcano island," said Hoek, beside me on the quarterdeck, peering through the mist, wiping his eyes, peering again. "The kind that gives out smoke and vapour but never erupts. As if it wishes to hide its secrets. So little wind. Hardly a breath! Would I could turn away from this—but we have need of water, we have need of supplies . . ." He looked at me as if he wanted to ask what I had learned in my foray the night before. But I shook my head and turned away, and he grunted as if in some personal confirmation.

I could not bear to talk of it. Only with an inner struggle was I able to force myself to make this written account.

One phrase keeps returning to my mind, this morning . . .

He will never die!

No. I will not listen to that voice. I would rather die than lose my humanity.

I attempted to seek counsel from the Reverend Mothe. But the pastor will not heed me; he kneels, praying—coughing and supplicating—beside the mainmast. He will respond to no one. He prays with the desperate ardor of one who begins to doubt that he is heard.

I feel safer in my cabin, now, scribbling away, though the candle gutters as if it might go out—but it is even harder to breathe here, somehow.

I will go on deck and see if, perhaps, the wind has changed.

*

I have been on deck, and I wish I had not gone. The sky was a little clearer—the wind blows from the east again, and has broomed some of the ashen sky. The island broods nigh, dominated by a dark cone nestled in jungle so green it is almost black; streams that emerge from the hills about the volcano run dark down through red soil; dark to the sea like streaks of blood.

We are still almost a mile out from the rocky cove. And we are moving in, despite all the captain can do.

For after the voice that came from the sea, Hoek wanted to move away from the island.

It was a feeble voice, a squeak and a hoarseness, but Hoek claimed he recognized it. "That is . . . that is Galange! One of those who was lost overboard! Do ye hear it?"

"In name of God, arête! Turn back, Hoek," came the voice. *"Nom de Dieu! Do not surrender. Do not listen. All here is poisoned! Go back, j'implore! In name of God . . . kill me! Fetch a musket and kill me!"*

I thought to see a man writhing in the dark waves, about a cable ahead of us, but then again not a man, for he had round yellow lidless eyes, and hands that were not hands. And then there was a great splashing about him, and the man gave a cry of despair as other hands, webbed and clawed—hands so dark-green they were almost black, like the jungle about the volcano—clutched at him from all sides, and dragged him under.

Then he was gone. But we seem to hear him still. *Fetch a musket and kill me!*

The captain, his face gone whiter than his vessel's sails, turned and shouted orders at the affrighted crew. "You there, wheel her about! We will tack, and turn about! We will lower a boat and pull the ship if we must . . . but we will not go to that island!"

So the few crewmen still willing to respond tried to turn about—and we had not gotten but a few strakes turned before there was a splashing and crackling from the rudder, and the captain made haste to aft. I followed him and looked over the rail . . . and saw that the rudder had snapped away. Or perhaps I should say, it *had been snapped* away. Something had torn it free. The ship was now drifting rudderless. And the wind was shifting, as if of its own accord . . . and driving us in toward the island.

Hoek went about the ship shouting orders, trying to steer the by adjusting the sails—but nothing availed us. There was another force pushing us in: swimmers, many swimmers, not quite seen in the murk and dark water; we saw only the splashing of their legs, the occasional glimpse of slick finny limbs, as they put shoulders to the hull of the ship and directed it into the dark stone arms of the cove.

"Do you fear this consummation?" Nukanga asked, as he joined me at the bow of the ship, the island looming near. "Do not fear it," he said earnestly. "You do not wish to die young, alone, coughing blood like your father! Surrender to the god whom my people once knew—who many worshipped, in many places, and knew by many names. Once we were a seafaring people, who lived on these shores. But seeking to end the surrender of certain our children to the dark gods of the sea, the village elders took us inland to the Uneasy Mountain. Yet even in the shadow of the mountain were rivers, and upwellings from the stone. And here Dagon called to us, and said, *Where you go, I follow!* And so it will be with you, Caleb Ward—and with Captain Hoek, and with all the others. Why do you think I brought this ship here? Do you suppose we were ever truly bound for Amsterdam? No, my friend. I have no interest in diamonds. My mother, my sisters, my only brother—all died in Galange's mines before I arrived! I swore revenge! And to kill Galange and his men was not enough! Galange has already gone to serve Dagon! For Captain Hoek once commanded a slave ship!"

As he went on, I was aware of a struggle behind us—Captain Hoek and a few others shouting, ordering muskets to be used, weapons to be fired, and then someone sobbing that the muskets would not fire for the ash in the air. I heard the slipping wet sound of slick limbs and flippers on the deck as something crawled onto the ship from the sea; I smelled that unholy reek; heard the sounds of struggle, and claws on wood; I heard Reverend Mothe shrieking as he was dragged to the side. . . . A sudden cessation of the shrieking, with the sound of two large objects splashing into the waves. . . .

I did not turn to look. I simply gazed at the great black cone of the volcano and listened to Nukanga.

"But you—you shall have an honored place at Dagon's side!" declared Nukanga eagerly. "Ha ha! You amuse the god! And it is your only hope . . . of life! Choose, Caleb Ward—choose! For those who do not submit to the transfiguration . . . will become food! And Dagon, and his minions, they eat slowly, my friend—so slowly! They take many months to consume a man—months of sleepless agony! Choose, Caleb Ward! Transfiguration and immortality—or the slow awful revenge of the people of the Uneasy Mountain! *Choose!*"

June 28 (?), 1806

Can scarcely write. Not sure how long ship aground. Others all taken. Scream in night. Some make other sounds. Soon, myself.

Difficult to write. She changed me. Change almost complete. Words come hard. Forgetting old language. H'Beth K'hrauh-sug-uth! New words—yet very old. They come instead. Cthulhu Yog-S'hruth Dagon!

Fingers changing. Hard to hold quill. Webbing between fingers; new claws. Eyes no longer focus well, out of water. The sea calls. Must answer.

The horror that is myself, my new self—is beyond expression.

Will seal journal in box. Place this account in ship's boat, set to drift. Perhaps warn others. Tell them: If choice given, choose well.

Choose not as I chose. Choose carefully.

Choose death.

THE RIME OF THE COSMIC MARINER

About, about, in reel and rout
The death-fires danced at night;
The water, like a witch's oils,
Burnt green, and blue and white.
　　　　—The Rime of the Ancient Mariner

Highgate
November 17, 1833

To Mr. Thomas Penson De Quincey
Glasgow, Scotland

My dear De Quincey!

I write to you in a curiously Arctic fever, cold and febrile at once, and on a cryptic mission of mercy. I would save you from the ponderous but imponderable darkness, indeed the cosmic chaos that descends upon me.

I can almost hear you laughing, my former friend, but this is no hyperbole and certainly no jest. You will, I trust, forgive this presumption after some years of silence, and forgive, too, my shaky hand, my lines as uncertain as rain patterns in sand—and doubtless as unwanted as an icy rain upon a walking tour. *Pace tua,* De Quincey, I am not insensible to our differences of civic philosophy; marching through the decades you have become the Tory's very own Tory, and at this remove it may be you think me a secret Jacobin, a Guy Fawkes reborn, despite the moderation I have shewn these many years since my boyish days of planning American Utopias. I have moderated my views considerably; but even so, we would strike sparks at disputation over a bowl of punch, I'm sure, within minutes after the nostalgic niceties concluded.

Despite our widening political divide, De Quincey, we yet have much in common: a love of the streaming effusion of language, the surge of contention like a river driven upon a boulder, the flow bifurcated by obstacle—by objection.

We are like brothers who are doomed to disagree, but brothers we are, in our tragic affiliation with opium. On our first meeting, in your youth, when you shewed such enthusiasm for my poetry, the poppy's poison was much upon my mind. I sought day by day to escape laudanum's warm embrace; but, more seductive than Calypso or Circe, opium would not let me go—not for long. Hence I spoke of it too freely, complaining to you quite tiresomely of the opium eater's burden of costiveness, of the erosion of the foundations of love, the sickness of withdrawal, certainly—but also I held forth about opium's revelatory powers. You were quite young, scarcely twenty and two! And it may be you absorbed the report of laudanum's good and shed the greater evidence of its evil; perhaps I tilted you toward opium. Much later I certainly read your *Confessions of an English Opium-Eater*: no man better comprehends the pleasures and pains of laudanum than you. But, quite beyond its known evils, opium leaves a man like you and I vulnerable to something cosmically ruinous . . .

In veritate, amicus, I have reason to believe you might be in danger of succumbing to something more than opium. You may find yourself visited by a Particular Something that intrudes itself into a narcotic dream; on occasion, it stops by in person, appearing to be Man. Once, in 1804, I glimpsed it while gazing raptly into the crater of Mt. Etna. It was as if the bottom dropped away from the crater; as if of a sudden its smoky depths plumbed infinity, passing through the whole earthly sphere; and for a few moments it shewed me an unspeakable heavenly oddity crouching within a cluster of stars visible from the unnatural opening on the other side of the Earth. Then it was gone; the infinite shaft snapped shut. But I had seen the Thing That Waits, and it had seen me.

Now, this Thing has an agent, a watcher; a servant, which appears to us as a large bird of no known species. It is the blacker, the *bloodier* albatross. It is the messenger, the deed-doer, of Nyarlathotep, arriving from a very great distance; it flaps wings broader even than the span of an great albatross. O, perhaps it's more like a gigantic raven than an albatross, yet it's not like an earthly bird at all, in truth. It has no true beak—and no true colour. Ever and again it's quite black; yet it ventures to shift, as the light does, and it becomes dark sea-green; and yet again it becomes dark purple, or a sanguinary crimson. It flies where no bird should be able to fly, pressing its wings against the fabric of space, instead of the air; it arrives upon the benumbed Earth, gazing down to consider, and then it soars away. But when the messenger has parted from the likes of thee and me, it is only biding its time.

Let us trek onward, De Quincey, and, I fear, downward . . .

It began when I met Al-Azizi. It was Carter, *Renwald* Carter, an importer of fine goods from the Levant and descendent of the magician Sir Randolph Carter, who introduced me to the curiously articulate and elegant Monsieur Al-Azizi.

Carter sent me a hasty note from his hotel; in sum, he would be honoured to introduce to me a wealthy admirer, one "M. Al-Azizi" who was drawn to my poetry, especially the epic verses. Al-Azizi, he said, was not a Mussulman, despite his Levantine heritage. Carter was perhaps sensible that, as I sink toward my own last judgment, my former deism becomes ever more Christian.

I welcomed Carter's missive. A wealthy admirer of my poetic amusements? I hastened to affirm the meeting for tea.

When Carter and his exotic companion arrived at Number 3, The Grove, Highgate, ushered in by our housekeeper Bethesda, I was, for a rarity, out of my dressing gown; I was almost splendid in red silk smoking jacket, matching trousers, and my eternal

down-at-heel slippers. I had even made shift to scrape my face of
superfluous foliage, for I had hope of a new patron—a final patron, I suspected, as my health has for a time been in leisurely
but steady decline.

Clutching his hat, looking appraisingly at the Persian carpet
in the drawing room, and then at me, Carter said, "Ah—
Coleridge. I have brought you a living marvel. May I present
Monsieur Feruz Al-Azizi, of Paris and Cairo."

I gave my bow and Al-Azizi returned it stiffly, the straight
line of his lips flickering with the most transient of smiles. Tall
and gaunt and dark, he wore a pristine white suit, a red necktie,
a red felt fez; even without the elongation of the fez, he was at
least a foot taller than Carter. He had a jet-black mustache, like a
line on aged foolscap, and once I thought it writhed quite apart
from the working of his face. I assumed this was a product of the
laudanum I had just taken as a restorative—the measured dose
left to me by Dr. Gillman.

"Dr. Gillman is not at home?" Carter asked, looking around
the drawing room, licking his thick lips.

"My host is with his patients," I said. I might have said "his
other patients"—Dr. Gillman has taken it upon himself, these
many years, to house me, to physic me, to dose me as he sees fit.
He is a man of great patience.

I glanced at Al-Azizi—and felt caught, for a moment, in the
gaze of his heavy-lidded, deep-black eyes, which seemed to regard me with a ravenous fixity.

I looked quickly back at Carter, marking that my old ac-
quaintance had changed since I'd seen him last: his face was now
blotchy, his lips bluish, his eyes yellow and flickering; he was hap-
hazardly unshaven, and his stubby fingers clasped over his stained
weskit in what appeared a failed effort to restrain their trembling.

Carter's gaze darted about the small sitting room. "So—we
are in essence quite alone here? I have no wish to be unsociable
but—Monsieur Al-Azizi prefers . . . a small party."

"We are alone but for the housekeeper. She keeps discreetly to the pantry."

I noticed for the first time that Al-Azizi carried a large bag of crocodilian leather, rather like a physician's satchel; I could have sworn he had not the bag when he first came in.

"Please sit down, gentlemen," I said, eyeing the bag.

They sat in Gillman's settee across from my armchair. Al-Azizi stroked the the settee's leather arm with a long-fingered hand. "What an exquisite piece of furniture," he said. "The skin of a fine animal—as comfortable as the arms of a beautiful woman." His accent was both Egyptian and French, to my ear, his voice by turns rumblingly low-pitched and intermittently high, and tremulous as if keeping laughter on a leash.

"Ah, yes," I said, "it is one of the original pieces designed by the Earl of Chesterton; it has resided for some time with Dr. Gillman's family."

My eyes returned to the black crocodilian bag on the Egyptian's lap, as Al-Azizi exclaimed, chuckling, "Why, it is my old friend George!" I thought at first he meant the crocodile, but then he gestured at the oval portrait of King George III on the wall to my right. "How well I remember our talks. George and I went to the roof and gazed upon the stars together—and they gazed upon us!"

"Did you, indeed?" I asked, smiling indulgently. "What year was your interview with the late king?"

"Why, it was 1788, I believe, on a previous trip to your jewel-like isle. Yes!" He flashed grey teeth in a smile that came and went like the tail of a Nile fish, surfacing and gone.

Carter visibly grimaced, and I raised my eyebrows. Of course this putative interview with the king would have been *forty-five years ago,* De Quincey—but this fellow looked no older than his middle thirties! Was it, I wondered, some dreamy vanity on his part, imagining an interlude with George III?

"Was it 1788, for a fact? Well! The very year His Majesty

first succumbed to the . . . to his malaise." I suppose I could have said *madness,* as he is long gone, but I am rooted in an earlier era of delicacy—when I am not in my cups.

"Al-Azizi," Carter began hoarsely, "perhaps this is not the time. I had hoped—"

His gaze still upon me, Al-Azizi raised a hand with the suddenness of a dagger raised to strike, and Carter fell silent, his sentence severed.

"So few men can survive gazing upon the stars with unveiled eyes," said Al-Azizi, shrugging. "Your king—sadly he could not bear it. But—" He put his hands on the clasp of his bag. "But you, sir! When I consider the letter you wrote to your *other* Sara, Sara Hutchinson, in 1802, Coleridge! Surely *you* would be capable of gazing past the veil and coming away whole!"

I fairly gaped at the man. "Letter, sir? 1802?"

"Why, yes." He closed his eyes a moment—how like parchment the lids of his eyes! He seemed to read out the words from some inner scroll.

> *"All this long Eve, so balmy and serene,*
> *Have I been gazing on the western Sky*
> *And its peculiar Tint of Yellow Green—*
> *And still I gaze, and with how blank an eye!*
> *And those thin Clouds above, in flakes and bars,*
> *That give away their Motion to the Stars;*
> *Those Stars, that glide behind them, or between,*
> *Now sparkling, now bedimm'd, but always seen . . ."*

He opened his eyes—yet his eyes seemed almost closed to the world, so empty were they of fellow-feeling. "Yes? Do you recall?"

I cleared my throat. "That letter—why, yes. That passage later became part of an ode. I believe I was on the pinnacle of a tor when I first . . . But Monsieur Al-Azizi, has the lady's family given over my letters to her? I don't recall their—that is . . ."

"Oh, they're written in the Akashic Record, as some call it, with all else, Mr. Coleridge!" he crowed, amused. "I looked them up!"

"He is a marvel indeed, as you said, Carter," I murmured. "However, I—"

That is when Al-Azizi opened his crocodilian bag, a flash of his hands opening it so quickly I thought of a reptile opening its mouth to snap at prey before it could escape. "Here, sir," he said, reaching into the bag, "I have three scientific instruments you will not have seen before, I wager."

He took up a device with his right hand, the instrument resembling a cut-glass doorknob but asymmetrically festooned with brass spikes—and I noticed, for the first time, the ring upon that hand, its large tablet-shaped face of carnelian engraved with the image of a double-headed crystal growing out of a snarl of serpentine shapes. I was distracted from the ring when he snatched the end table, on which stood the Argand lamp, nearly rocking the lamp onto the floor. I made to catch it, but the lamp settled down as he set the table in front of him and placed the instruments on in it the small pool of lamplight. There was the spiked, crystalline knob; beside the festooned crystal was something like a pair of spectacles made of twists of wire, possibly copper, but without lenses. The third instrument was in the shape of a serpentine figure of some silvery alloy; the figure was rather like the engraving on his ring. The instrument stood on one of its coils, its head pointed at the ceiling. Looking closely I saw that it was not precisely a serpent, for its head was eyeless and it seemed to have feathers instead of scales.

"This one," I said, indicating the coiled serpentine instrument, "more resembles jewellery than a scientific instrument. I fancy I have seen something of the sort on a lady's arm, by way of a bracelet."

"Oh, but no lady could long bear to wear this as a bracelet, Coleridge—and no bracelet will do this!" Al-Azizi reached out and carefully pinched the serpentine figure just under its jaws—and immediately the light in the room became a thick luminous liquid, as if amber had melted. The liquid light swirled about us, the whirlpool centreing on the serpentine instrument, and I saw, with gathering trepidation, the light was sinking away *into* the coil, as if the serpent were consuming it. At the ceiling and corners, darkness increased, itself a liquid, something heavier than light forcing it into the genii's bottle of the serpentine instrument. The lamp flickered and dimmed. Al-Azizi's eyes had quite vanished away; there was only a shifting blackness in the sockets, as in a skull seen by the feeble light of a taper.

Oddly enough, Carter had his own eyes covered by his trembling hands.

I felt a piercing coldness growing upon my back. I turned and saw the thick shadow increasing behind me, as if the suctioned light took all warmth and hope with it, and a vortex of black despair was rushing upon me.

"Al-Azizi!" I called out, turning to him with what must have been a shameful desperation—the dark pools of his eye sockets swirling with that same darkness as the living opacity gathering behind me. "Please . . . do reverse the phenomenon!"

Al-Azizi shrugged innocently. "Ah! If you like, Coleridge!"

He once more pinched the instrument, his fingertips pressing with practised exactitude, and light disgorged from the instruments, spiralling up from the serpent's mouth; the shadows wavered furiously a moment, like a flight of crows flapping away, and then the light in the room was restored.

Only a curious smell lingered, like stale frankincense mixed with the mineral reek of a deep, watery cavern. My feet seemed clammy in my shoes as if I'd got them wet.

And lingering, too, was that darkness pooling in the Egyptian's eyes. Then he leaned back a little, and I could see his eyes once more. He smiled thinly. "Mr. Coleridge—are you quite well? You look pale, sir. And I believe you are shivering."

I made myself straighten up and smile. "That was an impressive . . . *illusion,* sir. Something in the way of a magic lantern, perhaps." I licked my lips and wished I might slip off to my room for a brandy. Gillman keeps none in the drawing room. "How you managed it I am quite unsure."

"Illusion!" murmured Carter, rubbing his knees with his hands. "Would that it were so."

Al-Azizi turned a sharp look at Carter, who instantly compressed his lips and said nothing more. I was amazed at Al-Azizi's authority over him. Who had brought *whom* here?

I rubbed my hands together to warm them, wishing that we might have some more coal put in the basement furnace. I was about to call for the Bethesda when Al-Azizi picked up the brass-thorned crystal, tapped three of the spines in a distinct pattern, and whispered, "Listen!"

I heard nothing but Carter's heavy breathing. I leaned a little closer, and then . . . surely those were voices? They were coming thinly from the crystal. A man's voice wheedled, "Hullo, Freddie, old boy, how about spotting me a fiver! Here now, cully, I *needs* it!" Then a little girl said, "If Papa does not come home again tonight, we shall have to steal the cheese crusts from the kitchen rubbish again, and we are not to go into that part of the house with the better people!"

"Good Lord!" I said. "It is like a telescope for sounds! They must be speaking from the street below the hill!"

"They are rather more distant than that," said Al-Azizi.

Then I heard another voice, this one speaking in a foreign tongue. At first I thought it a language obscure to me, like Mongolian; but after a moment I supposed the chirping, clicking, almost insectile sound might not be a human dialect at all. Yet it seemed to be speaking in something like sentences. It set my teeth on edge, I can tell you, De Quincey.

I was about to ask him to put the instruments away when the door opened and Bethesda came in, carrying the tea tray.

Al-Azizi put the instruments back into the bag, his motions quick and neat, and closed it with a snap. His voice was a steely monotone as he said, "I was given to understand we would not be interrupted."

"I'm sure it will be but the interruption of a moment!" Carter assured him.

Bethesda O'Neill was, perhaps *is,* a full-bosomed woman of thirty and four, with frowsy brown hair, a pert nose, thick ankles, and powerful arms; she wore a white servant's bonnet, a black dress, and a white apron, and she bustled into the room in her prim, officious fashion, carrying a tray to the small tea table behind my chair. "Lor', but there's a chill on this room. Will the gentlemen take tea here, sir?"

"That will do very well, Beth," I said. "Will you see to the furnace? I will pour the tea."

"The furnace? Why, it has been burning coal by the ton all this day, sir. Are your registers not open? But they are! I shall have a look."

She turned to go—and stopped dead, staring at Al-Azizi. I supposed at first she was affrighted of this swarthy foreigner. But she had the look of a rabbit enrapt by the eyes of a snake. She opened her mouth as if to speak, but said nothing, merely worrying at her apron with her fingers.

"Beth? This is Mr. Al-Azizi, my guest."

"We met at the door," Al-Azizi said smoothly. "Beth . . . yes. Bethesda. She escorted us within."

"Yes. But was it *him* . . . ?" Beth breathed, as if speaking only to herself. "Was it *this* one then?"

Al-Azizi continued to look at her. Then he waved his hand dismissively, and she hurried, almost running, out of the room. She slammed the door in going.

I was puzzled. Al-Azizi had alarmed her overmuch, considering their harmless encounter—she had not seen the trick with the swirling light.

However, I myself had reason to be alarmed. I was thinking to myself that perhaps, after all, I should not like him to be my patron; that I would like him to take his leave. But I did not seem to have the inner strength to demand his departure. It was not fear of coarseness that held me back; it was something else I can only describe as a failure of my will.

"I could use some tea," I said, my own voice sounding hoarse in my ears. Somehow I knew that Al-Azizi would not choose to sit at the tea table. I know not how this knowledge came to me.

I went to the table and poured a cup, returned, and offered it first to Al-Azizi. He merely shook his head, gazing up at me. I avoided his eyes. I offered it to Carter. He took the cup gratefully.

"Something stronger would not go amiss, as well," Carter said.

"No," said Al-Azizi, his voice calm but firm.

"No, quite right, too early," said Carter hurriedly, sipping the tea.

I buttered Carter two biscuits, put them on a plate, and set it on the lamp table, but he ignored them.

I sat with a couple of biscuits and my tea, and had hardly begun when Al-Azizi said, "You have a stair that leads to the roof."

It was not a question.

"Yes," I said. "Dr. Gillman has an interest in meteorology."

"Let us repair to the roof. I have something to shew you—the very thing I came to lay before you."

I put my cup carefully upon its saucer. "You have shewn me a great deal, sir, quite a sufficiency for one afternoon. I do not wish to presume upon your generosity."

Then—I cannot recall, precisely, De Quincey, how it came to be that we removed from the drawing room to the roof.

I have a dim memory of walking out the back door, with Al-Azizi ahead and Carter behind, and the creaking of the spiralling iron staircase under my foot as we ascended three storeys from the garden to the step between the gables, onto the copper rooftop terrace, a wide flat place between sloping pantiles where the doctor makes his observations.

My next clear recollection is of holding the twisted-wire spectacles. Al-Azizi was standing before me, with the crocodilian bag gaping open in his bony hands. It was a chill, windless afternoon, the indefinite fog a kind of ever-changing lacework around us. The cups of the weather indicator above us did not turn at all.

"But only put them on," Al-Azizi said, "and the veil you wear all unknowing will be at last lifted; the blindfold will be tugged away from your eyes. You will see the stars."

"First, sir," I said, looking around as if I'd awakened here, "allow me to observe that it is not yet nighttime. The day is a trifle befogged and, though the dusk arrives, no stars are visible. And second, sir, seeing stars is in itself unremarkable. True, they may be seen more vividly with a telescope—yet that is often done . . ."

"I could shew you stars as you have never seen them," said Al-Azizi smugly; "but to be perfectly clear, I plan to reveal a planetary object largely unknown to astronomers. If they see it, upon occasion, it appears as star-like from Earth, just as Mars seems a star until gazed upon with a telescope. But you will see this Outer World more vividly than any man ever saw Mars—if you so choose! Of your own free will, place the instrument over your eyes—and thus remove the veil. Lift the blindfolds that perpetually dim your sight, Coleridge!"

It was partly curiosity, De Quincey, that led to my acquiescence. And I suspected he had beguiled me with illusions. As there were no lenses in the spectacles, I thus reasoned that in all probability their effect was to be sheer power of suggestion, mayhap enhanced by mesmerism. A suspicion had been growing upon me that the evident miracle I had perceived in the drawing room was the result of some form of hypnotism, combined with optical illusion. I thought my will strong—bending only to laudanum. Now forewarned, I intended to confront him with his own charlatanry.

I boldly secured the instrument over my eyes, just as a man slips on a pair of spectacles. I saw nothing but what I had seen before, truncated by the frames.

"Now, sir," said Al-Azizi, "we shall make all dark so that the stars present themselves."

I feared the coiling instrument and was about to object, but he quickly placed it upon the ground, activating it as he did so, and the light of the late afternoon began to thicken and spiral above us, compressing, leaving shadow as it declined.

In a moment, darkness had collected thickly above us, and the light of the day was pushed rudely aside. Gazing upward, I saw the stars shining within a circle of darkness directly overhead; it was as if they were seen from deep down a pit, a shaft plumbed into the Earth, much as I had imagined on Aetna.

The celestial array glittered with more presence of that unique starry blue-white than I had ever beheld before. It was honey-thick with it. But apart from that striking fulsomeness, they seemed as usual—a miracle of nature, no more.

Then Al-Azizi reached up and touched the spectacles with a forefinger, near my left temple.

Sparks flew, and arcs of electricity flashed across my vision, close to my eyes. Fearing to be blinded, I cried out and would have taken them off—but I also feared to touch them. Yet they were touching me . . .

Electricity flashed across the empty spaces over my eyes, as if its blue and yellow coursing had become the energetic lenses of the spectacles.

Then it cleared—and the veil was lifted.

A star thrust itself at me, as if hurtling meteorically toward us. It advanced with such malevolent determination that I wanted-ed to throw myself aside—but suddenly it stopped partway, and simply whirled in place. The shining planetoid—for so it was, churning with glowing gases—was so bright I could scarcely bear the sight.

The planet's whirling slowed, then ceased, and a black spot appeared on its face. This spot swelled and grew, consuming most of the shining planetoid, until all that was left was a kind of corona, and then something that cannot be described as *a shape* appeared within the coruscating circle. The apparition was a writhing *thought* made visual—a thought of annihilation, a thought of conscious mockery of all faith, a derision of all order; yet it had something of organism at its very centre. It reached out . . . And a horrible fascination took hold of me. I was shaking with fear, and yet I wanted to *know* . . .

"Behold Azathoth," Al-Azizi intoned. "Behold he who awaits when I have done with you, Coleridge! With your own free will have you gazed upon this majesty. Now—"

"No!" someone shouted.

It was Carter. A moment later I felt his spongy, pudgy hand slap my face—and the spectacles were knocked away.

Freed from the vision, if that is what it was, I was dizzy, nauseated, and my head throbbed. I saw that someone, probably Carter, had kicked over the serpentine instrument as well, and the dull late afternoon light was assaultive to my burning eyes in that moment.

Blinking, I turned, and saw that Al-Azizi, the crocodilian bag clutched in his hands, was stalking angrily toward Renwald Carter, who was backing away step by hesitant step toward the edge of the roof. He was about to pitch over backwards, off the roof to his death.

"You, sir! Al-Azizi!" I roared, putting all my will and volume into it. *"Stop!"*

Al-Azizi turned toward me, his face an icy mask of fury.

As if released from some unseen hold, Carter blinked and looked around, then turned and rushed to the stairs, clattering down them toward the garden. "I'm sorry, Coleridge!" he shouted as he went. "I'm sorry!"

Al-Azizi walked toward me—and seemed to come to some kind of decision. A most unpleasant smile appeared under his mustache. "Better to have one so choice as *you,* Coleridge, at a time of my own choosing. I have learned much about you today. Next time you will have no recourse. I will send my messenger to fetch you from your body. It matters not where you go. Verily, I can count on you to come to *me.* You hovered close to me many times, in years past, in what you supposed were dreams . . ."

Keeping his eyes upon me, he opened the crocodilian bag. I heard a hissing sound, and then he closed the bag and turned away. In a moment he had gone to the spiral stairs and descended them with no sound at all.

I looked at the rooftop. The Egyptian's instruments were gone. I have no doubt he had somehow gathered them into his bag.

My knees gave way, and I sank down to the cold metal roof. I found I was panting and close to weeping, trying to take it all in. The thing I had seen coming at me from the planetoid . . . another illusion?

But De Quincey, it was no illusion. You cannot look upon that entity and not recognise the dreadful thing for what it is.

I wish I had looked away. Carter saved me, in a moment of conscience—which can sometimes set a man free. I wonder what price he has paid for knocking those spectacles aside.

I wish I could say I removed those spectacles myself, De Quincey. I could not have done so, I fear, to my shame. Scientific knowledge is good; but I was nigh surrendering to a predatory alien mind, to an embrace of all chaos and a lust for entropy itself—and *that,* my old, disaffected friend, has not scientific objectivity. It is an insight of metaphysics alone.

Suddenly, kneeling there, I realised that I owed Carter a great debt. I forced myself to my feet and tottered to the stairs, hoping to find him, to draw him away from Al-Azizi. To pay the debt in kind.

I went with difficulty down the slippery iron stairs and stumbled through the garden. I saw that the garden gate was open to the lane.

I rushed to it, and through—and to my horror I saw not only Carter, trailing after Al-Azizi, but also Bethesda! The housekeeper was walking along without coat, or handbag, quite methodically following along after the Egyptian.

"Bethesda!" I shouted. "Come back!"

She did not respond, not a twitch.

"Carter!" I shouted. "Wait!"

Carter looked back—imploringly. He desperately wanted to come away from Al-Azizi. But he was drawn inexorably away. They were striding up into the fog, becoming less and less real with each step as the haze, coal smoke perfectly wedded with mist, strove to erase them.

My hands were cold, and so was my heart. But I gathered my courage and started after them. I took a score of steps, beginning to run—then saw a coach waiting for them, just under the gas lamp.

"Stop!" I called, as loudly as I might. "Bring her back, both of you—come back! Coachman, hold!" I stumbled on, almost falling on the slick cobbles.

I arrived in time to see the coach clatter away, taking Al-Azizi, Carter, and Bethesda with it.

I stood there for a minute, perhaps two, dazed and uncertain. At last I walked slowly back to the house.

Soon after Dr. Gillman came home for dinner, I tried to tell him what had happened; but he thought me addled by a delirium tremens, by delusion due to insufficiency of my habitual dose—for he was late in providing it. Wearily, he unlocked the medical cabinet and poured me twice my usual dosage. As for Bethesda, he supposed she had merely taken up with another "ruffian," as he put it. She had a weakness for sailors.

I thought to explain all to him on the morrow, as he was greatly fatigued and I could not fathom a means to convince him. I bowed, and went to my room with my double dose.

There I sank into a chair and looked dully around at the books covering every wall, their titles unreadable in the dim light of the lamp as if they were cryptic volumes seen in a dream. Before me on my little rosewood writing table lay pen, ink, and paper. I purposed then to write down the events of the day.

I reached for the laudanum before the pen and ink—and found I was reluctant to take the dose. As you know, De Quincey, this reluctance is an untoward turn of events with STC.

Why should I be afraid of something so familiar—so comforting?

The smell of the opiated brandy at last drew me to taking a sip, and then another. Soon it was all down. The increased dose induced me to nod in my chair.

A waking dream settled upon me. I saw a man sleeping in his bed—a man I knew. Then, standing beside the man, I looked through the dusty window and beheld the stars.

One of the celestial orbs rushed toward the window—and a spot appeared on the sphere. But this time the spot became a great black bird that soared toward me, its enormous wings ever so slowly flapping, each flap making the sound of a cracking whip. The messenger! It had not a beak—it had the mouth of a man. It spake!

Nyarlathotep, it said. *He calls you, Coleridge. Come!* And the bird spake again, quite clearly. *Nyarlathotep. He calls you.*

The giant bird, like a roc with a grin, rushed toward me—I struggled away from it, crying, "No!"

The vision suddenly flew asunder.

I sat up, sweating, and shook off the remnants of the dream. But it tried to reassert itself. Again—the bird was diving at me, coalescing from the shadows of the room.

I threw off the bedclothes, ran to the window, flung the sash wide, and breathed in great draughts of cold air. I refused to close the window till the vision had passed.

But the memory will not pass. I saw something more in that dream. That man in the bed—it *was you*, De Quincey—sleeping, doubtless in an opiated slumber. I am afraid that was an omen. He comes for you next!

And what of me? He said, *Verily, I can count on you—to come to me.*

Who is he I wonder? Who in actuality is Al-Azizi? The messenger told me the true name of the "Egyptian"—and I have verified it, of late, as I pore through certain tomes so old they fall apart at my touch.

He is *Nyarlathotep*. He appears in many guises, as a man. But he is not of humanity, De Quincey.

It is a man's mind he wants, you see. He feeds on madness; he profits by the madness he induces in men. A man he drives mad becomes his slave—his inwardly gibbering servant—and eventually what remains is fed to the *thing* I saw residing, for now, within that unknown planet on the far edge of our solar system.

And we give him a doorway to our minds, De Quincey, when we surrender fully to opium. In opiated dreams we go to his realm, you see. And once you have entered his realm, he knows forever where you are.

He has gone to ground, now that I have discovered him. But, in due course, he will find us both—in the astral realm. For we have journeyed there, like children wandering in a forest, often enough. If you do not suffer the pangs of setting opium aside—a terrible tribulation, I know—you will enter his world a step, and two steps, and then three, and he will send his messenger to bring you the rest of the way.

If you and I do not turn aside from the drug, then that predatory enormity, the black, beakless bird, will come to each of us crying its master's name. *Nyarlathotep!*

He has marked you, De Quincey. And if you do not turn away from the drug, as I struggle to do once more—he will claim you.

Every day I try not to take the infernal concoction—in moments of weakness I take a drop or two, but so little I am scarcely affected. This regimen cannot last, I fear. Even now I feel laudanum calling.

There is now no locating Al-Azizi—I have hired men to find him, along with Carter and Bethesda, and the searchers have failed utterly. It cannot be done.

But I know that Nyarlathotep will find me again, when I open the door of my mind to him.

I pray I die before I go to his realm . . . for there is another, far better realm waiting for me, if only I have the strength to get there.

Your Devoted Servant,
Samuel Taylor Coleridge

THE WITNESS IN DARKNESS

From the Division of Stealth Archaeology to Dr. Kyu Kim, Your Eyes Only, Class. Top Secret:

On October 20, 2011, a roughly cylindrical artifact of unknown metal, pentagonally five-sided in cross section, its outer surfaces imprinted with the dot-cluster writing of the Elder Culture, was found by DSA classification team 23, in the Eastern Quadrant Elder Ruins, Antarctica. Retro-analysis lends to the hypothesis that the artifact is an electronic telepathy device, enhanced by sound recording and playback.

Attached to the artifact by rubber band was a scribbled note in a handwriting thought to belong to the geologist William Dyer, who returned to the Antarctic on one additional occasion after his second visit to the so-called "Mountains of Madness."

The legible part of the note reads, "Final return to Antarctic ruins, encounter with Elder One—the creature applied this device from earlier phase of civilization. You'll hear my voice but it is not, ultimately, I speaking; the Elder One has simply used my mind and linguistic lexicon for telepathic translation so as to [water damage has erased the remainder]."

The artifact, when activated by a flow of electricity, produced sound, a playback that seems to be a recording, which is transcribed below.

The recording gives the listener the distinct impression that William Dyer is telepathically channeling a narrative provided by an Elder Thing, a.k.a. a "Great Old One":

I never anticipated being wakened by a blade—by vivisection. Even after my body had been shifted, transported, and exposed to much colder temperatures, I continued my trance.

Reluctant to emerge from my warm suspension, in which I'd been immured for immemorial ages, I slept onward, despite the interference of the pink primates, until the blade wielded by the intruder began to saw away at my skin. My race evolved to be not only beautiful, but tough as tree bark; still he persisted, and finally broke through, digging ever deeper into my flesh with his cold, unrelenting knife-edge, gouging and probing. The exquisite agony, the sheer unthinkable intrusion of it, burst the bubble of my dream.

When the outrage at last forced open my eyes, the pink primate made a pathetic squalling noise and backed away. My tentacles lashed about his forelimb, and I snatched the edged probe from him, immediately giving him a taste of his own vivisection. He did not survive the process.

If he'd only left me in slumber! Had I awakened in my own good time I would have treated him more kindly. He was descended from some of our creations, after all. Abandoned, the primates developed without guidance, and he knew no better. Tragedy upon tragedy might have been averted if he'd left me to my limitless contemplation in the dark place where I lay rooted, enraptured, deep under the polar crust of this world. . . .

I know now that this world has circled the sun millions of times since first my people came here. I should explain that I did not come to this world with our pioneers—I was spored here, gestated on this world, after the wars reduced our numbers, the diminution making reproduction necessary.

How I long to see the homeworld! But it seems unlikely now. The art of traveling between worlds has been lost to those of us who survive on this outpost. It is true that we can *prepare* ourselves to travel in the great void; we can increase the density of our inward pockets of hydrogen and helium, so that we rise up and up; we can unfurl our dazzling wings and take the energies of the sky within them and so move on into space. But to open the portals through which we travel the interstellar gulfs—

to enter the tunnels through space itself, wending between star systems—that method is lost to us. Nor do any live, to my knowledge, who can locate the homeworld—who know clearly where it lies. Still, the murals of history give hints. Perhaps someday I will try to find that storied paradise. . . .

Hoary eons have I lived already—and re-lived, in my dormancy. The dreams of my people are not the muddle that I perceive yours to be; instead, they are the revisiting of our lives and the lives of our ancestors, an exploration of the genetic wisdom hidden within our birthing spores.

So vast an account kept me amazed, hypnotized with its epic intricacy. It is an inspiring odyssey to contemplate, from the seas to the swamps of that far-away homeworld; to the grand heights of the mountains and then to the skies, as we developed flight— and thence, when instinct told my ancestors it was time to move on to new worlds, to the Great Migration: soaring through intricate tunnels in space, past networks of effulgence, followed by the anticlimactic descent into the primeval seas of the world you now call "Earth."

Our first residence was in the great, warm oceans of Earth. Only the most primitive organisms had developed in this world, on that long bygone day—my people took those simple one-celled organisms into engineering-skeins and shaped them, nudging their evolution. Over many millennia, we created a variety of creatures; we then let evolution have its head for a time until, judging that primitive primates would be the best clay from which we might sculpt simple servants, we created the ancestors of mankind. Some we allowed to roam, as part of our sprawling scientific experiment; others were turned to simple tasks. Who knew that one day, a descendant of those primitive primates would wrench me from the sacred sleep with a cutting blade?

For the great tasks my people created the shoggoths [*note: approximate transcription of term*]. They were misbegotten, though we didn't know it then. We made them too facile, too adaptable, and too swift. We used hypnotic suggestion to control them, a control that was all too uncertain. Even so, they served us well for millennia: gorgeous creatures they were, fascinatingly odoriferous, their gelatinous bodies capable of startling speed. A most impressive sight with their splendid display of protoplasmic bubbles, their self-luminosity, their myriad eyes capable of forming and unforming as needed. But even then, some of us, shifting our gaze into the infrared and ultraviolet, saw the emotional desperation of the shoggoths; we could see the plangent hunger of their desire to pervade, to dominate, to infuse themselves in all they saw.

Radiated in many spectra, our hypnotic beam bent their will to conform to ours. And so they constructed the great undersea galleries at our behest and later emerged from the depths to erect the façades and beetling walls, the soaring towers and ramparts of our city upon the crags at the southern pole of this world; exuding acids, the shoggoths shaped the stone of the mountains themselves, in any contour that pleased us; they lifted great blocks of hollowed-out stone into place on the shoulders of snowy peaks; they dug hallways and chambers, stacked massive blocks of granite to our specification. We fed them with the abundant creatures feverishly arising within the warm incubator of the nascent world; we praised our servants and perhaps spoiled them, for they forever wanted more—ever more, of everything.

I was there, a part of it all, for the erecting of that Cyclopean splendor, our five-sided metropolis—I myself, though alive for less than a half a million turns about the sun, at the time, was thought gifted enough to design a great deal of it. We called the great colony [*name sounds like a dying man's cough, quite untranscribable*] and we took unspeakable pleasure in its creation. I myself insisted on the five-sidedness, in honor of our ancestors, of the city itself, and in praise of the Five-Sided Eye at the center of the cosmos. Fiveness is consciously replicated in many of the city's structures, and indeed, in other creations, as in our design of a creature you call the "starfish," and in the five fingers we placed on our primates. This motif does more than echo the five-pointedness of our bodily head and basal forms, the perfect, star-like extremities of our physical beings; it was also reverentially resonant of the five-sidedness of the creative principle emanated by the Five-Sided Eye, the Law of Five in vibratory repetition throughout the universe: Step One, the active vibration pulses forth; Step Two, the passive reflects it back; Step Three, the reconciling force arises from the two—thesis, antithesis, synthesis, as your human philosopher had it—and then the reconciling force spins and splits into the active, the passive; Steps Four and Five . . . which again generate the third force, which in turn gives birth to the fourth and fifth—and on, *ad infinitum,* ultimately creating all cosmic phenomena. We hoped to cover much of the surface of this world with five-sided paeans to the Law of Five, but it was not to be.

Still, our capital city, nestled amongst the world's steepest peaks, was the materialization of our shared inner worlds, a reverberant revisiting of the galleries of our ancestors—and too, it spoke of our response to the world you call "Earth"; the entire city was the hallmark, the stamp of our collective identity. It sang of our nature, of course, as well as standing for it; the fluting hollows and tubes we introduced, with exactitude, within the high faces of the mountains, caught the furious perpetual breath of the wind and turned it to traditional melodies we'd brought with us from the homeworld: as if the very atmosphere of this world was chorusing its submission to the greatness of our culture. We often sang along with it, of course, fluting with exquisite harmony; even now the mountains sing, with a melancholic sadness in their voicings . . . of what might have been.

Now all is crumbled; all has become mere ruins.

It was vanity, and an illusion of invulnerability: these were our undoing. Certainly the shift of the planetary axis contributed, along with the subsequent coming of the ice age. Yet we'd have adapted well enough to the encroaching cold were it not for the war with the rebellious shoggoths. . . .

In later times we suffered further attrition in the conflict with the Cthulhuites, those ancient competitors from the stars whom at last we trapped in the glaring asymmetry of R'lyeh beneath the polar seas. For a time the spawn of Cthulhu allied itself with the Mi-Go, further eroding our power, until we drove the vicious, buzzing Mi-Go back to their outpost on that icy world at the outer fringe of this solar system; there they doubtless crouch and murmur still, in subzero, fungally furred warrens under the frozen surface.

But damaged as we were, many of us half-mad with privation and desperation, tormented by the depredations of rebel shoggoths, we failed to prepare properly for the age of ice. Some of our technology was destroyed in a particularly vicious Cthulhuian battle: technology we had no clear memory of having created, after so many long millennia. We could no longer effectively reproduce it, since much was corroded. Those of us who knew the secret of travel between the stars were among the first killed when the shoggoths overran our city—leaving us no escape. In our own dogged time we defeated the shoggoths, but we made the mistake of keeping several rebels for study, to try to understand how the beasts had gone awry. The captive shoggoths pretended to a simplicity that deceived their keepers—and one of them worked out the combination of its energy-prison. The rebels broke free and went on a rampage. There were few of us left to resist. . . .

The memory of that rampage and massacre remains vividly within me—sometimes it seems to cut me from within as the pink primate cut me from without.

I had been meditating on the looping mosaics in the great gallery of remembrance, in the 13th-degree trance, when the breakout happened. I was ecstatically intoxicated by the history panels, seeing them in all five dimensions, including the animated segments hidden from eyes as simple as those of the pink primates, and thus did not hear the first concussions of the latest attack. . . .

And then a shriek of pain penetrated my dreamy musings—and another. I tore myself from my entrancement and turned to the entrance of the great gallery. An overwhelming wave of sheer *reek* swept in first—the rage of the shoggoths expressing itself in malodorous venting—and then a ragged column of my people scurried into the gallery: refugees from the shoggoths, who fumed through the tunnels in pursuit, eye-sprouts flailing as they hooted their mocking cry, *Tekeli-li!* First one shoggoth, then another, squeezed its gelatinous bulk through the entrance; extending plasmic tentacles to entwine their victims, they combined acid secretions with ripples of inner force to rip my fellows to oozing, twitching pieces.

The refugees wailed in poignant despair as the shoggoths dismembered them. Once-beautiful eyes glazed as they rolled across the floor after being torn from five-pointed heads, and souls splashed like oceanic muck, green and sparkling with dying life, puddling on the stone floors. . . .

It was this vision, seared into memory, that drove me into the sleeping trance of hibernation; in the depths of the cavern where, ages later, I was found by the pink primates; for there I fled, a coward but not a fool. Before the shoggoths could reach me I slipped through a narrow side passage and down into the depths, scurrying away with a few others. We impregnated the walls of the hibernation cavern with prickly energies to keep the shoggoths away, but this precaution had no overt effect on the insensitive pink primates, ages after.

At first I hunched in the hibernation cavern, trembling in the blackness, shaking with horror at what I'd seen. It was as if the arrogance of my people had taken physical shape, had materialized and come in person to kill us. In memory, I watched the massacre again and again, in excruciating detail, as each elegantly columnar, fluted five-pointed body of the shoggoth's victims was torn asunder; I saw the viscous shoggoths plucking off wings out of sheer cruelty, before the crunching decapitation . . . I could not bear it. I writhed at the recollection.

So I extruded my vestigial roots and took hold of the cavern's fundament, drawing my nutrient—as the most ancient of the ancients did—directly from soil; in this case, from well-aged bat guano. And rooting myself first in loam and then in slumber, I escaped into an endless procession of glorious ancestral memories. . . .

*

I might have slumbered there—my body muted to survive in the cold, my pulse so slow it barely pulsed at all—until, perhaps, the bloated sun expanded to engulf this world with fire, a billion years hence.

But my trance was weakened by the invasion of the pink primates; by "men" like you; by their uprooting of me, and by the unbidden transport. My dream was stabbed, slashed by a knife blade. And I took command of the blade, returning slash for slash ten times over, in my mind somehow slashing at shoggoths as well as the pink primate. When the "human" at last lay still, I called out a sub-vocal vibratory alarum to my fellows; for others had been transported to the primate's camp.

Spurred by my call, those who had survived this latest atrocity woke. And we might have made our way peacefully back to our cavern. After all, the other pink primates had withdrawn, seeing that I and the others were moving about. One of them carried a weapon and seemed to argue with his companions. There was time to depart. . . .

But then one of us discovered other bodies, the mangled corpses of my people, who'd been sliced open, and who hadn't survived the vivisection, so weakened were they by the ages. One was sliced into sections. Clearly, our dead had suffered hideously in the process—the contortion of agony was there to see in their twisted limbs as they were vivisected, cut apart while alive and paralyzed, till the loss of emerald-tinted lifeblood set them free at last.

That's when the shaggy four-legged ones broke loose from their corral of ice: the furred, raucous creatures you call dogs. Driven mad by some primal response to our smell, they came at us snapping and snarling . . .

The remains of old friends who'd been tortured to death, and the onslaught of the dogs—it was all too much. In fury, and perhaps addled by disorientation, the others went on a rampage. I could not restrain them. They rushed the group of pink primates and dogs, tentacles whipping. A primate used a tubular weapon to fire a lead projectile, injuring one of my fellows, but that was the only damage done, and it was not mortal.

Most of the dogs, then the remaining pink primates—all but one—were torn asunder, shrieking and gasping, then left to bleed out their lives upon the snowy ground. . . .

It all seemed a terrible waste to me. Clearly the pink primates had evolved a rudimentary intelligence. They had developed scientific curiosity of a crude sort, the ability to command lower species, some fairly impressive technology—I discovered a device that transmitted radio waves, probably for messages, in one of the structures of cloth you call tents. We should have been able to communicate with them.

After the attack, I did some dissecting of my own and examined many of the instruments in the tent; I experimented with their primitive devices for making fire and created some heat in the operating tent for other investigations.

Then it was discovered that one of the primates had escaped on a sled, with a surviving dog. (Gedney, the creature means Gedney!) [*Note: this naming of Gedney is the only expostulation from William Dyer himself in this account, the remainder seems to be the "Elder One" resuming Dyer's voice.*] But one dog pulling his sled could not get him far, certainly not rapidly—the primate was forced to help push the sled, piled with his supplies—and we had no difficulty in overtaking him. By this time I was able to persuade the others to allow him to live, for a time. He and the dog were returned to the camp for examination, just as a fierce blizzard commenced. We had to break the dog's neck—it would not be restrained—but the primate did not die immediately. He made some rather loud noises when we allowed him to personally experience vivisection. We bandaged his remains, to preserve him for later dissection.

The weather cleared, and soon we were able to perform the rituals of burial. Digging through the hard snow with tools left by the primates, we buried our dead companions as well as we could. In keeping with the right afterlife preparation, we buried them with their feet pointed to the center of the world, and their heads pointed toward the stars. Over them we inscribed, in ice and snow, the sacred five-pointed symbol, and their names. Some of us left a few traditional artifacts there, to remember them by.

Then, having eaten of the flesh of the dog creatures, and having tasted the primates—we found them less palatable—we hurried back to the city, drawing the sled with us and carrying a few primate artifacts for later examination.

It was an arduous journey. We were glad when we arrived—little did we know what awaited us. We had thought the shoggoths long gone; had passed away or departed. . . .

Most have gone. Not all.

We rested in one of the great chambers, and there I examined the primate artifacts. We attempted an assessment of the ruined city, to see if it might be rebuilt, in the event we chose to spore offspring, but the more we looked at the ruins the more a restoration seemed an unappealing, discouraging task. Quite depressing. And of course, it had been defiled . . .

My own idea was to return to the deep sea, for we are more than an amphibious race, our gills can become operative as needed. And there we could spore freely, build up our population, and construct a new city, a homeland to compete with the civilization of the pink primates. But before we could agree on a plan, one of us probed the depths under the old city too deeply. For there, in an underground sea, lurked the remaining shoggoth, grown gigantic, feeding on the enormous, lumbering, eyeless penguins peculiar to that place. And it did not remain sequestered below.

When I heard the screams and the mocking *Tekeli-li!*, I thought, at first, it was a traumatic memory resurfacing; I could not accept my own perceptions when I saw body parts flung before the furious, oncoming shoggoth: a particularly bloated specimen, its huge gelatinous mass heaving and quivering as it came, its sprouting eyes goggling madly about.

Suddenly I perceived the truth: this was no trauma-spawned memory, but a quivering rebirth of the old horror, a true return of an isolation maddened rogue shoggoth. On it came, raking serrated tentacles among us, hulking implacably toward me . . .

A few of us were able to escape, just as before—but this time, I vowed I would not hide in the caverns—this time I would have my revenge.

My companions retreated into the hibernation cavern, where, so far, the shoggoth dared not go, but at my urging they taunted it, hissing and vibrating on many levels and calling out *Tekeli-li!*

Enraged, the bloated, ancient shoggoth ranged back and forth near the entrance to the hibernation cavern, depositing a great trail of slime—the gleaming muck reeking horribly of its rage. Like a mad sentry it paced, afraid to enter the chamber, kept at bay by the stinging energies we'd impregnated into the rocky walls, restrained by the ancient hypnotic suggestion that made such energies an effective shoggoth repellent.

It continued its stalking, shrugging its heaving body this way and that, slobbering furiously about the entrance—as I busied myself back at the pit it had climbed from.

It was about this time I became aware that two more pink primates had found the city, that they were exploring it. I observed them ogling the history displays in the gallery of remembrance, and watched them from the shadows as they probed more deeply.

Meanwhile, the shoggoth was becoming hungry . . . and at last it put off its vigil and grudgingly returned to the pit for food, seeking after a quick dinner of blind penguins, reaching its den not long before the primates discovered it. It was not far down in its lair when their muttering and flickering lights caught its attention. It swarmed from the depths and pursued them, doubtless driven to mad rapacity at the thought of soft-fleshed primates to feast on, a delicious novelty after countless centuries of fish and penguin.

The primates escaped, with a little help from me, of which they were unaware. I had an intuition that I would one day communicate with one of these primates. I had seen their respectful fascination as they viewed the history panels in the gallery of remembrance. I thought that perhaps one of these "men" might be worth speaking to . . . if a means could be found.

And so it was I who distracted the shoggoth—I called out to it as it pursued them, confusing it, making the rogue turn toward me long enough for the men to find a branching tunnel for escape.

I myself then slipped away, withdrawing up a winding ramp too small for the shoggoth, barely large enough for my own bulk. I had taken the same ramp earlier, preparing certain devices in the maintenance passages over the vast chamber that contained the entrance to the pit.

The frustrated shoggoth returned to its cold, lonely, meal of eyeless penguins—just as I'd hoped. It descended once more into its den. . . .

I had no doubt the shoggoth would be back, if I allowed it. The rogue would eventually work itself up into a fury that might well carry it past the prickling energies of protection in the walls of the hibernation cavern. And it would tear my companions to pieces in its madness.

No. I had vowed it would not happen again.

Thus I activated the simple devices I'd placed around the roof of the chamber. The two primates had long since left the city when I triggered the vibratory cannon I'd brought from our ancient storeroom. The reverberatory blasts went off in a carefully placed ring of detonation, to my great relief, for I was afraid the ancient devices would fail to trigger. But as if expressing long pent-up fury, they roared out on schedule, and stone that had hunched over the pit for more than a million years crackled and buckled, then tumbled, in great slabs, into the pit, with a titanic roar that shook the city, and spurred many a landslide.

The great galleries, the tunnels shuddered and the passageways trembled, so that I was afraid the ruins would collapse in their entirety; the very air groaned, choking with dust as boulders fell from above.

But at last the ruins subsided into silence, with the occasional whisper of trickling debris.

I had to pick my way through the wreckage, but reached the entrance to the pit—and confirmed that it was quite choked with stone, as planned. The way was sealed, and the shoggoth was trapped, far below.

Or so I pray! I call out to the Five-Sided Eye to make it so. Will it in time find its way through some unknown subterranean pathway to invade the upper world and wreak vengeance on us? It's possible.

For it lives down there, still. I can occasionally feel its mind thrumming from the depths.

Those few of us who survive plan to return to the deepest trenches of the sea, to the dark, unfathomable places where warm sulfurous vents create a swarm of primal life to feed upon. . . .

There we will root, and ponder, and strengthen, until the time has come at last to spore. Do not seek us there. We have learned to value our privacy, and we will fight for it.

One of the pink primates who viewed our history panels did indeed return to the ruined city; he returned a final time, long after he penned the account I perceive in his mind: his apologia for the invasion of our hibernation cavern, for the murder of my people. I confronted him, and we chose communication over violence.

I had long carried the telepathic translation device with me, in anticipation of this moment. The primate allowed me to apply it to his mind, to delve into his brain, use his language and manner of speaking for this communiqué, this account of myself—this warning:

Do not disturb our city again. The shoggoth lives! It may have learned how to reproduce, despite the inhibition we once placed in it against the process. There may be more of them now.

Disturb them, probe where you are not wanted, and they will arise, and spawn, and spread. And you will suffer as we did.

I have seen that your primate race, descendants of those we created, are perhaps advanced enough now to have stored up a little wisdom. Thus I leave you this device, and its message to your higher selves. May the Five-Sided Eye guide you; may the Law of Five unfold for you.

May you understand when to leave well enough alone.

There, Dyer's voice comes to a stop, the recording ends, and we end our transcription of it. As to Dyer, he died in obscurity, in a remote New England village. No other account by him of his final journey to the "Mountains of Madness" has been discovered. . . .

This department can only recommend that the long-maintained suppression of public knowledge of the Antarctic ruins be continued indefinitely; that we take the Elder One's advice.

And we remember these words by the philosopher Schopenhauer: "The fundament upon which all our knowledge and learning rests is the inexplicable."

Perhaps the final learning is this: leave some dark corners of the inexplicable . . . unexplained.

HOW DEEP THE TASTE OF LOVE

Sid Drexel was just totally into it. He was so fucking happy it stank from him. Just coincidentally, his wife was dead.

He was sitting in the bar of Tuffy's, the "Hottest Little Singles Bar in the Bay Area," and the place was jiggly with women. Some already had men talking to them, but there were women sitting in twos and threes who were only marking time with each other while they waited for a Sid Drexel to make his move.

Drexel could barely keep himself glued to his barstool. He bobbed his head to the MTV stuff coming from the hidden speakers near the big-screen TV, he chewed handfuls of twig-like pretzel sticks, and he made rude noises with his straw in the soupy dregs of his second strawberry daiquiri.

Drexel decided to wait till it was time to make his move. Having no one to talk to, he spoke to the bartender, an almost unnaturally good-looking guy with a golden tan, wearing an odd sleeveless tuxedo. The bartender had pumped-up arms, and he moved with no wasted motion as he poured things, shook things, gave things, accepted things, wiped things; Drexel admired the way one smooth action became another.

"Tom Cruise's got nothing on you," Drexel said.

The bartender glanced at him as he opened a glass-washing machine. The look seemed to ask if Drexel was in the wrong kind of bar.

"I mean," Drexel hastened to explain, "that movie *Cocktail*—Tom Cruise played this slick bartender—"

"Oh. Yeah. Thanks." The bartender did a sort of glissade to the Jack Daniel's bottle, sweeping it off its rack and pouring all in the same motion.

"My wife's dead," Drexel announced, beaming at him. "I mean, it's a shame and all. But, tell you the truth—"

"Oh, I understand," the bartender said. He took someone's money for the Jack Daniel's. There was a small tattoo of a $ inside a toothy mouth on the bartender's tanned forearm.

"You understand?" Drexel asked, rhetorically. "You know what I mean? Twenty-one and a half years married, my friend! You know what else?" But Drexel decided not to say it: that he had once considered killing Helen. Not too long ago, either. But—too risky. And divorce? Jeez, with his contracting business and California's community-property laws, she'd take him for half of everything, but *this* way . . . Boom! A car accident! And none of his doing. It was so sweet that the cops had checked her car to see he hadn't messed with the brakes or something. But he hadn't, really hadn't; he'd just been lucky. And he still felt lucky.

"Maybe it's the dance training," the bartender said, with narcissism glazing his eyes. He looked at Drexel. "The reason I can do the Tom Cruise behind the bar."

"You're a dancer?"

"Why you think so many ladies are here? To see you?" A crooked grin said he meant no offense. He nodded toward the small, circular, tinsel-curtained stage. "Male dancers for the ladies. My bar shift ends in twenty minutes. Five dancers in all."

"Oh." Thud. There it was. The ladies were here to see guys undulating their muscle tone on the stage. "And I got to leave?"

"'Fraid so. In twenty minutes it becomes ladies only. But come back after showtime." He winked. "At eleven." He drifted over to talk to a tall, busty blonde woman with skin that looked faintly blue in this light. The bartender looked directly at Drexel, then back at the blonde.

Eleven, he'd said. *Eleven?* Drexel would be half in the bag by then, or half asleep. He had to get something *going* with someone. Helen was in the ground a month now; he had given himself a week's vacation, he had plenty of money, he had that pricey Mercedes convertible that Helen had bitched about, and he had his looks. Okay, sure, his face was sagging around the edges, and he had that pattern-baldness thing starting up, but he was still a good-looking guy . . . Maybe he should have had his teeth cleaned.

Don't worry about it, he told himself. Just—*go for it.* Life is short. And Helen had been very particular. Everything had to be just *so* when she did it.

Except for a couple of whores watching the clock the whole time, and Billy Jane Dotts in her parents' garage, Helen had a corner on Drexel's sexual experience. And Helen was not into . . . exploring. You read those magazines—*Forum,* things like that—people wrote in all kinds of letters about every damn kinky thing in the book. Like there was nothing weird about it, in particular. Like it was okay. But Helen wouldn't even talk about it, let alone—

"Excuse me. Is this seat taken?" It was that blonde . . .

No, came the reply in Drexel's head, is yours? But he was savvy enough to say, instead, "Nope. Have a seat."

She was damn good-looking. Smooth skin—still looking blue-black—beautifully Asiatic eyes, the shape of her face maybe Hispanic, some kind of foxy crossbreed. The hair looked like a wig, but so what? And those *tits.* God! She sat with her shoulders thrown back, chest jutting in her tight cream-colored sweater. It was sewn with black beads in an odd pattern he almost recognized but knew he'd never seen. He didn't spend much time looking at the beads. Her breasts were almost too magnificent to be real. Then, too, she had that wig. And she was tall. *Maybe . . .*

He looked at her closer. *Some kind of transsexual?*

He looked at her neck, her lips, and her cheekbones. No way: this was a woman.

She looked frankly back at him. "Aren't you going to offer? I mean, here's the first guy I've met all night I'd like to buy me a drink, and he's the only one not offering."

"Oh—well, shit, I mean—yeah! Bartender! Hey, pal, anything this lady wants. I'll have another . . . right?"

She said her name was Sindra. She had some kind of slight accent he couldn't place, maybe Middle Eastern. She sat very quietly, but he had a feeling she was just bursting with something inside, like him. *We're two of a kind.*

He prided himself on his sense of humor, so he tried telling her a joke. The bartender listened in, wiping the bar. The only one that'd come to mind was: "So this guy comes into a bar with a frog growing out of his forehead! A whole, live frog! And the bartender says, 'Hey buddy, how'd the hell that happen?' And *the frog* says, 'I dunno, it started out as a wart on my butt.'"

She stared at him for a moment; he seemed to have startled her, somehow. She and the bartender exchanged looks.

Then she laughed politely. "Do you believe in omens, Sid? Hmm?"

Drexel shrugged. "Sure. I hope it's a lucky omen, whatever it is. Say, pal, can I get another?"

He got only halfway through the daiquiri before an amplified voice interrupted the MTV T&A to announce the men had to leave in five minutes for the ladies only show. The ladies clapped and whooped.

"Well hell! I guess you're waiting for the show, huh, Sindra?" Drexel asked. He thought that was a pretty smooth segue.

"Actually, no," Sindra said, adding gravely, "No, I'm . . . waiting for you, I think. I need someone to live out some dreams with. Tonight."

He felt his groin churn with blood. "Yeah? Man, I've been waiting for someone like you for . . ." And it all came tumbling out. She listened, nodding, as they put on their coats, and without ever having to discuss it, walked out to the parking lot to his car. On the way out, Drexel absently noticed the bartender up onstage, half nude, throwing his muscles suggestively around, and she didn't even glance at the guy, *not once,* and the bartender gave them a long look that might have been a kind of resentment.

"I understand exactly what you've been going through," she told Drexel, holding his gaze with hers as they stood by the white convertible, in the monoxide velvet of the warm Indian summer night.

He hadn't noticed, in the bar, how golden her eyes were. Golden—or almost lemon-colored.

"I was in the same position—in more ways than one—with my husband of many years," Sindra said. "He would try nothing new. And sex is like a continent. A tropical continent. It must be explored to be appreciated. Don't you agree?"

"Hey, listen, I—Okay, maybe it sounds like one of those things that's just ... that everyone ... that's—What's the word?"

"Trite? Cliché?"

"Right! Trite, like, but Sindra, I couldn't agree more. I am just totally there with you."

They got into the car and he started it up, drove out into the street. Glancing at her from time to time ... in wonder.

He hadn't gotten to his forties without knowing when something was too good to be true. If some guy wanted to pay you three times the rate to build something that was too easy to build, it was always too good to be true. The mob was covering up something, or there was some other hassle behind it.

And he knew Sindra was too good to be true. Women like her just didn't come at you this easily.

"Don't they?" Sindra said.

"What?" He did a double take.

"I can see it in your expression. You don't trust me. 'People don't do this sort of thing.' There are some one-night stands, but women who ... well ..."

"Women as good-looking as you don't offer to, you know, uh—"

"Fulfill a man's every fantasy within minutes of meeting him?" She smiled. "I didn't offer that."

"Oh. Right. I, uh—"

"But you're right: I was going to. I still am."

"Uh, is there, I mean—"

"No charge. Unless you cost something."

He laughed. "Hey—for you, it's free."

They both enjoyed that. He was having one motherfucker of a good time. He really was.

"How would you know if things like this never happen?" Sindra asked. "Living with your Helen, you'd be out of circulation. But you must have heard about it happening to other people." She was slightly hunched down in her seat to keep her wig out of the wind streaming over the open top of the convertible.

They were tooling down the 580 toward the turn-off that'd take them into the Berkeley Hills, where Sindra lived. Drexel replied, "I've heard of people having encounters like that, but you always figure those stories are bullshit."

"No. It's simply . . . rare. Rare that it comes true. See, it only comes true for *special people,* who are into *special things.* And those people are rare. They're *select.* A kind of sexual elite. And they're carefully selected."

"You *selected* me? Like you've been watching me?"

She hesitated. "No. No, but—I have a special instinct for these things. That's why they send me."

His hands got sweaty on the steering wheel. "They?"

"Here's the exit."

He took it, mechanically. "You said *they?* Who's *they?*"

"Perhaps I should have said we. You did say you wanted to experiment. To really live. Go into some new directions. Why don't we talk about it frankly? You can tell me: what sorts of things did you want to try?"

"Uh . . . well . . ." Could he really tell her?

"Tell you what; I'll go first. Turn right at the next light. Best get in the right lane. That's it. I'm into being tied up with my own panties, given golden showers, then covered in fragrant oil and gang-fucked. Among other things."

If he'd been in a cartoon, his lower jaw would have bounced on his lap.

"Jesus," he said, shaking his head in admiration. "'Among other things'? I really—I admire that. How you can just come out and talk about that and . . . and not only talk about it. This is great. I always wanted to . . . well, lots of stuff. Two girls. And being . . . being spanked by two girls. And they make me do things. Then I spank them. And make them do things."

"Turn right again. Up the hill here. Turn left at the corner."

"Up near the big burn-out, huh?" They were driving through the hills charred by the Berkeley-Oakland fire of '91. The black ash had seeped away in the rains, except along the concrete foundation lines of the burned houses most of the ground was gray and muddy and erosion-raked. Chimneys jutted here and there like those termite towers you see in pictures of arid African plains.

He drove onto her cul-de-sac. The fire had been a windfall for Drexel's contracting business, but he hadn't been on this particular street. All the houses were burned away except one, with thick brush around it. Brush that should have burned, he would have thought.

"Yes, we were lucky in the fire. The neighbors were crowding us." She smiled distantly. "'Make people do things,' you said. What sort of things?"

"Hm? Oh, God."

"Come on. I told you mine."

"Right. Chewing on people. Chewing on feet. Clean feet, of course. Chewing on private parts. Not . . . not hurting anything but . . . sucking and chewing on fingers and toes and nipples, really *chewing* . . . God, it feels good to just . . ." He shifted in his seat. He hadn't been this hard since his teens.

He parked in front of her house. Drexel had flirted with archi-tecture in his one year of community college; he recognized the house as an old Maybeck, heavy on the dark wood, the intricate levels and the big windows. The yard was overgrown; he didn't recognize most of the plants. There were pines encircling the place, and more pine and fir, singed survivors of the fire, march-ing down the hill behind it. Berkeley, much of Oakland would be visible on the other side of the house, maybe even San Francisco.

They went up the mossy flagstones; brown pine needles fringed the stones, and stiff silvery-green brush pressed in from both sides of the winding path. Sindra stepped over something on the porch—something that made Drexel backpedal a few steps. A large gray tarantula. It made tentative, feathery move-ments, like the fingers of an anxious piano player, and slipped in-to the succulents lining the porch. "It's that time of year in the East Bay hills," Sindra said, noticing his reaction. "It gets warm and they come out and mate." She unlocked the door and they went in. It was cool and moist here and smelled of mildew. They passed along a dim hallway to a living room. There were picture windows that should have looked down on Berkeley—but they were covered with red cellophane. There were large, shapeless cushions on the hardwood floor. Nothing else to sit on.

He stood awkwardly in the flushed light by the window as Sindra went to the built-in bar. There were paintings on the walls, but standing here he couldn't quite make them out.

Sindra knelt beside a small refrigerator—the movement tightened the skirt around her rump. She took out a Mason jar of dark liquid and poured some into two cups with a little cola. "I make a mind-fuck of a cocktail," she said. "I keep it pre-mixed."

She brought the glasses back to him, and they each drank. The stuff was both sweet and acrid. He couldn't quite . . .

"What is it?"

"Tarantula venom, partly," she said, as he began to twitch.

Even in his toxic delirium, he thought passingly: Her breasts must be silicone. Too perfect, too firm.

She was on her back, nude, legs spread, her whole body beckoning. Her breasts looked violet in this light, with purple-brown nipples. They were vast, jutting, round, perfect, and just impossible.

But they weren't silicone. One of the whores had been silicone-enhanced that time. Kneeling between her legs exploring with his hands, he knew: This wasn't the same. This was . . .

Her breasts were meaty. They were *big* breasts, not like enhanced pectorals, and she had a real vagina; it wasn't as if she were some kind of transsexual, no. But her breasts seemed utterly filled with muscle. Meat. Which was impossible, wasn't it?

He thought about all of this for maybe two and a half drugged seconds. Then the convulsions hit him.

*

After a while the convulsions stopped scaring him. And not long after that they stopped entirely.

It was all the same to Drexel: he had gone through the panic and sickness stage, and now, with the psychedelic effects of the high-dose venom, he was riding waves of psychotic exultation through a storm of light. The storm's colors were sultry shades of the primaries, with neon variants of violet and emerald and gold, whipping past him in arching, interweaving wires, like lasers gone rubbery. The wires of light dove into him and careened down his spine, each color a different sensation; other lights arched over him like the buttresses of some infinitely refined cathedral, where even the building stories were of stained glass. And occupying completely the floor of the cathedral was the naked Sindra and her impossibly perfect breasts.

He'd twitched his clothes off, and his manhood was hard as teak. She took him immediately into yielding slickness, and his face into her cleavage.

There was a delightful scent off her that was like venison and gardenias with just a touch of frying trout. It translated into taste as he thrust his tongue into her meaty cleavage; he rocked back from her a little with the intensity of the feeling, a sexual sensation as palpable as the heat waves you felt rolling off the tarmac when you stepped off a plane in hot-season Florida. "Jezzusyeah . . Jezzusyeah . . ." His heart felt like a molten lump. He couldn't quite talk. "Jezzusyeahfuggincredibuh . . . Yuhincredibuh . . ."

"Why, thank you, Sid," she said quite clearly, her voice chiming against the incandescent glass of the air.

He shoved up into her and he seemed to go farther than was physically possible—as if the cleft of her kept parting, wider and wider, as if he were wading into her, as a man might wade into a swamp.

And her nipple in his mouth—it moved, the nipple *probed* in his mouth . . .

"Bite it, sweetheart," she said, sweetly and lucidly.

"Yuhruhllywahmuh?"

"I really do. Bite it hard."

He bit down, and forty years of frustration came rollicking out of him, singing. A lifelong weight he'd taken for granted simply curtsied and left him. This was *way* better than he'd hoped for.

"Bite harder, much harder. Yes. Now harder still." Her voice was quite clear and insistent, there was no mistaking it, but it was hard to believe she wanted . . .

"Harder."

"Yuh sure?"

"Oh, yes."

He bit down as hard as he could, and if he hadn't been in unspeakable ecstasy he would have screamed in revulsion as her skin parted under his teeth. As his teeth sank into the meat of her.

"Now chew it up."

Oh, no. But he could no more spit it out than a two-year-old boy could spit out his first taste of real candy. Maybe he'd be sorry later, maybe he'd be explaining it to the police and the *National Star* and specialists in criminal psychiatry, but right now was *right now* more than it ever had been, and this was the most delicious bite he'd ever taken; it was the most satisfying oral sensation he'd ever felt. Her flesh was drugged. It was cocaine and heroin and Quaaludes, oozing velvety fingers of electric delight into his brain.

As he chewed, he waited, rather abstractedly, for her to scream and push him away. But after he swallowed—that itself a deeply satisfying act, awakening unheard-of erogenous zones in his esophagus—she demanded, *"Take another bite. A big one."*

When he hesitated, she said, "Bite and chew it up and swallow! *It doesn't hurt me."*

He ate most of her right breast and was working on the left before he began to feel full. And even then he could feel the bitten-off breast *melting* in his stomach . . . dissolving into him, more rapidly than with anything so banal as digestion. The taste was of meat, almost a sausage but more delicately flavored, and some sort of exotic fruit pie, and just a *faint* touch of blood, hardly any at all, and a faint under flavor of something he'd had at a Japanese restaurant. Roe? Sea-urchin eggs?

And the texture: wonderfully creamy, but with just the right meaty resistance to his mastication.

He could hardly breathe, with his sticky face thrust deeply into the rind of her left breast. But he couldn't get enough; he was infinitely hungry, endlessly consumed by lust. His hips thrusting, his maleness working almost incidentally in her (orgasm was not an issue, so to speak—he was far beyond that), he devoured the pulpy wet blue-violet glory, working his way greedily down into the breast, down to a sort of root . . . like the little nubbin one finds at the inside bottom of a pumpkin, a kind of internal stalk. He gnawed at the stalk, sucking away the last of the drugged flesh around it—and she said, "That's about right, I'd say."

The stalk opened and took hold of his tongue.

Someone in the background said, "Are you in full contact?" A man's voice.

"Yes," she said. "I have him."

He tried to pull free, of course; both extensions of him were pinned, and pain warned him not to try again. The pain was as intense as the pleasure. It commanded him to stillness.

He was still drunk on her; the high had programmed a profoundly somatic trust in him. He was hers.

A man squatted behind Drexel and thrust something in Drexel's ass.

But he knew from the shape of it—it hadn't been a penis. It was a rounder, more truncated shape. It dissolved, like the stuff in his stomach, and seeped into him.

He saw someone else out of the corner of his eye—another man, kneeling by Sindra's head. Bending, thrusting his hips toward her face.

She bit off the man's penis and chewed it up, her smile droopy with euphoria.

The man arched his back, but not in pain. This wasn't something masochistic. There was no blood at the bitten-off root between his legs. Only the same bluish pulp at the stub.

Drexel couldn't see the man's face clearly from this awkward angle. But he recognized the tattoo on the muscular arm: *the bartender*.

He felt something flush into him through his tongue; tingling, interpenetrating. Something else warmly *hissing into* his trapped genitals, like a backward ejaculation. Some secretion entering him from her. He sensed that the seeming penis that Sindra had bitten off, the flesh of the bartender, had been *processed through her* somehow and was now entering Drexel, fertilizing the meaty secrets he'd swallowed.

*

Most of the time he would lie passively in the low, bowl-shaped bed, squirming only occasionally, when the internal sensations unsettled him. Now he reposed dreamily, listening to her soothing. Sindra was standing over him, telling him a few things just to keep him quiet, so it would all seem natural. So he wouldn't struggle, though there was little struggle left in him. His limbs had merged arm into arm, leg to leg. There wasn't much he could do. The inhabited flesh he'd swallowed, with the secretions that she and the men of her peculiar species had mixed into it, were changing him; were guiding him, on a cellular level, along some metamorphic byway of synergenesis.

She remained nude when she was in the house; so did the "bartender." So did the others: the women with the slightly blue skin, their heads, when they'd removed their wigs, furred with the faintly waving blue polyps; the men with golden polyps on their craniums, their skin softly gold. It was not a tan.

The bartender's penis was growing back.

As Sindra stood beside Drexel, gazing at his changing body and smiling beatifically, he could see that her breasts were already rapidly growing back as well; the little stalks were covered over, the rinds of the old breasts fallen neatly away. At this rate she'd be back up to size in a week.

A little boy came to the incubator bed—a boy of about five, nude and golden-skinned but without the quivery polyps on his scalp the others had. More than once he'd come to look at Drexel with some unspoken personal fascination.

Sindra shooed the boy away with a murmur, then turned to the bed, reached in, and stroked Drexel as she spoke. "It's all a cycle, a natural, beautiful cycle, Sidney. We have a pact with them—we call them the Guests. They are the brethren of the Akishra; they are a branch on the family tree of the Old Ones. Their world intertwines with ours in places; we've always had a sort of overlapping ecology with it, with their dimension. A lot of the Old Gods were just people altered by the Guests, Siddy.

We had to leave Dunwich, to find those suitable . . . new blood . . ." She cocked her head thoughtfully, looking for the most calming way to explain: "Some of us are suitable to be hosts to the Guests—and others are to be incubators for their young. It's to do with your DNA, I suppose, and your spiritual type. It's something we can sense. Carl and I sensed you were perfect incubator material—and so you are! Not everyone is suitable, so it's fortunate the Guests only need to lay once or twice a year.

"The Guests use us as hosts—people like me, and Carl, your 'bartender'—and they change us and give us life. A very, very long life with many pleasures. They pass through us to you incubators, and we feel no pain, and our lives are sweet and varied." She paused to stroke his swelling belly.

"They've passed fully into you, Sidney; *you* brought the *layings* of the Guests in, hungrily, and willingly. I used the venom of our pets to make it faster. And because I enjoy it. But we didn't really need the drug. *You wanted me that way, Sidney*—and now you're fulfilled!"

She crouched beside the incubator bed, letting him try out his feeble protest, which came out as unintelligible mutterings. She stroked him and pinched one of her own nascent nipples thoughtfully as she went on.

"Hush, hush, and lay still, Sid. The real miracle is still to come. We fertilized that which you devoured from me; from my breasts; it's growing in you. You won't be one of us; they need you differently. But you'll have your own rewards . . ."

She bent near him with a sponge of nutrients, sweet and syrup-thick, blowing kisses at his muted lips.

*

At the *Feedtime,* the time of reconfiguration, they no longer had to soothe him. The unneeded part of him was gone. It was displaced when the one who had grown in his belly moved up, through the passages within, and entered his skull for its first feeding.

Sindra and Carl and the boy and the others knelt beside the incubation bed. Hugging one another in excitement, they watched as the transformation achieved its penultimate stage.

The Guest had moved into Drexel's head like a hermit crab into a seashell. Now the onlookers gasped in wonder and joy, like anyone privileged to watch a birth, as Drexel's head detached itself from his neck and crawled—*the head crawled*—on its gastropodic underside down the length of Drexel's body. It began to graze contentedly, nourishing itself on his flesh. It would fill itself thus until the *Growtime* should come, and then the bonding with a host: the little boy who watched eagerly and happily beside his parents, Carl and Sindra. The boy had been instructed in what to expect; he would not become an incubator like Drexel—he would become a carrier for a Guest, like Carl and Sindra, immortal and perfect.

The boy watched rapturously as the Guest in Drexel's head fed on the body it had quit; he watched in a glow of anticipation, eager for the day the Guest should be ready to join with him, to bring him into the manhood of his people.

BURIED IN THE SKY

"If he didn't kill Mom, then why are we moving away?" Deede asked.

"We're *moving* because I have a better job offer in L.A.," Dad said, barely audible as usual, as he looked vaguely out the living-room window at the tree-lined street. Early evening on a Portland June. "I'll be working for a good magazine—very high-profile. See those clouds? Going to rain again. We won't have all this rain in L.A. anyhow, and Hanging Gardens will be a nice change. You'll like L.A. high schools—the kids are very . . . uh . . . hip." Wearing his perpetual work shirts, jeans, and a dully stoic expression, he was a paunchy, pale, gray-eyed man with shaggy blond hair just starting to go gray. He stood with his hands in his pockets, gazing outward from the house. In a lower voice he said, "They said it was an accident or . . ." He didn't like to say suicide. "So—we have to assume that's right and, well, we can't harass an innocent man. Better to leave it all behind us."

Deede Bergstrom—waist-length sandy-blond hair, neo-hippy look—was half watching MTV, the sound turned off; on the screen a woman wearing something like a bikini crossed with a dress was posturing and pumping her hips. Deede's hips were a shade too wide and she'd never call attention to them like that.

Deede knew Dad didn't want the travel writer job in L.A. that much—he liked Portland, he didn't like Los Angeles, except as a subject for journalism, and the travel editor job with the Portland newspaper paid their bills. He was just trying to get them away from the place where Mom had died because everything they saw here was a reminder. And they had to get over it.

117

Didn't you have to get over it, when someone murdered your mother?

Sure. Sure you do. You just have to get over it.

"You think he killed her too, Dad," said Lenny matter-of-factly, as he came in. He'd been in the kitchen, listening. The peanut butter and jelly sandwich dripped in his hand as he looked at his dad, and took an enormous bite.

"You're spilling blueberry jelly on the carpet," Deede pointed out. She was curled up in the easy chair with her feet tucked under her skirt to keep them warm. The heat was already turned off, in preparation for the move, and it wasn't as warm out as it should have been, this time of year.

"Shut up, mantis-girl," Lenny said, the food making his voice indistinct. He was referring to her long legs and long neck. He was a year older than Deede, had just graduated from high school. His hair was buzz-cut, and he wore a muscle shirt—he had the muscles to go with it—and a quizzical expression. His chin was a little weak, but his features otherwise were almost TV-star good-looking. The girls at school had liked him.

"Lenny I've asked you not to call your sister that, and go and get a paper towel and clean up your mess," Dad said, without much conviction. "Deana, where's your little sister?"

They called her Deede because her name was Deana Diane. Deede shrugged. "Jean just leaves when she wants to . . ." And then she remembered. "Oh yeah, she went rollerblading with that Buzzy kid."

Lenny snorted. "That little stoner."

Dad started to ask if Lenny a good reason to think his youngest sister was hanging with stoners—Deede could see the question was about to come out of him—but then his lips pinched shut. Decided not to ask. "Yeah, well, Buzzy won't be coming with us to L.A., so . . ." He shrugged.

Dad was still looking out the window, Deede mostly watching the soundless TV.

And Lenny was looking at the floor while he listlessly ate his sandwich, Deede noticed, looking over from the TV. *Dad out the window, me at TV, Lenny at the floor.*

Mom at the interior of her coffin lid.

"I think we should stay and push them to reopen it," Deede said, doggedly.

Dad sighed. "We don't know that Gunnar Johansen killed anyone. We know that Mom was jogging and Johansen was seen on the same jogging trail and later on she was found dead. There wasn't even agreement at the coroner's on whether she'd been—"

He didn't want to say *raped*.

"He was almost bragging about it," Lenny said tonelessly, staring at the rug, his jaws working on the sandwich. "'Prove it!' he said." Deede could see the anger in his eyes, but you had to look for it. He was like Dad, all internal.

"It was two years ago," Deede said. "I don't think the police are going to do anything else. But we could hire a private detective." Two years. She felt as if it were two weeks. It had taken almost six months for Deede to be able to function again after they found Mom dead. "Anyway—I saw it . . . in a way."

"Dreams." Dad shook his head. "Recurrent dreams aren't proof. You're going to like L.A."

She wanted to leave Portland—and she also wanted to stay here and make someone put Johansen in jail. But she couldn't stay here alone. Even if she did, what could she do about him, herself? She was afraid of him. She saw him sometimes in the neighborhood—he lived a block and a half down—and every time he looked right at her. And every time, too, it was as if he were saying, *I killed your mom and I liked it and I want to kill you too and pretty soon I will.* It didn't make sense, her seeing all that, when he had no particular expression on his face. But she was sure of it, completely sure of it. He had killed her mom. And he'd liked it. And he had killed some other people and he'd liked that too.

She had no proof at all. Recurrent dreams aren't proof.

". . . the movers are coming in about an hour," Dad was saying. "We're going to have a really good new life." He said it while looking out the window and he said it tonelessly. He didn't even bother to make it sound as if he really believed the part about a really good new life.

*

Two days later, they were ready to go to Los Angeles—and it had finally started to warm up in Oregon, as if it were grudgingly admitting it was the beginning of summer. "Now that we're leaving, it's nice out," Jean said bitterly, from the back seat of the Explorer. The sky was showing through the clouds, and purple irises edging the neighbor's lawn were waving in the breeze. Then, as Deede just sat in the front seat of the car, waiting for her Dad to drive her and her brother and Jean to the I-5 freeway, she saw Johansen walking down the street toward them, walking by those same irises. Dad was looking around one last time, to see if he'd forgotten to do anything, making sure the doors to the house were locked. He would leave the keys for the Realtor in some prearranged place. The house where Deede had grown up was sold and in a few minutes would be gone from her life forever.

Jean and Lenny didn't see Johansen. Lenny was in back beside Jean, his whole attention on playing with the PSP, and Jean was looking at the little TV screen over the back seat of the SUV. Fourteen years old, starting to get fat; her short-clipped hair was reddish brown, her face heart-shaped like Mom's, the same little dimples in her cheeks. She was chewing gum and fixedly watching a Nickelodeon show she probably didn't like.

Deede wasn't going to point Johansen out to her. She didn't much relate to her little sister—Jean seemed to blame Deede for not having the same problems. Jean had dyslexia and Deede didn't; Jean was attention deficit and Deede wasn't. Jean had gotten only more bitter and withdrawn since Mom had died.

She didn't want anyone acting protective. Deede felt she had to try to protect her anyway.

Johansen was getting closer.

"This building we're moving into, it's, like, lame, living in a stupid-ass building after living in a house," Jean said, snapping her gum ever few syllables, her eyes on the SUV's television.

"It's not just any stupid-ass building," Lenny said, his thumbs working the controllers, destroying mordo-bots with preternatural skill as he went on, "it's Skytown. It's like some famous architectural big deal, a building with everything in it. It has the Skymall and the, whatsit, uh, Hanging Gardens in it. That's where we live, Hanging Gardens Apartments, name's from some ancient thing I forget . . ."

"From *Babylon,*" Deede mumbled, watching Johansen get closer. Starting to wonder if, after all, she should point him out. But she grew more afraid with every step he took, each bringing him closer, though he was just sauntering innocently along, a tall tanned athletic man in light blue Lacrosse shirt and Dockers; short flaxen hair, pale eyes, much more lower lip than upper, a forehead that seemed bonily square. Very innocently walking along. Just the hint of a smirk on his face.

Where was Dad? Why didn't he come back to the car?

Don't say anything to Jean or Lenny. Jean would go back to not sleeping at night again, if she saw Johansen so close. They all knew he'd killed Mom. Everyone knew but the police. Maybe they knew too, but they couldn't prove it. The coroner had ruled "accidental death."

Johansen walked up abreast of Deede. She wanted to look him in the eye and say, with that look, *I know what you did and you won't get away with it.*

Their gazes met. His pale blue eyes dilated in response. His lips parted. He caught the tip of his tongue between his teeth. He looked at her—

Crumbling inside, the fear going through her like an electric shock, she looked away.

He chuckled—she heard it softly but clearly—as he walked on by.

Her mouth was dry, very dry, but her eyes spilled tears. Everything was hazy. Maybe a minute passed, maybe not so much. She was looking hard at the dashboard.

"Hanging Gardens," Lenny said, finally, oblivious to his sister's terror. "Stupid name. Makes you think they're gonna hang somebody there."

"That's why you're going to live there," Jean said, eyes glued to the TV. "'Cause they're going to hang you."

"*You're* gonna live there *too*, shrimpy."

"Little as possible," Jean responded, with a chillingly adult decisiveness.

Deede wanted to ask her what she meant by that—but Jean resented Deede's protectiveness. She'd called her "Miss Protective three-point-eight." She resented Deede's good grades—implied she was a real kiss-ass or something to get them. Though in fact they were pretty effortless for her. But it was true, she was too protective.

"Deede?" Dad's voice. "You okay?"

Deede blinked, wiped her eyes, looked at her Dad, opening the driver's side door, bending to squint in at her. "I'm okay," she said.

He never pushed it, hadn't since Mom died. If you said you were "okay," crying or not, that was as good as could be expected. They'd all had therapy—Lenny had stopped going after a month—and it had helped a little. Dad probably figured it was all that could be done.

He got in and started the car and they started off. Deede looked in the mirror and she saw Johansen, way down the street, his back to them. Stopping. Turning to look after them . . . as they drove away from their home.

*

"This place is so huge . . . so high up . . ." Deede, Lenny, and Jean were in the observation deck of the Skytown building, up above Skytown Mall and the apartment complex, looking out at the clouds just above, the pillars and spikes of downtown L.A. below them. They were in the highest and newest skyscraper in Los Angeles.

"It's a hundred-twenty-five stories, fifteen more than the World Trade Center buildings were," Lenny said, reading from the guide pamphlet. "Supposed to be 'super-hardened' to resist terrorist attacks . . ."

Deede remembered what she'd read about the *Titanic,* how it was supposed to be unsinkable, too. Skytown, it occurred to her, was almost a magnet for terrorists. But she wouldn't say that with Jean here, and anyway Lenny had been calling her "Deana Downer" for her frequent dour pronouncements. *"Just an inch the wrong way on that steering wheel and Dad could drive us under the wheels of a semitruck,"* she'd told Lenny, when they were halfway to L.A. Jean had been asleep—but Dad had frowned at her anyway.

"When's Dad coming back?" Deede asked, trying to see the street directly below. She couldn't see it—the "hanging gardens" were in the way: a ribbony spilling of green vines and lavender wisteria over the edges of the balconies encompassing the building under the observation deck. Closer to the building's superstructure were rose bushes too, but the building was new and so were the rose bushes, there were no blossoms on them yet. The building had a square base—filling a square city block—and rose to a ziggurat peak, a step pyramid, the lowest step of the pyramid containing the garden, the penultimate step the observation deck.

"Not till after dinner," Lenny said. "He has a meeting."

"Is this part of, what, the Hanging Gardens Apartments?" Jean asked, sucking noisily on a smoothie.

"No, that's actually down," Lenny said. "This is the observation deck above Skymall. Whole thing is actually called Skytown. The apartments are under the gardens but they're called the Hanging Gardens Apartments anyway, just to be more confusing."

Feeling isolated, lonely, gazing down on the tiny specks that were people, the cars looking smaller than Hot Wheels toys, Deede turned away from the window. "Let's go back to the apartment and wait for Dad."

"No way!" Jean said, talking around the straw. "The apartment smells too much like paint! I want to see the Skymall! We're supposed to have dinner there!" She sucked up the dregs of her smoothie. "And I'm still hungry."

*

At first it was like any mall anywhere, though it was so high up they felt a little tired and light-headed. Deede heard a security guard talking about it to the man who ran the frozen yogurt shop—the young black guard had a peculiar uniform, dark gray, almost black, with silver epaulettes, and the shapes of snakes going around his cuffs. "Yeah, man, we're so high up, the air's a little thin. They try to equalize it but it don't always go. They're working out the bugs. Like that groaning in the elevators . . ."

Windows at the end of the mall's long corridors showed the hazy dull blue sky and planes going by, not that far above, and the tops of high buildings—seeing just the tops from here made them look to Deede like images she'd seen of buildings in Egypt and other ancient places.

There were only a few other customers; they were among the first to move into the building and the mall wasn't officially open to the public, except for the apartment owners. Walking along the empty walkway between rows of glassy storefronts, Deede felt like a burglar. She had to look close to see shopkeepers inside—the ones who noticed them looked at Deede and her siblings almost plaintively. *Please give me some business so I feel like this new invest-*

ment isn't hopeless and doomed to failure. "Sorry, Mister," she muttered, "I don't want to buy any NFL Official Logo gym bags."

"What?" Jean said. "Lenny she's mumbling to herself again."

He sniggered. "That's our Deede. Hey what's that thing?"

He pointed at a window containing a rack of objects resembling bicycle helmets crossed with sea urchins. The transparent spikes on the helmets seemed to feel them looking and reacted, retracting.

"Eww!" Jean said. "It's like critter antenna things!"

The store was called INTER-REACTIVES INC. There was a man in the back, in a green jump suit, a man shaped roughly like a bowling pin, who seemed to have a bright orange face. It must be some kind of colored light back there, Deede decided, making his face look orange. The man turned to look at them. His eyes were green—even the parts that should be white were green.

"Is that guy wearing a mask?" Jean asked.

The man looked at her and a rictus-like grin jerked across his face—split it in half—and was gone. From expressionless to grin to expressionless in half a second.

Deede backed away, and turned hastily to the next store.

"That guy was all . . ." Jean murmured. But she didn't say anything more about it.

You got weird impressions sometimes in strange places, Deede decided. That's all it was.

The next shop was a Nike store. Then came a Disney store, closed. Then a store called BLENDER. Jean stopped, interested: it seemed to sell things to eat. Behind the window glass, transparent chutes curved down into blenders; dropping through the chutes, into the intermittently grinding blenders, came indeterminate pieces of organic material Deede had never seen before, bits and pieces of things: they weren't definitely flesh and they weren't recognizably fruit but they made you think of flesh and fruit—only, the colors were all wrong, the surface textures alien. Some of them seemed to be parts of brightly colored faces—

which seemed to squirm in the blender so that the apparent eye would line up properly with a nose, above lips, the disjointed face looking at her for a moment before being whirred away into bits. But the parts of the faces, when she looked closer, weren't noses or eyes or lips at all. "What *is* that stuff?" Deede asked.

Lenny and Jean shook their heads at once, staring in puzzlement—and the blenders started whirring all at once, making the kids jump a bit. In the back of the store was a counter and someone was on the other side of the counter, which was only about four and a half feet high, but you could just see the top of their head on the other side of the counter—a lemon-colored head. The top of the head moved nervously back and forth.

"Some kid back there," Jean said. "Walkin' back and forth."

"Or some dwarf," Lenny said. "You want to go in and see?" But he didn't move toward the shop. The other two shook their heads.

They moved on, passing an ordinary shop that sold fancy color photo portraits, a store that sold clothing for teenage girls that neither Jean nor Deede would be interested in—it was for cheerleader types—and then a store.

It was filled with birdcages and in the cages were birds that didn't seem to have any eyes and seemed to have beaks covered with fur, from which issued spiral tongues. They moved around in their crowded cages so fast it was hard to tell if the impression Deede had of their appearance was right. A woman in the back of the shop had a fantastic piled-up hair style, an elaborate coif with little spheres woven into it, reminding Deede of eyes, randomly arranged into the high hairdo; she turned around . . .

She must have turned all the way around, really quickly, so quickly they didn't see the turn, because they saw only the elaborate coif and the back of her head again.

"This place is making me feel, all, sick to my stomach," Jean said.

"I think it's like . . . not enough oxygen . . . or something," Lenny said. decisively: "Yo look, there's an arcade!"

They crossed into the more familiar confines of an arcade, its doorway open into a dark room, illuminated mostly by light from the various game machines.

"Lenny, give me a dollar!" Jean demanded.

"Stop ordering me around!" But he gave her a dollar, mashing it up in her palm, and she got a videogame machine to accept it. Deede had never seen the game before: it was called KILLER GIRL and it appeared to show a girl—so low-res she had no clear-cut features—shooting fiery red bullets from her eyes and the tips of her fingers and her navel—was it her navel?—toward dozens of murkily defined enemies who cropped up in the windows of a suburban neighborhood, enemies with odd-looking weapons in their pixilated hands.

The neighborhood was rather like the one they'd left in Portland. As Jean played, Deede and Lenny watching, the video figure that Jean controlled changed shape, becoming more definite, more high-resolution—looking more and more like Jean herself. Then a videogame "boss" loomed up over a building in the game, a giant, somewhat but not quite resembling Gunnar Johansen.

"What are you kids doing in here?"

All three of them twitched around to face him at once, as if they'd rehearsed it. A security guard was scowling at them—a man with small eyes and a flattened nose in a chunky grayish face that looked almost made of putty. He wore a peculiar, tight-fitting helmet of translucent blue that pressed his hair down so that it looked like meat in a supermarket package. There was a smell off him like smashed ants. He wore the almost-black and silver uniform with the snake cuffs.

"What you mean, what're we doing?" Lenny snorted. "Dude, it's an arcade. Work it out."

"But the mall's closed. Five minutes ago. Closes early till full public opening next month."

"So we didn't know that, okay? Now back the fuck off. Come on, Deede, Jean."

"My game!"

"Forget it. Come on, Deede. You too, Jean—now."

The guard followed a few steps behind them as they headed for the elevators leading out of the mall. Deede thought Lenny was going to turn and hit the guy for following them, his fists clenching on rigid arms, as he did before he hit that Garcia kid—but he just muttered "Fuck this guy!" and walked faster till they were in the elevator. The guard made as if to get in the elevator with them, but Lenny said, "No fucking way, asshole," and stabbed the elevator "close doors" button. It shut in the guard's face, on a frozen, minatory expression that hadn't changed since he'd first spoken to them.

Jean laughed. "What a loser."

The elevator groaned as it took them down to the apartments—as though it were old, not almost brand-new. It groaned and shivered and moaned, the sound very human, heart-wrenching. Deede wanted to comfort it. The moans actually seemed to come from above it, as if someone were standing on the elevator, wailing, like a man waiting to be executed.

*

It was a relief to be back in the apartment, the doors locked, in the midst of thirty floors of housing about halfway up the building: a comfortable, well-organized three-bedroom place—the bedrooms small but well ventilated. No balcony but with a view out over the city. They had cable TV, cable modems, a DVD player, big LCD screen, an Xbox, and a refrigerator stocked with snacks and sodas. Dad finally came home with pizza. Life was pretty good that evening.

A few days later, though, Dad announced he was leaving for five days. He had an assignment for the magazine, had to fly to Vancouver, and they'd spent too much money getting here that he couldn't afford to bring the kids with him, though school was out for the summer. Jean refused to respond to the announcement with anything but a shrug; Deede found herself almost whining, asking whether this was going to be a regular thing. As a travel editor in Portland, Dad hadn't left town all that much; mostly he just edited other people's articles. Standing at the window, a can of Diet Coke in one hand, he admitted he was going to be gone a lot in the new job.

"Yeah, well, that's just *great*," Lenny said, his mouth going slack with disgust, his whole frame radiating resentment—and he stuck his fists in his pockets, the way he always did when he was mad at his father, so that the seams started to pop. "I need to get my own place. I can't be babysitting all the time, Dad."

"Well, until you do, you've gotta do your part, Lenny," Dad said, gazing out the window at downtown L.A. "Just—just help me out this summer, while you figure out what college you want, get a day job, and all . . . all like that. And—and you're re-sponsible, while I'm gone, for your sisters: you have to be, I just don't have time to find anyone reliable."

"Like we need *him* to take care of us," Jean said. "Like Mom would leave us this way."

They all looked at her, and she stared defiantly back. Finally Dad said, "This building is very safe, really safe. I mean, it's high-security as all hell. You have your door cards. But you shouldn't even leave the place while I'm gone if you can help it. Everything you need is here. Supermarket, clinic, it's all in the building. There's even a movie theater."

"It doesn't open till next week," Lenny said bitterly.

Dad cleared his throat, looked out the window again. "There are kids to meet here."

"Hardly anyone's moved in," Jean pointed out, rolling her eyes.

"Well," Dad hesitated, taking a pull on his Diet Coke, "only go out in the day and . . . and don't run around in downtown L.A. Downtown L.A. is dangerous. You can go to Hollywood Boulevard and go to a movie. Lenny can drive the car, I guess. But just . . . try to stay . . . to stay here . . ."

His voice trailed off. He gazed out the picture window, watching a plane fly over.

*

She met Jorny in the Skymall when they got their iPods mixed up in the frozen yogurt shop.

"Yo, girl, that's my iPod," Jorny said, as Deede picked it up from the counter. He had blue eyes that glimmered with irony in a V-shaped face, dark eyebrows that contrasted with his long, corn-rowed, sun-bleached brown hair, a tan that was partly burn. He was slender, not quite as tall as she was; he wore pants raggedly cut off just above the knees, with *ANARCHY? WHO THE FUCK KNOWS?* written on the left pants leg in blue ballpoint pen, and a way-oversized T-shirt with a picture of Nicholas Cage on it hoisting a booze bottle, from *Leaving Las Vegas.*

He had various odd items twined around his wrists as im-provised bracelets—twist-ties worked together, individual rings of plastic cut from six-packs. He wore high-topped red tennis shoes, falling apart—probably stressed from skateboarding: a well-worn skateboard was jammed under his left arm.

"No, it's not your iPod," Deede said, mildly. "Look, it's play-ing The Hives' 'Die All Right,' the song I was listening to."

"That's the song *I* was listening to. I just set it down for a second to get my money out."

"No, it's—oh, you're right, my iPod's in my purse. I paused it on 'Die All Right.' I thought I—Sorry. But that really is the same song I was listening to—look! Same one—at the same time!"

"Whoa, that's weird. You're, like, stalking me and shit."

"I guess. You live in the building?"

"You kids want these frozen yogurts or what?" asked the man at the counter.

They bought their frozen yogurts, and one for Jean, who was in the Mall walkway looking in store windows. It turned out that

Jorny lived downstairs from them, almost right below. He was three weeks younger than Deede and he mostly lived to do skateboard tricks. His Dad had "gone off to live in New York, we don't see him around much." When she said her mom was dead he said, "Between us we almost got one set of parents."

Jean told him she did rollerblading—he managed not to seem scornful at that—and he and Deede talked about music and the odd things they'd seen in the mall shops and how they didn't seem to be the same shops the next day.

"One place seemed like it was selling faces," Jorny said. "Latest Face."

"I didn't see that one. They must mean masks or maybe makeup."

He shook his head but didn't argue and tried to show her some new skateboard ollies right there in the mall; but the putty-faced guard began jogging toward them from the other end of the walkway, bellowing. "You—hold it right there, don't you move!"

"Security guards everywhere hate skateboarders," Jorny declared proudly, grinning. "Fucking hate us. Come on!" He started toward a stairwell.

"Jean—come on!" Deede shouted, starting after him. Sticking her tongue out at the security guard, Jean came giggling after them as they banged through the doors into the stairwell and the smell of concrete and newly dried paint, and pounded down the stairs, laughing.

"Hey, you kids!" came the shout from above.

They kept going, Jorny at the next level down jumping a flight of stairs on his skateboard, and landing it with a joint-jarring *clack*. "You actually landed that!" Deede shouted, impressed—and privately a little dismayed. It was a big jump, though skateboarders did that sort of thing a lot. She was also pleased that he was evidently showing off for her.

"Yeah, huh, that was tight, I landed it!" Jorny called, clacking down the next group of stairs, ollying from one stair to the next. Jean squealed, "Agggghhh! Run! He's coming! That blue helmet weirdo's coming!"

They ran down the stairs, easily outdistancing the security guard, and bolted onto the mid-level observation court and community center. They took the elevator to the Hanging Gardens, where they went to check out Jorny's place, an apartment almost identical to their own. Deede didn't want Jean to come but couldn't think of way for her not to.

Jorny's mom was there for lunch. She was a lawyer, the director of the county Public Defender's office, a plump woman in a suit with a white streak in her wooly black hair, and a pleasantly Semitic face. She seemed happy to see Deede, maybe as opposed to some of the rougher people she'd seen her son with— all that was in her face when she looked at Deede. She smiled at Deede, then glanced at Jean, looked away from her, then looked back at her, a kind of double-take, as if trying to identify what it was about the girl that worried her.

It had only just recently occurred to Deede that what she saw in other people wasn't visible to everyone. It wasn't exactly psychic—it was just what Deede thought of as "looking faster." She'd always been able to look faster.

"Come on," Jorny said, as his mom went to make them sandwiches. "I want to play you the new Wolfmother single. It's not out yet—it's a ripped download a friend of mine sent me."

*

The notice was there on Saturday morning, when Deede got up. Dad had left at six that morning, not saying goodbye—they all knew he was going to be gone several days—and he wouldn't have seen the notice, she thought. Someone had slipped it under the door from the hall. It read:

NOTICE
DUE TO SECURITY CONCERNS ONLY AUTHORIZED
PERSONNEL WILL BE ALLOWED TO LEAVE THE
BUILDING THIS WEEKEND, AS OF 8 A.M., SATUR-
DAY MORNING, EXCEPT FOR DESIGNATED EMER-
GENCIES (SEE SKYTOWN MANUAL PAGE 39 FOR
DESIGNATED EMERGENCY GUIDELINES). RE-
STRICTIONS WILL BE LIFTED IN A FEW DAYS.
PLEASE BE PATIENT.
THANK YOU FOR YOUR COOPERATION.
SKYTOWN OFFICE OF SECURITY

"What the fuck!" Lenny burst out, when Deede showed it to him. "That is totally illegal! Hey—call that kid you met, with the lawyer mom."

"Jorny?" It would be a good excuse to call him.

Jorny answered sleepily. "Whuh? My mom? She left for . . . go see my aunt for breakfast or something . . . s'pose-a be back later. Why, whussup?"

"Um—check if you got a notice under your front door."

He came back to the phone under a minute seconds later. "Yeah! Same notice! My mom left after eight, though, and she hasn't come back. So it must be bullshit, they must've let her go. Maybe it's a hoax. Or . . ."

"We're gonna go to the bargain matinee over on Hollywood Boulevard. You wanna go? I mean, then we can see if they really are making people stay."

A little over an hour later they were all dressed, meeting Jorny downstairs outside the elevators at the front lobby. They walked by potted plants toward the tinted glass of the front doors . . . and found the doors locked from inside.

"You kids didn't get the notice?"

They turned to see a smiling, personable, middle-aged man standing about thirty feet away. He wore a green suit and tie—

maybe that was why his face had a vague greenish cast to it. Just a reflection off the green cloth. Behind him were two security guards in the peculiar uniforms.

"That notice is bullshit," Lenny said flatly. "Not legal."

"You look a little young to be a lawyer," said the man in the green suit mildly.

"Your face is sort of green," Jean said, staring at him.

But as she said it, his face seemed to shift to a more normal color. As if he'd just noticed and changed it somehow.

"Or not . . ." Jean mumbled.

The man ignored her. "My name is Arthur Koenig—I'm the building supervisor. I'm pretty sure of the laws and rules and I assure you kids, you cannot leave the building except under designated emergency conditions."

"And I'm pretty sure," Jorny said, snapping his skateboard up with his foot to catch it in his hand, "that's what they call 'false imprisonment'—it's a form of kidnapping."

The security guards both had the odd translucent-blue helmets. They stood behind and to either side of Koenig—one of them, who might have been Filipino, stepped frowning toward Jorny. "That's the boy who was doing the skateboarding in the Mall—I saw him on the cameras. Boy, you give me that skateboard, that's contraband here!"

"Not a fucking chance, a-hole," Jorny said, making Jean squeal with laughter.

"Come on," he said to Lenny, "we'll go to my place and call around about this."

"Building phone line's being worked on," said Koenig pleasantly. "Be down for a while. Building cable too."

"We've got cell phones, man," Lenny said, turning toward the elevators. "Come on, you guys."

As they went back to the elevators, Deede glanced over her shoulder, saw that Koenig was following at a respectful distance—and while they were walking at an angle, the shortest way to the elevator, he seemed to be following a straight line—then he turned right, and she realized he was following the lines of the square sections of floor. And she saw something coming off his right heel—a thin red cord or string, like a finely stretched-out piece of flesh, that came from a hole in his shoe and went into the groove between the floor tiles . . .

A thread stuck to his shoe, is all, she told herself. *It's not really a connection to something inside the floor.*

"That skateboard!" the blue-helmeted security guard yelled, following Jorny. "Leave it here! I'm confiscating it!"

But Koenig reached out, put his hand on the guard's arm. "Let him go. It doesn't matter now. Let him keep it for the moment."

Deede followed the others into the elevator. She didn't mention the red cord to them.

*

"This is 911 emergency. May I have your name and address?"

Lenny gave his name and address and then said, "I'm calling because we're being held against our will by the weirdoes in this building we live in. The manager, all these people—no one's allowed to leave the building! It's totally illegal!"

"Slow down, please," said the dispatcher, her voice crackling in the cell phone, phasing in and out of clarity. "Who exactly is 'restraining' you?" The skepticism was rank in her voice.

"The building security people say we can't leave, *no one* can leave, there're hundreds of people who live here and we can't—"

"Was there a bomb threat?"

"I don't know, they didn't say so, they just said 'security concerns.'"

"The security at that building interfaces with the police department. If they're asking people not to leave it's probably so they can investigate something. Have they been . . . oh, violent or—"

"No, not yet, but they . . . Look, it's false imprisonment, it's—"

"They are security, we'll have someone call them—but they're probably doing this for your protection. It could be a Homeland Security drill."

"Oh, Jesus, forget it." He broke the connection and threw the cell phone so it bounced on the sofa cushion. "I can't believe it. They just assumed I was full of crap."

Jorny was on his own cell phone, listening. He frowned and hung up. "I can't get my mom to answer, or my aunt."

"Jorny?" said Deede thoughtfully, looking out the apartment's picture window at the smog-hazy sky. "You think maybe they stopped your mom—took her into custody 'cause she tried to leave?"

Jorny stared at her. "No way." He shot to his feet. "Come on, if you're coming. I'm gonna ask if she's at the security office."

Deede looked at Lenny to see if he was coming, but he was on the cell phone again. "I'm trying to call Dad . He's not picking up, though."

"Lenny—where's Jean?" Deede asked, looking around. It wasn't like Jean to be so quiet.

"Hm? She left. She said she's going to that coffee lounge where those kids hang out."

"What kids?"

"I don't know. She started hanging with them yesterday sometime. She came back at three in the morning. I think she was, like, stoned."

"What? I'm gonna go get her. And help Jorny!" She called this to Lenny as she followed Jorny out the door. Lenny waved her on.

*

Another notice had been taped up on the wall next to the elevator call buttons.

NOTICE
ELEVATOR MOVEMENT HAS BEEN RESTRICTED TO THE
UPPER SEVENTY FLOORS UNTIL FURTHER NOTICE.
ELEVATOR WILL NOT DESCEND FROM THIS LEVEL.
THANK YOU FOR YOUR COOPERATION.

"What the fuck!" Jorny said, gaping at the notice.

"I wouldn't have put it that way," said a white-haired older woman standing a few steps away. She wore thick, horn-rimmed glasses and a long blue dress. "But that's generally my feeling too." She had her purse over her shoulder, as if she had planned to go out. "I was going to the Farmer's Market but . . . I guess not now." The woman went back toward the doors to the apartment complex, shaking her head.

Jorny shook his head as the woman walked away. "Everyone just accepts it."

"Security office is downstairs," Deede said. "We can't get to it on the elevators. But we could take the stairs. Only, I want to find my sister. But then she could be down there too . . ."

He was already starting toward the door to the stairwell, skateboard under his arm—you can't skateboard on carpet.

But the stairwell door was locked. "What about the fire laws and all that?" Jorny said, wondering aloud. He looked toward a fire alarm, as if thinking of tripping it. Deede hoped he wouldn't.

"Okay," he said, "let's go upstairs on the elevators to that lounge, see if we can find some way from there to go down. There must be a way—the security guards must be able to do it."

"I want to get my brother to go with us."

They went back to the apartment—and found the apartment door standing open.

Inside there was a lamp knocked over. Lenny was gone. He'd left his cell phone where he'd thrown it and he was just—gone. She looked through all the rooms and called up and down the halls. No response except that a Filipino man looked out a door briefly—then hastily shut it when Deede tried to ask him a question. They heard him lock it.

"I'm sure he's okay," Jorny said.

Deede looked reproachfully at him. "I didn't say he wasn't."

"You looked worried."

"I . . . I'm worried about Jean and this whole weird thing. That's all. Lenny gets in a snit sometimes and goes off and says 'Screw everybody' and wanders away . . . gets somebody to buy him beer somewhere and he gets a little smashed and then he comes home. But leaving the door open that way . . ."

Jorny was on his cell again, trying to call his mom. He called his aunt, spoke to her for less than a minute in low tones—and hung up. "She never showed up. She was supposed to meet my aunt—and she never got there."

"It's too soon to call it a 'missing persons' thing. We could look for your mom in the building. And Jean."

"You want to try the lounge?" Jorny asked. She nodded and they went to the elevators and rode up toward the lounge. On the way he tried to call his mom on the cell phone again—and gave up. "Doesn't work at all now. Just static."

"There are places in the elevators for keys," Deede said, pointing at the key fixture under the floor tabs. "The security guards must have keys that let them go to restricted floors."

That's when the moaning started up again, in the elevators above them—and below them too, as if the one down below were answering the one above. A moan from above, the ceiling shivering; an answering moan from below the elevator, the floor resonating.

Jorny looked at her quizzically, but said nothing.

They got out at the coffee lounge, a big, comfortable cafeteria space spanning most of one side of the floor, with a coffee shop and a magazine stand. Both were closed. But there were kids there, about nine of them, five boys and four girls, middle-schoolers like Jean, in a far corner, crowded together in a circle near the restrooms. Deede hurried closer and found they were standing in a tight circle around Jean, circling, and each one pointing an index finger at her, one after the other, as if they were doing "the wave," the fingers rippling out and pointing and dropping in the circle, and each one pointing said, "Take a hit."

"Take a hit . . ."

"Take a hit . . ."

"Take a hit . . ."

Like that, on and on around the circle, and when Deede and Jorny got there, Deede looked to see what Jean was taking a hit of, what drug or drink, but there was nothing there—no smoke, no smell, no pipe, no bottle, only the pointing fingers from the rapt, feral faces of the other kids, their eyes dilated, their lips parted, saying, "Take a hit, take a hit, take a hit . . ." And Jean was swaying in place, rocking back, staggering in reaction from each pointed finger, each 'take a hit,' her eyes droopy, her mouth droopier, looking decidedly stoned. Was she playacting?

"What're you guys hitting on?" Jorny said, laughing nervously.

All nine of them turned their heads at once to look at them. "You can't join," the tallest of the boys said. An acned face, a spiky haircut. "You can't. You're not trustworthy."

"We don't want to," Deede said. She waved urgently at her sister. "Come on, Jean—let's go. There's some weird stuff going on. We've gotta find Lenny."

Jean shook her head. She was swaying there, hyperventilating. "I'm not feeling any pain at all and I'm between the suns. I'm not going, going to stay here."

"Jean—come on!" Deede tried to push through the circle— and someone, she wasn't sure who, shoved her back, hard, so she fell painfully on her back. "Ow!"

"This way," said the big kid with the acned face, leading the group around Jean into the men's room, taking Jean with them. Both males and females filed, without a word or hesitation, into the men's bathroom.

Jorny helped Deede up. "That was fucked up," he said, shaking his head in disgust. "I'm going in there."

"I'm going too. I don't care if it's the men's room. They took my sister in there."

"She went on her own. But fuck it, let's go."

He led the way into the men's room—which was empty.

Not a soul in it. Jorny even opened the toilet booths. No one. There was only one entrance. There was no way out of the bathroom except the one door. There were no ventilation shafts. There was just the big, overlit, blue-tiled, and stainless steel bathroom and their own reflections in the mirrors over the metal sinks.

Jorny gaped around. "Okay, what uh . . ." His voice seemed emptied of life in the hard space of the room. "We were right in front of that door. They didn't get out past us."

"Look!" She pointed at the mirrors. They were reflected in a continuum of mirrors, as when mirrors are turned to other mirrors. Only there was only one set of mirrors on one wall. There were no mirrors opposite—yet the reflection was the mirror-images-within-mirror-images telescoping that happened only if you turned mirrors to mirrors . . . And Deede saw hundreds of Deedes and Jornys stretched into infinity, each face looking lost and shocked and scared. Lost and shocked and scared endlessly repeated, amplified.

And then she saw Jean in the mirrors, about thirty reflections down the glassy corridor, passing from one side to the other, glancing at her as she went past.

"Jean!" She turned from the mirror, looking the other way as if she might see Jean throwing the reflection there—but saw nothing but a row of toilet booths and urinals. She looked back at the mirrors. "Jorny—did you see someone in the mirrors beside us?"

Jorny's endlessly repeated reflections nodded to her. "Thought I saw your sister."

Feeling dizzily sick, Deede turned away. "It's like there's another room in this room."

She noticed an outline, about the size of a door, on the farther wall between the urinals and the corner, etched with what looked like red putty along the joins in the tiles. She walked over to it. "There's a door-shaped mark here. But . . ." She touched the puttied areas. "This gunk is hard here, like it's been this way a long time. It couldn't be where they got out."

Jorny came over and battered at the marked section of wall with his skateboard; they pushed at tiles but could find no way of opening the door, if it was a door. And when they touched it there was a sensation like a very weak electric shock—not enough to make them jump but just enough to give a feeling of discomfort. Electrical discomfort—and the hairs rising on the back of their necks. And chills too, sick chills of the kind you get with the flu.

"It's like a warning," she whispered. "Come on—I want out of here."

Jorny nodded, seeming relieved, and they hurried out of the men's room, back into the lounge area—where they were entirely alone. "I've been thinking about some of the shops we saw," Deede said, as they walked over to the elevators and the door to the stairwell. The stairway door was locked. "And—it was like something was influencing stuff around here, something changing the way things . . . just the way they are." Should she tell him about the cord connecting Koenig's foot to the floor tiles?

"I know what you mean," Jorny said absently as he fiddled with the door to the stairway. "Locked. But yo—*that* door's open."

The door he was pointing at, between the stairs and elevator, was marked MAINTENANCE 47-17. It looked as if it hadn't quite closed—as if the doorframe was slightly crooked and it had stuck with the door just slightly ajar. You had to look close to see it was open.

She went to it and put her hand on the knob.

Jorny whispered, "Be careful—you could end up locking it."

She nodded and turned the knob while pulling hard on the door—and it swung open.

Inside, it was an ordinary closet, containing a new vacuum cleaner with the price tag still on it, and bottles of cleaning fluid, all of them full, and a push broom; and another smaller door, in the wall of the closet to the right. She bent over and turned the little chrome handle it had in place of a knob—and it opened on-to the stairway. "Cool! Come on!"

Hunching down to fit, they went through—and found them-selves in the main stairway. It was dimly lit, echoing with their every movement, a smell of rot overlaying the smell of new con-crete and paint.

"Smells like roadkill," Jorny said. He turned to look at the door they'd come through—which shut behind them into the wall, hardly showing a seam. "Weird that they put that door there."

"It's for *them* to use—in case of emergency," Deede said. "And don't ask who *they* are—I don't know."

"Deede—there's something moving down there . . . and it doesn't seem like people."

She leaned over the balcony and looked. Something slipped across the space between flights about four stories down—a transparent dull-red flipper . . . feeler . . . tentacle? She couldn't get a clear visual picture of it from where she stood. But it was big—maybe three feet across and very long. Slipping by, like a giant boa constrictor. She could just make out that it was con-nected to something bigger, something that stretched down the open space between the descending flights of stairs.

And as it moved she heard the familiar moaning. That sob-bing despair.

She stepped back and said, "Jorny—punch me in the shoul-der."

"Really?"

"Yeah. I'm pretty sure I'm not dreaming. But only pretty sure. So go ahead and—ow!"

"You said to! Okay—do me now. Right there. Stick out your knuckle so it—shit!"

"So what do you think?" he asked, rubbing his shoulder, wincing. "Damn, you hit hard for a girl!"

"That's sexist. And I think we're awake. We have to decide."

He surprised her by suddenly sitting down on the steps and taking a cigarette out of his shirt pocket. "I've been trying not to smoke. Promised my mom I'd give it up." He took a wooden match out with the cigarette and flicked it alight on his skateboard—Deede thought it was an admirably cool thing to do. He lit the cigarette and puffed. "But right now I don't care what my mom thinks about cigarettes."

"So what're we gonna *do?*" She was thinking of going back to the apartment again and seeing if Lenny had come home. She'd made excuses for him, but under the circumstances she thought he'd have left her a note or something if he'd left . . . voluntarily.

Don't think about Lenny, too, she thought, sitting on a step a little below Jorny. *One person at a time. Get Jean. She's younger. He's older and he can take care of himself.*

Jorny was blowing smoke rings and poking at them with his finger—he was absentmindedly running his skateboard back and forth on its wheels with one foot.

"One time two or three years ago," he said, his voice a dreamy monotone, "when my dad was still living with us, I was worried about where he was all day. See, he was a photographer, and he worked at home. So he was usually there. But one summer he just started being gone all day and there was a lot of . . . I dunno, him and my mom were arguing all the time about little things. About bullshit. Like there was something else . . . but they weren't saying. I was feeling like he was doing something—and it was gonna make them break up. So anyway I followed him. I didn't even think about why. I borrowed my sister's car—she's moved out now—and I followed him. He didn't notice I was following. He was really into where he was going, man. He went to a motel. I should've left it there, but I saw which room he went to and after awhile I went up and they had the windows curtained, but there was a place where if you bent over and looked at the corner, you could see in."

"Oh, Christ, Jorny."

"Yeah. He was doin' it with some woman I never saw before. They had champagne and stuff. Later on he left my mom for her."

"That must've been . . ." She couldn't keep from making a face.

"It was. I wished I hadn't gone, wished I hadn't looked. It's different, really seeing it. Worse. He was still married to my mom, and . . . Anyway, since then, I figure there's things I don't want to find out about. And if we go looking down there, we'll see things we don't want to know about." He flicked his cigarette away half smoked. "I'm not scared. Not that much. I just . . . don't want to see anything else that I don't want to know about. Especially since my mom might be in any one of a million places."

"But—" Deede heard the moaning again from below. She just wanted to go back to the apartment and wait there with the doors locked. But that hadn't helped Lenny.

"You okay?" Jorny asked, looking at her closely.

"I'm just worried about my brother. And Jean. I'd like to go back to the apartment, but—" She sighed. "No one did anything about my mom being killed. No one . . . no one *pursued* it." Deede felt her hands fisting—and she couldn't prevent it. "They said it was suicide or an accident. But there was a man who scares people—he was following some girls in the neighborhood, and there's rumors about him—and he was there that day, he was seen on the same trails, and then there was the dream. The dream seemed almost as real as . . . as today is."

"What dream?"

"It was one of those dreams you get over and over—but the first time I got it was the morning my mom was killed. She was out jogging early and I was still asleep. Our house was out on the edge of town, by this sorta woodsy area with an old quarry. And in my dream I saw her jogging along the edge of the old quarry, where there's this little pond, jogging like she always does on the trails there, and I saw Gunnar Johansen watching her and he looks like he's been up all night, he's sort of swaying there, and then he starts following her and then starts running and she turns and sees him and stumbles and falls on the trail and then he throws himself on her and she struggles and hits him, and he laughs and he knocks her out and then he . . . plays with her body kind of, with one hand on her throat, squeezing and the other hand in his pants, and then she kicks him in the groin and he gives a yell and picks her up and throws her down in the quarry, and she falls face down and she hits hard in that shallow water down there. And . . . bubbles come up . . . *And that's exactly how they found her.*"

"They found her like that, in that exact place? And you hadn't heard about it yet?"

Deede nodded. "I tried to tell them, but they said dreams don't count in court. I had that dream again, I had it a lot. I was afraid to go to sleep for a long time."

She put her face in her hands and he came and sat close beside her, not touching her, just being there with her. She appreciated that—the sensitivity of it. Him not trying to put his arm around her. But coming to be right there with her.

A few seconds more, and then a moan and a long, drawn-out scraping sound came from below. Deede decided she had to make up her mind. "I have to go down there. No one found out about my mom. I'm going to find out about Jean. You can go back."

He cleared his throat, then muttered, "Fuck it." Nodded to himself. He stood up and offered his hand to help her up. "Okay. Come on."

They descended. Jorny carried his skateboard for two turns, and then decided to do a jump, as if some kind of oblique statement of defiance of whatever waited below. He jumped a whole flight—and the skateboard splintered under him when he came down, snapped in half, and he ended up sliding on his ass. "Shit god*dammi*t!"

She helped him up this time. "Sorry about your skateboard. You going to save the trucks?"

"I don't know. I guess." Disgustedly carrying half a skateboard in each hand, he led the way downward—and they stopped another floor lower to peer over the concrete rail.

Something slipped scrapily by thirty-five feet below, something rubbery and transparently pinkish-red. It made her think of the really big pieces of kelp you saw at the shore, thickly transparent like that, but redder, bigger—and this one had someone swallowed up in it: one of the kids, a young boy she'd seen in the lounge. The boy was trapped inside the supple tree-trunk-thick flexible tube, trapped alive, squeezed but living, slightly moving, eyes darting this way and that, hands pressed by the constriction against his chest . . . and moaning, making the despairing moan they'd been hearing, somehow louder than it should be, as if the thing that held him was triumphantly amplifying his moan.

"You *see* that?" Jorny whispered.

She nodded. "One of those kids who was with Jean . . . in a . . . I don't know what it is." And then it moaned again, so loudly the cry echoed up the shaft of the stairway.

It's calling to us, she thought. *It's luring us. Saying "Come and save him, come and save them all. Come down and see . . ."*

The slithering thing, connected to something below, itself descended—or, more accurately, was pulled down—ahead of her and Jorny, themselves going down and down, the light diminishing ever so subtly toward the lower floors. The transparent red tubule drew itself down, like an eel drawing itself into a hole, pulling the boy—and others, too, squirming trapped human figures glimpsed for a moment enveloped in other thick tendrils, moaning, down and down. Did she see Jean, caught down there? Deede wasn't sure. But she felt that sick flu-chills feeling again and she wanted to turn and run up the stairs and—

"I saw my mom down there," Jorny said, his voice cracking. Inside that thing. "Now I've really got to go."

Deede wanted to run. *Don't let them scare you into not going.* She almost thought she heard her mom's voice saying it. Almost. *He needs someone to go with him. And Jean . . . don't forget Jean.*

"Okay," Deede made herself say. She started down, following the slithering descender, following the moans and the moaners, following the trapped squirmers . . .

Down and down till they got to the dimly lit bottom floor. And to the basement door.

Deede had expected to find the squirming thing at the bottom, but it wasn't there, though there was a thin coating of slushy red material on the floor—like something you'd squeeze from kelp but the color of diluted blood—surrounding the closed basement door. The thing had gone through the door—and closed it behind.

She half hoped the door was locked. Jorny tried it—and it opened. He stood in the doorway, outlined in green light. She looked over his shoulder.

About forty feet by thirty, the basement room contained elevator machinery—humming hump-shaped units to the right—and cryptic pipes along the ceiling. But what drew their eyes was a jagged hole in the floor, right in front of the door, about seven feet across, edged with red slush—the green light came from down there. From within the hole.

She followed Jorny into the room, and—Deede taking a deep breath—they both bent over to look.

Below was a chamber that could never have been made by the builders of Skytown. It was a good-sized chamber, very old. Its stones were rough-carved, great blocks set by some ancient hand in primeval times, way pre-Columbian. Grooves had been carved in the stone floor by someone with malign and fixed intentions. They were flecked with a red-brown crust that had taken many years to accumulate.

"It looks to me like they dug this building in real deep," Jorny said in a raw whisper. "I heard they dug the foundation down deeper than any other building in Los Angeles. And I guess there was something down there, buried way down, they didn't know about . . ."

She nodded. He looked at the fragments of skateboard in his hand and tossed them aside, with a clatter, then got down on his knees, and lowered himself—

"Jorny!"

—through the hole in the floor; into the green light; into the ancient chamber.

"Oh, fuck," she groaned. But she lowered herself and dropped too, about eight feet to a stinging impact on the balls of her feet.

Jorny caught and steadied her as she was about to tip over and they looked around. "Some kind of temple!" he whispered. "And that *thing* . . ."

The grooves cut into the naked bedrock of the floor, each about an inch deep, were part of a spiral pattern that filled the floor of the entire room—and the gouged pattern was reproduced on the ceiling, as were the dais, the spirals, above and below, converging on the circular dais and the translucent thing that dwelt at the room's center. Spiral patterns on ceiling, spiral patterns on floor; between them, a thing hung suspended in space—suspended between the space of the room and the space between worlds: an enormous, gelatinous, transparent sphere containing a restless collection of smaller iridescent spheres, like a clutch of giant fish eggs. Were they smaller than the encompassing sphere, or were they of indefinite size, perhaps both as small as bushels and as big as planets?

The iridescent spheres shifted restlessly inside the enveloping globe, changing position, as if each sphere were jostling to get closer to the outside of the container, the whole emanating a murky-green light that tinted the stone walls to jade. The light was a radiance of intelligence, a malign intelligence—malevolent relative to the needs and hopes of human beings—and somehow Deede knew that it was aware of her and wanted to consume her mind with its own . . . She could feel its mind pressing on the edges of her consciousness, pushing, leaning, feeling like a glacier that might become an avalanche.

And then as her eyes adjusted she saw what the green glow had hidden till now—its extensions, green but filled with diluted blood, stolen blood, the tentacles stretching from the sphere-of-spheres like stems and leaves from a tuber, but prehensile, mobile, stretching out from thick tubules to gradually narrow, to thin, very thin tips that stretched out red cords, like fishing line up into the grooves on the ceiling, and from there into minute cracks, and, she knew—with an intuitive certainty—up high into the building, where they reached into people, taking control of them one by one, starting with those who'd been here longest, Skytown's employees. And some of the tentacular extensions had swallowed up whole people, drawn them down and into itself, so that they squirmed in the tubes, dozens of them, shifting in and out of visibility . . .

She saw Koenig, drawn down in one of the transparent tentacles, sucked through it, his face contorted with a terrible realization . . . blood squeezing in little spurts from his eyes, his mouth, his nose . . . And then he was jetted back up the tentacle, becoming smaller as he went, transformed into a transmissible shape that could be reconstituted up above . . . And all this she glimpsed in less than two seconds.

Visibility was a paradox, a conundrum—the tentacles were visible as a whole but not individually: when you tried to look at one it shifted out of view, and you just glimpsed the people trapped inside it before it was gone . . . And the moaning filled the room, only they heard it more in their minds than in their ears . . .

"It's like this thing is here but it's not completely here," Jorny said, wonderingly. "Like it's . . . getting to be more and *more* here as it . . ."

"The people look pale, some of them like they're dying or dead," Deede said, feeling dreamlike and sick at once. "I can't see them clear enough to be sure but it's like they're being drained real slow."

Jorny said, "It's not coming at us. Why?"

"It's waiting," she said. It was more than guessing—it felt right. The answers were in the air itself somehow; they throbbed within the murky green light. Her fast-seeing drew them quickly into her. "It wants us to come to it. It's lured the others in some way—we saw how it lured Jean. Everyone's been lured. It wants you to submit to it."

"Look—there's something on the other side."

"Jorny? How are we going to get out of here? There's no way back up."

"There has to be another entrance."

"Okay, fine." She felt increasingly reckless—she felt so hopeless now that it seemed as if little was left to lose. She led the way herself—she was tired of following males from one place to the next—and edged around the boiling, suspended sphere-of-spheres, getting closer to it and learning more about it with proximity.

It was only partly in their space; it was in many spaces at once. There was only one being: each sphere they were seeing was another manifestation of that same being, one for each world it stretched into. It slowly twisted things in those worlds to fit its liking. And they were only seeing the outside of it, like the dorsal fin of a shark on the surface of the water. It had many names, in many places; many varieties of appearance, many approaches to getting what it wanted. Its true form—

"Look!" Jorny said, pointing past her at a jagged hole in the floor—a hole that was the *exact duplicate* of the one in the ceiling they'd dropped through on the other side of the room. Its edges were shaped precisely the same . . .

The tentacular probes of the sphere-of-spheres teased at them as they passed, almost caressing them, offering visions of glory, preludes of unimaginable pleasure . . .

But the creature frightened her more than it attracted her—it was somehow scarier for its enticements. It was as malevolent to her as a wolf spider would be to a crawling fly. Or as a Venus fly-trap would be.

"Jesus!" Jorny blurted, hastening away from the thing. "I almost—Never mind, just get over here!"

She wanted to follow him, but it was hard to move—she was caught up in its whispering, its radiance of promise, and the undertone of warning. *Run from me and I'll be forced to grab you!* Jorny ran to her and grabbed her wrist, pulled her away from it. She felt weak, for a moment, drained, staggering . . .

He knelt by the hole in the floor and dropped through. "Come on, Deede!"

After a moment she followed, almost falling through the hole in her weariness. He half caught her, as before—and she felt her strength returning, away from the sphere-within-spheres.

"Look—we're on the ceiling!" Jorny burst out. "Aren't we?"

They were on a floor—with pipes snaking around their knees—but above them was the machinery of the elevators, affixed upside down on . . . the ceiling. Or—on the floor that was now their ceiling. There was a door, identical to the one they'd come through to find the hole into the temple room above—but it went from a couple of feet above the floor to the ceiling. The knob seemed in the wrong place. The door was related to the ceiling the way any other door would be related to the floor—it was upside down. Jorny went to it and jumped to the knob, twisted it, pulled the door open, and scrambled through, turned to help her climb up . . . and then he yelped as he floated upward.

They both floated up, tumbling in the air . . .

They were floating in space for a moment, turning end over end, in the bottom level of the stairway they'd come down. It was the very same stairway, with the occasional cabinet with fire extinguishers and floor numbers painted on the walls—only it stretched down below them, instead of up above them. They instinctively reached for a railing, Jorny caught it . . .

A nauseating twist, a feeling of turning inside-out and back right-side out again, and then they were standing on the stairway, which once more was zigzagging upward, above them. Only—it couldn't be. It had been below the temple room. Or had they been somehow transported back above?

"What the fuck?" Jorny said, pale, fumbling for a cigarette with shaking hands. "Damn, out of smokes."

Deede stared. Someone was up above—crawling down the walls toward them. Two someones. A man and woman. Coming down the walls that contained the stairs, crawling like bugs, upside down relative to Deede.

"Jorny—look!"

"I see 'em."

"Jorny I don't know how much more I can—"

"I'm not feeling so good either. But you know what? We're surviving. Maybe for a reason, right? Hey—they look . . . familiar."

They were about thirty-five, a man and woman dressed in what Deede could only describe to herself as dark, clinging rags. The man had a backpack of some kind tightly fixed to his shoulders. They approached, crawling down the wall, and Deede and Jorny backed away, trying to decide where to run to—up the stairs past them? And then the strangers stopped, looking at them upside down, the woman's hair drooping down toward them . . .

And the woman spoke. "Jorny—it's us, me and you as kids!"

"What—from earlier somehow? But we never discovered the temple as kids!" said the man. "We just found out about it last year!"

"They're us in one of the other worlds—younger versions . . . and they found their way here! Just like in my dream, Jorny! I told you, there was something here—something that would help us!"

Jorny—the younger Jorny standing at the younger Deede's side—shook his head, stunned. "It's us—in, like, the future or . . ."

Deede nodded. "Would you guys come down and . . . stand on the level we're on? Or can you?"

"We can," the older Deede said. "The rules shifted when Yog-Sothoth altered the world, and gravity moves eccentrically."

She crept toward the floor, put one foot on it, then sidled around on the wall like a gecko, finally getting both feet on the floor and standing to face them; the older Jorny did the same. His blond hair was cut short and beginning to recede, his face a trifle lined, but he was still recognizably Jorny.

Deede found she was staring at the older version of herself in fascination. She seemed more proportional, more confident, if a bit grim—there were lines around her eyes, but they looked good on her. But the whole thing was disorienting—was something she didn't really want to see. It made her want to hide, seeing herself, just as much as seeing the thing in the temple.

"Don't look so scared, kid," the older Jorny said, smiling sadly at her.

Deede scowled defiantly at him. "Just—explain what the hell you are. I don't think you're us."

"We're *another* you," the older Deede said. "And we're connected with you. We all extend from the ideal you, in the world of ideas. But this sure isn't that world. Time is a bit in advance in our world, I guess, from yours, for one thing."

"Come on with us," the older Jorny said. "We'll show you. Then we can figure out if there's a way we can work together . . . against *him*."

They turned and climbed the stairs—after a moment's hesitation, Jorny and Deede followed. They went up eleven flights, past battered, rusting doors. "Your building," the older Deede said, "extends downward from ours—but to you it will seem upward. Ours is downward from yours. They're mirrored, but not opposites—just variants at opposite poles from one another. Jorny and I found out that the primary impulses were coming from the basement of our building, so we cut the hole in the sub-basement floor—that's the ceiling of the other room."

"I think it's the other way around," said the older Jorny.

"I don't know, it depends. Anyway the Great Appetite—that's what we call it, though some call it Yog-Sothoth—he reaches out through the many worlds through that same temple . . . and he changes what he comes to, so the beings on that world become all appetite, all desire, and nothing else—so he can feed on low desires, through beings on those worlds."

"You say *he?*" the younger Jorny asked. "Not *it?*"

"Right—he has gender, but little else we can comprehend. Once he's changed a world enough, he can eat what you eat, feel what you feel. Some he will already have changed, in your world—the rest he will change later. He changed our world about eighteen years ago. We've resisted—but most people don't. They get changed—the Great Appetite removes whatever there is in them that checks appetites and desires and impulses. Any kind of strong controlling intelligence, he takes it out. Makes psychopaths of some people, and zombies of just *feeding,* of different kinds, of others—"

"Like Gunnar Johansen!" Deede burst out.

The older Deede stopped on a landing and turned to look at her. "Yes," she said gravely. "He killed my mother too—before the Great Appetite took over. Like him. He was already under Yog-Sothoth's control . . . without knowing it."

She looked as if she wanted to embrace the younger Deede—but Deede was afraid of her and took a step back.

The older Deede shrugged and turned to follow the older Jorny through a doorway—the door at this landing had been wrenched aside, was leaning, crumpled against the wall, hinges snapped. They passed through and found themselves in the lower mezzanine lounge, exactly like the one they'd left—sterile in its furnishings and design.

They walked over to the window and stared out at the world—the transformed world.

There was no sky. Instead there was a ceiling, high up, just above the tallest building, that stretched to the horizon. And the ceiling was covered with images, enticing objects and enticing bodies flashing by and intermingling and overlapping.

She saw an advertisement for BLENDER—and the indeterminate segments of fleshy material that she'd seen in the Skymall shop window. She saw an ad for something called BRAIN BLANKER: *For* really *changing your child—remake it exactly as you please!* She saw an ad for INTER-REACTIVES, INC., the sea urchin helmets she'd seen in Skymall. She saw an ad that said simply, WE ELIMINATE PROBLEM NEIGHBORS—GOVERNMENT CERTIFIED AGAINST RETALIATION; another ad asked, WANT A PET THAT REALLY SCREAMS? ORDER LITTLE PEOPLE! And there was an image of a frightened, dwarf-sized semi-human figure lifted by its neck from a "home-grow vat"—by a grinning man holding a two-by-four with nails sticking out of it in his other hand. There was an ad for LATEST FACE: THE TOP TEN FACES, WITH NEAR-INSTANTANEOUS TRANSFER GUARANTEED, AT REDUCED PRICES.

The images were sometimes blurred by great gray clouds of smog—clouds pierced by people who flew through them, people mechanically enhanced to fly, their bodies pierced by pistons and wires, shrieking as they went; other people crawled up and down the sides of buildings like bugs; clusters of junk material floated by, clouds of metal with people clinging to them, wailing and tittering and fornicating; unspeakably fat people drifted by on flying cushions tricked out with pincers and mechanical hands; emaciated people drifted by too, their heads penetrated by wires, their faces twitching with pleasures they no longer really felt, their vehicles suddenly spurting with speed to deliberately crash headlong into other vehicles, going down in spinning, flaming wreckage to join the accumulation of twisted metal and weather-beaten trash that filled the streets hundreds of feet deep, black with insects . . .

"That's pretty much the way the whole world looks," the older Jorny said, his voice cracking. "There are attempts at changing it in places—but the influence of the Great Appetite is too strong—unless you have with you . . ." He turned to his younger self. "What you are supposed to have."

"What? What do you mean?"

"You have something I need." The older Jorny removed his backpack and took out a boxy device that had speakers at both ends, like a boombox, but no place to put in CDs or an iPod—only a small recess at one end. "You see? It goes here."

"You're expecting something from us?" Deede asked, confused.

The older Deede looked out the window. "When we found the locus of the Great Appetite in the temple, we found I had a kind of . . . a sensitivity to it. I could pick up information from it. By something I think of as 'looking fast.'"

Deede nodded. "I'm like that too."

"I saw you then—saw that you were coming and that you carried something the Great Appetite is afraid of. A many-voiced note of refusal."

"A what?"

"Do you have a recording device with you?"

Jorny stared at them . . . then slowly reached into his pocket and drew out his iPod.

The older Deede frowned. "That's not what I saw."

"It's inside it!" the older Jorny said. He snatched the iPod from Jorny's hand and, ignoring Jorny's protests, smashed it again and again on the metal window frame till it burst open.

"There it is!" the older Deede shouted, pointing at the wrecked device. "That thing!"

"It's a microdrive!" the older Jorny said excitedly. "We use them to make sounds too—but we put them directly in our sound machines. We have only sounds that have been appropriated, co-opted by the Great Appetite. Now . . ."

"This better work," Jorny grumbled.

The older Jorny plucked the microdrive from the wreckage and pressed it in the recess of the alternate boombox. It fit neatly in place. He hit a switch and the box boomed out—with a roaring cacophony.

"Shit!" the younger Jorny yelled, reaching over to snap the boombox off again. "It's not picking out any one song—it sounds like it's playing all of them at once! There's more than a thousand songs in there!"

"So that's it," the older Deede murmured. She looked at the older Jorny. "Remember? 'A thousand voices will silence his roar!' That's what I heard from the green light—it tried to cover it up, but I saw it! *It's supposed to play them all at once!*"

A vast moaning shook the floor then, and the ceiling shed bits of plaster. It was coming from the elevator banks.

"We've frightened *him* with the sound—for just that one second!" the older Jorny said. "He's coming for us!" He handed the younger Jorny the boombox. "Play it as loud as possible in the temple! Go on! It'll make everything possible! We'll draw it off!"

They he looked at the older Deede—and, to Deede's exquisite discomfort, the two adults kissed, kissed hugely and wetly. She looked away—so did Jorny. Then the older Jorny and Deede turned and ran past the elevator. The elevator doors opened and something red and green and endlessly hungry reached from it, stretching after them . . .

"Oh no!" Deede said.

"We'd better try this," Jorny whispered. And they turned and pounded down the stairs.

In minutes they'd reached the upside-down basement room

and dropped through the ceiling, coming up, spinning in space with momentary weightlessness, in the temple room.

Deede found herself on the floor, with the sphere-within-spheres, the Great Appetite, Yog-Sothoth looming over her, reaching for her, making its unspeakable offering. . . .

And then Jorny reached to switch on the boombox, at full volume.

"Jorny!" His hand hesitated over the boombox and he looked up to see his mother, trapped in one of the transparent tentacles, compressed and terrified. *"Jorny—wait! I don't know what you're doing, but it'll punish me if you do it! Stop!"*

He drew his hand back. Deede knew she had to trigger the box—but she was afraid of what she'd see if she reached for it. This thing had the power to hurt, to punish, beyond time. It could reach into your soul. It was evil times evil. It was the dark side of pleasure and it was the green light of pain. It wasn't something to defy . . .

But she remembered what the world looked like after the Great Appetite was done.

"I don't know what to do," Jorny said, covering his eyes with his hands.

Deede knew what to do. She reached for the box . . .

"Deede—don't!" Jean's voice.

"Deede, wait!" Lenny's voice. *"Look—we're here—you can't—"*

Deede refused to look. In defiance, she stabbed her fingers on the play button.

The sound that came out of the box was the joint booming of a thousand songs at once, the sort that Jorny would choose—a thousand songs of angst, rebellion, uncertainty, insistence, fury. Everything but a certain kind of surrender. They all had one note in common—a sound that was a refusal to be anything untrue.

One great thousand-faceted roaring white noise, black noise, every noise of the sonic spectrum . . . roaring. Roaring refusal—roaring defiance!

And the sphere-of-spheres withdrew into itself, dropping everything it touched in the two worlds connected by the temple, retreating to other planes, where it could find surcease from the amplified, crystallized sound of refusal to surrender to its dominance.

The temple shuddered, and the spiral grooves seemed to spin for a moment like an old-fashioned record—then the ceiling tumbled down and smashed the boombox. Came tumbling toward Jorny—

Deede pulled Jorny aside at the last split-second, and the great ceiling stones tumbled down in the center of the room, leaving a crust of chamber, the edges . . . and a pile of stone that blocked off the hole into the other Skytown and rose in a cluttered knob into the basement room above . . .

"You did it?" Jorny asked, coughing with dust.

"I had to. It couldn't have been worse for anyone."

He nodded and they climbed, together, silently, through the dust cloud, and up into the basement room. They found their way to the stairways, where they found dozens of people, clothes soaked and skin wet with blood. They were weak—but most were alive, lying one to a step, up and up and up the stairs, feebly calling for help. Among them, they found Lenny and Jean and Jorny's mother. They couldn't remember where they'd been. No one could quite remember it.

Not all of them were alive. Koenig was there—crushed almost flat.

The elevators were no longer blocked, the security guards were gone—except the ones who were dead. The front doors were wide open. When the ambulances came, no one could completely explain where they'd been or what had happened to them. Some internal disaster was inferred, and explanations were generated. Deede's father returned that night, summoned to deal with the emergency, and they moved out to a hotel on the other side of town—the same one that Jorny and his mother were staying at. He asked remarkably few questions.

Lenny and Jean spent most of the second day away from the Skymall in the hospital, getting transfusions, getting tested. They seemed dazed, slowly coming back to themselves.

It was just three days later that Deede set out for Portland to visit her cousin. "Just need to get away from this town, Dad," she said. "Just for a few days. I want to go to Mom's grave."

He simply nodded and helped her pack—and he put her on a plane.

*

She had to go to the trail by the old quarry for three days before Johansen showed up. She'd let him see her go there, every night, but he'd been cautious. Still, since she was wearing as little as she could get away with, he couldn't resist.

That night he followed her along the trail under the moonlight.

She went to the precipice, where her mother had taken her fatal plunge. She waited there for Johansen, humming a song to herself. No particular song—bits of many songs, really.

Johansen came up behind her, chuckling to himself.

She turned to face him, feeling as if she were made of steel. "No one's here—I'm sure you checked that out. And you can see I'm not wired. Not wearing enough to cover up a wire. You may as well say it. You killed her. You want to kill me."

"Sure," Johansen said. His hair was a jagged halo in the moonlight; his teeth seemed white in a face gone dark because the light was behind him. His eyes were two dark holes. "Why shouldn't I kill the little slut as well as the mama slut?"

"I don't think you can, though," she said calmly. "You know what? I used to be afraid of you. But I'm not now. I'm not afraid anymore! You're small-time. *I* stopped what made you. I can stop you easily—you're so very small in comparison, Johansen, to the Great Appetite itself."

"You're babbling, kid."

"Yeah? Then shut me up. If you can. I don't think you can, you limp-dicked jerk. You're nothing!"

His face contorted at that, and he rushed her—and she moved easily aside, drawing the razor-sharp buck-knife she'd hidden in her belt under her blouse in back. Then his ankle struck the fishing line she'd stretched, taut and down low between the roots, over the little peninsular jut of the cliff. And he stumbled and plunged, headlong, into the quarry, just as she'd known he would. She wouldn't need the back-up knife after all, she decided, pleased, as she watched him fall wailing into the shallow water, to break on the jagged rocks she'd arranged down there.

He lay face down in the shallow water on the rough-edged stones, struggling, calling hoarsely for help, his neck broken, unable to lift his head but a few inches . . . finally sagging down into the water. Drowning.

Smiling, she watched him die.

Then she stretched and waved cheerfully at the moon. She cut the fishing wire, put it in her pocket, tossed the knife into the quarry, and, humming a thousand songs, trotted back along the trail to the street. When she got to the sidewalk, she called first her dad, then Jorny, on her cell phone, saying she'd be coming back soon.

And then she caught a bus to the cemetery to have a talk with Mom.

WINDOWS UNDERWATER

Dagon his name, sea-monster, upward man
And downward fish; yet had his temple high
Reared in Azatus, dreaded through the coast . . .
—John Milton, *Paradise Lost*

1. Gilberto Lopez, Lymon Barnes. Summer 2014.

Lymon and Gil, both twenty-one, stood in the shade of the canopy over the festival picnic tables. Gil looked around with disgust.

Summer sunshine, green lawns, the smell of the marshes coming faintly from east of town. Tittering children eating frozen yogurt with sprinkles.

Gil was repelled by it.

"I'm sick of Rowley, man." He didn't say it too loud. That dickhead Curston was sitting at one of the picnic tables, maybe forty feet away, jawing about baseball. Deputy Curston was all full of smiles because his Red Sox had a clear road to the playoffs. He'd given Gil at least two completely unnecessary traffic tickets.

Lymon shrugged. "Rowley's okay." He was thoughtfully eating his extra-large sprinkled cherry-chocolate frozen yogurt. He was the kind of guy who could eat anything and never get fat. Freckled, "pale as fishbelly, skinny as an eel" was what Lymon's dad said. He had hinted that Lymon wasn't actually his kid. True, Lymon didn't look like his pop. Recessive genes, is all.

Gil was half Mexican, ran to chubby, and was always fighting it. "You got to eat that giant triple cone in front of me?"

"Surrender, surrender to the lure of the fro-gurt, Gil!"

Gil snorted. "Hell, it's not just Rowley. I'm sick of Massachusetts too. I don't like the cops, I don't like the tourists, I don't like the ocean—especially around here. Water's too fucking murky and dark. I want to go to one of those islands where the water is crystal clear. You can see whatever's down there. And there's some kinda real culture going on. You know? Like in Hollywood."

"Kind of boring here," Lymon admitted. "Nothing to do but—"

"But *this*," Gil said. He waved a hand at the little tents and canopies and shade structures of the Rowley Arts and Crafts Festival. His other hand was holding a plastic wine glass from the "tasting booth." Eight dollars for one glass of lame wine from Virginia.

"If you left Rowley where would you go? You got free rent with your folks here."

"I'd go to California. Maybe L.A. Or San Diego. Get into filmmaking or . . ."

Lymon looked at Gil and raised the red-blond eyebrow that was always half raised anyway. "Filmmaking. Really."

"Okay, *listillo*. I'll start small—work for a videogame company. Do design, maybe direct-cut scenes." Gil drank some of his wine. "I got an uncle in L.A. He's kind of a dick, but he offered me a job. I could work there while I was getting my shit together to apply to Pixil Arts."

"You mean that uncle who has the car repair shop? You don't know anything about cars either. You've been studying to be a pharmacist, man."

"He'd teach me. I hate being in a classroom. I want to be out doing something."

"You could go back to work for your Pops."

Gil made a face. "I don't want to touch another goddamn fish. That's why I took pharmacy—there's nothing to do with fish. Dad still tries to get me to go out on Eddie's boat." His brother's name was Edwardo, but he went by Eddie. "I get seasick. And it's all fished out anyway around here. Mostly jellyfish out there. Eddie's getting desperate—starting to fish around Innsmouth. Those reefs out there."

Lymon blinked at him, genuinely startled. "That even *legal?*"

"Sure it's legal. Nobody does it much, is all—just a tradition not to fish there. I'm not going out on the boat, no way. I'm not even working at his fish market—the smell makes me sick."

"Everything makes you sick today, man. I like fish."

"I know you do. You and your fish tanks. Come on, Lymon, we should both go to L.A. Your dad's trying to get you to move outta his place anyway. We can stay with my uncle."

"I'm doing pretty good with the bookstore. Assistant manager."

"They're gonna close that store, man. Chain's downsizing."

"Maybe." Lymon ate some more frozen yogurt. "You wanna come over, play some Skyrim? You can use my sister's computer, we can meet online."

Gil sighed. He drank a little wine. It was supposed to be cabernet, but it tasted vinegary to him. "You and me used to talk about working in gaming. Gotta go to New York or L.A. for that. You can code. I can draw. We can get a job at Pixil Arts."

"Yeah, right. And we could date Natalie Portman and Mila Kunis, drive 'em around in our new Porsches. Sure. You want some of this fro-gurt stuff? I bought too much."

"No."

"I'm playing Skyrim. You coming?"

Gil sighed. "I guess so. It's that or this. But I'm telling you—"

"I know. You're leaving town."

2. Gilberto Lopez, Lymon Barnes. October 2028.

"How long you back for this time, Gil?"

They were standing on the top of the dike protecting Rowley from the ever-rising sea. Lymon had taken up cigarettes, Spirit Naturals, and he was blowing smoke upward to go with the breeze sucked toward the Atlantic as the tide went out.

Gil made a faint groan. "I don't know. Maybe a long time. Lost that gig at Vapor Arts. Actually—I got mad and quit."

"You ever got past designer assistant?"

"No. Finally they offered me a job in the cafeteria."

"Christ." Lymon shook his head. "Assholes. You're a good artist."

"I don't know how to use the new e-pens, all that stuff." Gil shrugged and admitted, "That technology's been around twenty years—I could've learned. I got all caught up in Melda and that just didn't work out. Nothing much worked out. I feel like growing up here just sapped all the life out of me. And L.A. couldn't give it back."

"Well, zip up your coat, and I'll show you something to take your mind off all that."

Gil zipped up his coat—not that easy to do. He was getting into his late thirties now and putting on significant weight, like his Pops. He glanced at the sky. "Getting dark."

"Naw, won't be dark for like three hours. It's just how it *is* now, lot of haze all the time, makes it murky out. Climate change. Florida's half underwater, north Georgia's turning into a desert. In the Carolinas it's storms all the time. Here it's like this. And the ocean slopping right at our feet. But do not despair, Gil, I got a pint of Hennessy on me too."

"You know how to get to me: offer me liquor. I'm a cheap date. It's sad, dude."

"*Dude,* he says. The legacy of L.A. Come on."

Gil let himself be drawn along with Lymon. They tramped along the curving seawall that kept Plum Sound from flooding the lowlands. The dike was high and strong, the best the Army Corps of Engineers could put up as the rising seas threatened Rowley. But if the stone and concrete wall cracked open, Rowley would be drowned.

Lymon handed him the pint of brandy. For something to say as he unscrewed the top—so he didn't feel like such an alky—Gil asked, "So your job's still going good?"

"Yeah. Have to learn new coding languages sometimes but—I like coding. Keeps my mind busy."

Gil glanced at Lymon and thought, *Getting fifteen years older hasn't helped him out much.* Lymon's profile seemed bloated; his lips thicker; eyes popping. Did he have some kind of thyroid issues?

Walking along the top of the dike as if it were a sidewalk, they passed the pint of brandy and looked out over the water. Up ahead, the dike curved to follow the contours of Plum Island Sound; on their right, the mirror-like water of the marshes reflected the dull sky; a seagull skated through the reflection.

Soon they'd left the sound behind. Now the sea gnashed close to hand to the left; it churned slowly, like a colossal ruminant chewing at something. The dike curved on between sea and marsh, squeezed to a thin charcoal-colored line that pointed at Innsmouth Harbor.

Gil glanced at his watch. It was low tide—but the water washed against the wall just ten feet below them. "How high's it get on the dike when the tide's full?"

"Runs over the top, sometimes, if there's a storm." Lymon sniffed, and wiped his nose with one hand. "So far, not enough to do much damage. But that dike wasn't ever high enough. Sea's rising even faster than they expected."

He passed the brandy bottle.

They fell silent for a time. The dike was flat, the brandy warming, and the miles seemed to melt away. Finally Gil said, "I kind of wonder, sometimes, why I always hated living out here. Rowley's not so bad, I guess. People treated me okay. Mostly. But something was always telling me I didn't belong and—how many Mexican families in Rowley? Almost none. A few Puerto Ricans, a few Cubans. Me, I'm half—neither fish nor fowl. And I don't like the fish part."

Lymon gave him a sharp look.

Gil went on: "I had this, like, fantasy, when the ocean was

rising and all the dikes were being built . . . that Rowley would screw up and the whole town would be sunken. I figured my folks would get away on their boats and—" He shrugged and chuckled in a nervous kind of way. "Sick, I know."

"Huh. 'Kay. Kind of weird that you mentioned that, but then again—You want to see a sunken town? You can pretend it's Rowley."

Gil started to answer—then his cell phone rang. He dug it out of his pants pocket, glanced at it, saw it was his brother's number. He thumbed answer. "Eddie?" Gil listened. The phone crackled, then Eddie's voice cut through. "Gil? The . . . don't . . . If they . . . that side . . . stay away . . ." Every third syllable was swallowed in a void. "They're looking from . . ."

"Eddie, what's up, I'm losing your signal, here, man. Can't make out what you're saying."

". . . looking up at me . . . windows underwater . . . their mouths . . . windows under the . . . just don't . . . not with . . ."

A furious crackle arose on the phone, as if something in the air was angrily drowning the voice out. "Eddie?"

Eddie's voice had fallen into a void of static. Then the static ended—there was only silence. *Call ended,* it said on the screen.

"Lousy reception out here. Don't even bother trying to call him back, it's hopeless, man," Lymon said. "Hey—you see that? Over there, look! There's your drowned town, man."

The sun was going down behind them; the sea in front, in this light, was strangely translucent here; as if for a moment, just before it got dark out, it had chosen to disclose what was normally hidden.

They were looking out at the sunken harbor of Innsmouth; the water had covered the old ruins. The high, razor-wired fences that had kept people out were fallen and rusting; between the remains of the fences the old brick and granite buildings were mostly tumbled into shapeless heaps. Here and there in the ruins were recognizable constructions: peaked gables and gambrel roofs, a few chimney pots, something that might have been a warehouse. A narrow shape almost like an obelisk was poking out of the water, just its sharp peak showing. Gil realized, as he stared at it, that it was the top of an old church spire. No cross adorned its tip.

The warehouse, if that's what it was, had some recognizable windows, though their frames were skewed by the partial collapse of the building into rhomboids. Something moved inside one of them—a large fish of some kind, looking back at him. Might be the face of a big moray eel.

"Holy fuck," Gil murmured. "The water's so clear! That's . . . really not normal around here!"

"Normal for the time of day," Lymon said. His voice sounded low, croakingly low, oddly melancholy. "It's just—a trick of the light. The old town shows itself as the night comes."

"I didn't know the water had, like, totally swallowed it up. You remember when we used to come and look at the town through the fence?"

"Sure. The ruins of Innsmouth. Try to figure out which story was true. Some kind of dumping place for World War One mustard gas—that's the story my old man used to repeat. Toxic dump. People had to be evacuated and the place destroyed, so stay away."

"I always liked the devil worshipper story. That was cooler."

Lymon chuckled—again his voice had that oddly low, silky intonation Gil wasn't used to. "Devil's Reef is just out there past the harbor . . . so maybe that's how the story got started. But it was never about worshipping the Devil, whoever that may be."

"I don't think it was the Devil, like Lucifer. But—some other 'devil.' Half fish and half man. From the Bible."

"Sure. He was mentioned several times in the Old Testament. Like from Judges: *Now the lords of the Philistines gathered to offer a great sacrifice to Dagon their God . . .*"

Gil glanced at him. "Impressive, dude! You memorized it!"

Lymon gazed fixedly into the sea. "My favorite is from 1 Samuel: *Then the Philistines took the ark of God and brought it into the house of Dagon and set it up beside Dagon . . . But when they rose early on the next morning, behold, Dagon had fallen face downward on the ground before the ark of the LORD, and the head of Dagon and both his hands were lying cut off on the threshold . . .*"

Gil stared. "That's . . . a long passage to memorize. When did you get all, uh, theological?"

"It's nothing to do with theology. It's about things that are old and powerful and different. Some creatures were simply powerful enough to be worshipped. That Bible story—a lot of propaganda. I don't imagine the Ark of the Covenant would have bothered Dagon much."

Gil licked his lips—and looked at his watch. "We got a long way to go back. I need to find out what Eddie was all worked up about."

"Sure. Here—you finish the brandy. I'm going out on the fishing platform for a minute."

He handed Gil the brandy bottle and walked off down the dike, toward a flat wooden structure Gil hadn't seen before. It was a kind of short jetty cantilevered from the dike, jutting out over the sunken remains of Innsmouth. The support beams were bolted into the dike below the water level.

As the sun went down, the sea breeze was rising, wet and cold, making Gil shiver. *Good excuse as any,* he thought, opening the brandy bottle. He drank down the last quarter of it, tossed the bottle in the water, and stuck his hands in his coat pockets to warm them as he walked over to the platform.

Lymon was standing right on the edge, looking down, as Gil joined him.

"What's up with this thing, Lymon? Something for tourists?"

"It's for fishing."

"Fishing *here?* Supposedly all the fish from here is toxic."

Lymon didn't respond. He just stared down into the water.

After a long moment he said, "You ready, Gil?"

"Yeah. We should get back. Hey—when the tide goes out, does it expose the town?"

"Only some of the higher bits. The water's getting darker but you can still see . . . there! Look—you see that?" Lymon pointed.

"What?"

"Over by the spire."

Something was moving toward them, making a rippling wake as it came. Gil thought it was a sea lion, probably. That was a head, sticking up out of the water, approaching them, not a fin.

"Is that a—?" He broke off, and stepped closer to the edge to peer at the thing. "No. Not a seal—maybe a dolphin?"

"No. That's my cousin," Lymon said. "She's been down there for years."

Then Gil was punched painfully in the middle of his back— as Lymon knocked him headfirst into the water.

Gil's mouth was open to shout and it filled with saltwater as he plunged down through the foul seawater; sinking toward sunken roofs, toward darting black shapes and rippling columns of yellow-red light.

He felt saltwater burning his throat, searing his lungs. *Drowning. Got to get to the surface.*

He flailed, but thrashing only sent him deeper.

A thick-bodied, naked woman rose up before him, a graceless blue-white shape, intermittently scaly—was it a woman?

She was looking unblinkingly at him from enormous, bulging eyes set a little too widely. He could see the pink and blue gills respirating on her neck; he could see . . .

Nothing.

Could see nothing . . .

Darkness swirled ever more thickly around him, icy cold penetrated to his bones, water pressure squeezed him—and something gripped him tightly by the ankles, pulling him deeper, and he thought, *Strange way to die* . . .

*

Gil woke and, after awhile, decided he was alive—after a fashion.

The six-sided chamber, perhaps thirty-five feet long and twenty wide, was cut from ancient layers of coral and stone; the smell made him think of his father's fish market on a hot day. But it was cold in there, and misty.

Gil raised himself on one elbow to look around. Where was the light coming from? It pulsed softly from the corners of the room, hand-sized growths shaped something like mushrooms but filmy, transparent, laced with veins that glowed roseate-tinged blue.

On the wall to Gil's left was a bas-relief carving of a sort of bearded merman wearing a crown, rising up from the sea and spreading his brutish claws in perverse benediction.

Dagon, Gil thought.

Now and then the walls shivered with a soft hollow boom-ing—the sound of the sea up above. Cracks in the ceiling dripped in rhythm with the boom.

Gil sat up and, after the throbbing in his head subsided, found he was naked, except for a clean dry blanket. He had been laid upon a wet, plastic-wrapped mattress, probably dragged from some sunken boat; the mattress lay upon a stone slab. Where was the door to the room? He couldn't see one.

"Hey!" he called out—his voice was raspy from salt He noticed a plastic bucket on the floor holding what looked like fresh water. And a terrible thirst took hold of him.

It could be drugged . . .

But he was soon crouching beside it, drinking clean water, clearing his throat.

"I'm glad you're up," said Lymon. Gil turned to see Lymon sauntering in. There was a deep shadow behind him that emitted a grinding sound as it closed behind Lymon. Some sort of hidden door.

Gil stared at Lymon. A kind of slippery membrane oozed across his otherwise naked skin. Gill-slits had opened in his neck; his face was more elongated now, his mouth rounder, thicker; his ears seemed to have vanished entirely; most of his hair was gone. There were only wisps of his orange hair remaining, hanging lankly to his thin shoulders. Some of the membrane had been pulled back from his head, flopping down his back like a hood made of jellyfish stuff. There were webbings of skin between his fingers.

Gil shook his head. "Jesus fuck, Lymon."

Lymon smiled. His teeth had become needle-like. "Do you like my second skin? It's alive, you know. It's a symbiotic organism, feeding off wastes from my skin and body. It protects me from cold and water pressure and salt damage. For genetic humans like you, we have another sort of second skin. It extracts oxygen right from the water, takes your carbon dioxide and—"

"Lymon—shut the fuck up! You're . . . you've . . ." Gil felt sick and the feeling overwhelmed him. He had to turn and heave out a bellyful of water.

"Yes," Lymon said, calmly, as Gil coughed and spat. "I've changed." His voice had that odd low silkiness as he went on. "The faithful of Innsmouth were not all exterminated. Some were able to escape. They were not entirely changed themselves. They intermarried . . . and those of us in whom the recessive gene is active—well, after a certain amount of time, as adults, we are called to the sea, and we begin to change." Lymon took Gil's elbow, helped him to sit on the mattress again. "He calls to us, Gil, and we hear him, when no one else does."

The door grated again, and the female came into the room— the one who'd approached Gil underwater. She was carrying a stone jar; she wore the living ooze just as Lymon did.

"That is Darla Jane," said Lymon.

"Eat," she said, proffering the jar. Her voice had a reverberant lisp to it.

Gil looked into the jar. It looked like boiled spinach, with bits of fish; there was a rusty spoon in the jar too.

"Seaweed, a variety that will restore your strength," Lymon said. "And some fish. You'd better get used to fish. I must insist you eat—otherwise certain persons will enter, and you will be force-fed in a particularly unpleasant way."

Gil felt heavy, weighted down by disorientation and despair. He had no strength in him to fight. He reached into the jar, scooped up some of the warm food with the spoon, and ate. It was salty and its texture was revolting, but it restored hope and strength almost immediately.

Lymon and Darla Jane watched in silence. When he'd eaten enough, Lymon took the jar away and Darla Jane pushed him back onto the mattress.

"Breed," she said. "We breed."

"Oh . . . no, no, really, that's not going to work," Gig sputtered, looking away from her. The smell; the membrane slopping over her—unbearable. He tried to push her away. But it was like pushing away a mudslide.

"You don't understand," Lymon said. "It's not . . . about arousal, really. Not at first. But—she will show you. We need your seed, Gil. We need human seed; we only do hybrids, as children, you see. That's what works best."

"But *me*—Lymon? I'm your friend!"

"And I would miss you, Gil! So you'll be here with me. I wanted to give you a chance to live your dream. To be something that matters. To really have an impact on the world. We've been preparing the planet—encouraging climate change deniers through our intermediaries . . . and certain industries. The damage humanity was doing to the sea could not be tolerated. We'll end it our way. And yet, ironically, global warming is to our benefit! The sea rises! What it consumes, we too will consume. Now let Darla Jane have her way, Gil."

"No—that's completely . . . no."

"It's all right. You don't have to kiss her."

Lymon walked away, and the thing calling itself Darla Jane pressed him back and straddled him—and the membrane parted at her groin.

Something emerged from her there. From between her legs. *Tendrils,* thin and whipping and transparent, restless and seeking, tickling up his belly; then a red, hose-like organ extruded from under the tendrils. The living hose opened itself wide and, slowly but inexorably, sucked his private parts into itself—clasping testicles and all.

Gil writhed and shrieked and tried to push her away, but she was far stronger than he was and he could get no grip on her slick limbs.

The hose-like organ squeezed peristaltically, *milking* his blood up into it, forcing his organ to become rigid. There was a kind of sickening pseudo-pleasure in the process, but he was gagging at her subaquatic reek, struggling against her clamp-like hands.

The tendrils to either side of the hose extruded spines that stabbed into his thighs.

The pain was piercing, attenuated—but almost immediately vanished. Some biological anesthetic, he thought. *Like what mosquitoes use so you don't feel them bite.*

Then he felt a cold pulsing from the spines and knew he was being injected. A thick, glutinous fluid was forced into his muscles. It carried a ghastly ecstasy, a vile delight that expanded through him from his pierced thighs . . . and he found himself bucking his hips, forcing his reproductive organs deeper into the externalized genitalia of the thing that held him down until . . .

3. Gilberto Lopez, Lymon Barnes. June 2037.

Gil delighted in the feeling of being a hand in the glove of the sea. He loved being out here, free of the oppressive weight of the temple hidden under the reefs—the freedom of the open sea, the infinite possibilities. He loved kicking easily along, warm and safe within his second skin. He envied Lymon his ability to breathe directly in water—Lymon didn't have to look out through a bubble of the membrane. It blurred his vision around the edges. But he could see well enough: the light wavering down from the surface; a school of striped fish swimming by. How had he ever felt that fish were repellent? They really were lovely—the way they all moved as one in their school. Someday the interspecies council would move with such graceful unanimity.

The Atlantic Ocean had regained much of its ancient vitality with the awakening of Dagon and the hard work done by His people. The acidity from global warming had been much reduced, with the cultivation of the undersea forests of specially bred kelp. Mercury and other toxins were being sponged away. The council had destroyed many of the ships that had done so much damage; they had blocked the outflow from dirtwalker cities—all that had helped. The wars, too, on the surface, had helped. Struggling for resources in an overheated world, the dirtwalkers were reduced in numbers and thus in power to do harm.

It really was becoming a kind of paradise along the northeast shore, underwater. But a number of foul dirtwalker settlements still festered on the coast.

Swimming toward the Plum Island Sound, Gil sighed, thinking that perhaps his father would have been proud of him after all, if he could have shown him all this—his father had always loved the sea. But Pops and Mom were dead. Eddie too—Eduardo had gone a bit mad after seeing Lymon and his brother Gil on the trawler that day.

I thought of him as my stronger older brother, but Eduardo was weak and foolish, Gil thought. A person of no vision.

Eddie had refused to be recruited. And Lymon's spies on the surface had reported his demise. Dead of a heroin overdose. Gil's parents had each taken their own lonely path to death. Pops had died of cancer, Mom had crawled into a bottle and never gotten out. They'd wasted away in Rowley.

As he gazed out across the underseascape, Gil's only real regret was that he had no artist's supplies. How he'd love to find a way to paint this! The kelp forests; the sliding shark, the nosing dolphin. Blue-green water and diffused golden light; green going to black farther down. And the work crew, swimming briskly to the dike. What a sight they were—men and women transformed, merged with the sea.

The work was almost done, he saw, as they approached the dike. The undermining was finished. The chains were being locked into place.

Soon the head engineer signaled to Gil—who was now high-priest of the interspecies brotherhood—asking for permission to proceed.

Gil looked around, saw that the tide was high as it was going to be, and the others had drawn back to safety. He gestured, *Proceed.*

The engineer signaled Darla Jane—who gave that high keening call she had, which came from her vibrating gill-slits . . .

And soon the kraken came from their deep place of slumber.

Their massive oblong bodies stretched out; they turned in the water, their multiple limbs seeking, reaching for the chains; their tentacles entwined the thick steel bands. And the giant squids, bigger than any known to dirtwalker humanity, began to pull . . .

It took almost ten minutes, but the underpinnings at last collapsed, taking the dike with them. A great rumbling shuddered through the sea as the dike fell into it, ragged boulders of asphalt streaming bubbles as they plunged down.

But Gil was lifted up. With a cry of joy he felt himself carried up, bodily sluiced toward the land as the dike disintegrated into the Atlantic Ocean.

The great wave lifted him ever higher, over the sinking debris; up and up so that at last he broke the surface, and with Lymon and their companions he rode the tsunami in at dawn, the servants of Dagon astride the great wave that would be the first of many to crash down on Rowley, Massachusetts, drowning it as Innsmouth had been drowned, crushing buildings and choking the squirming dirtwalkers, so that the triumph of Dagon, and the glory of Gilberto Lopez and Lymon Barnes was complete.

AT HOME WITH AZATHOTH

". . . that last amorphous blight of nethermost confusion which blasphemes and bubbles at the centre of all infinity—the boundless daemon-sultan Azathoth, whose name no lips dare speak aloud, and who gnaws hungrily in inconceivable, unlighted chambers beyond time . . ."

—H. P. Lovecraft
The Dream-Quest of Unknown Kadath

When Frederic DuSang saw the eye text from Filrod, he knew the bait had been taken. He knew it before he even read the eye-t. He had that tingle, as when code was about to become a program; that particular shiver of closure.

But it wasn't over yet. He still had to reel him in . . .

Walking down the Santa Cruz Beach boardwalk to the VR ride on a wet September morning, Frederic tapped the tiny stud under the skin beneath his right eye, the contact cursor in his fingernail telling the device to transcribe a subvocalization—he had learned to subvocalize his voice-recogs for security. And he subvocalized, "Text, 'Come over at seven tonight if you want it, FilRod. FdS.'"

The head chip heard and obeyed, sending the text to Filrod's palmer.

The guy's name was Rodney Filbern, but everyone called him by his screen name, and Filrod replied almost immediately, *Not a good time 4 me. Just tranz it?*

Frederic responded, "Tough, sorry, leaving town. Not offering it any other way. Wouldn't work. Need you there in person."

Filrod bit down harder on the hook. "OK Fred U dick, will be there."

Frederic snorted. He hated being called Fred.

He reached the perpetual carnival on the boardwalk, waved to his manager, a bruise-eyed, rasta-haired old surfer, and went to work at the VR ride, putting pallid teenagers through full-body virtual experiences and cleaning up the stalls afterward. As always, as he mopped, thinking, *I need a new goddamn job. Vraiment, yo.*

*

Frederic's thoughts were sometimes in French because his parents were French and they'd tried to make him bilingual. Never quite got there, but they left their mark.

His mom had left his four years earlier, after Jackie killed himself. Jackie was . . . had been . . . Frederic's younger brother.

Frederic's *père* was a thin man with shoulder-length white hair and an eaglebeak nose. When Frederic came home that evening, he looked at Frederic over his glass of Bordeaux with that familiar dull wince, that "depression nerveuse" expression he got when he thought about his son.

Okay, Frederic thought, *so I'm almost twenty-six and still living with you, so what? I know what you don't know, you old fils de pute.*

He nodded to his dad, in honor of the free rent, and started for the basement door.

"Frederic," Dad said muzzily, "a moment, eef you please. We should talk about . . . Oh, I don't know, somezing . . ."

Frederic paused and looked back at his dad. There was a little extra slurriness, a particular mush in his father's voice, and more French accent than usual, too much for a bottle of wine. Probably he was back on the OxyContin. Supposedly he took it for a work-related injury. Right, Dad. Frederic's father had been a computer programmer in Silicon Valley. Made good money, too, till Jackie died and Mom left, and then Dad started sinking, slowly sinking, and now they were living mostly on his disability, since Frederic spent most of his money on AI and chip augs.

"Dad, I thought you weaned off that shit."

Dad opened his mouth to deny he was on it, but Frederic looked at him evenly—and his *père* gave him the ol' Gallic shrug. He licked his lips and articulated more carefully. "Oh, well, you know, zuh scan . . . the scan, it said the crack in the vertebrae was open again, so—"

"Whatever. Come on. You're just . . . It's about Mom and Jackie. So if you gotta self-medicate, whatever. You do that, go ahead. I've got my own thing. Okay?"

Frederic turned and went down into the basement, thinking he should probably get his old man to go to a therapist, but Dad hated shrinks and Frederic just couldn't carry the weight of dealing with Dad's stuff. He did, in fact, have his own thing.

He veered between storage boxes and went to his basement room.

Once his father's den, the room was now Frederic's own little soundproofed warren of linked-up used hard drives, monitors, transervers, low-grade floating AI, a desk he used for extra shelf space. In a corner, almost an afterthought, was an old futon with yellowed sheets reeking of mildew. *The skuzz den,* Frederic's mom had called it. Laughing, though, as she said it. That was something he loved about her—that she laughed at you in a way that meant she didn't care if you had failings, it was all good, no one's perfect. Now he hardly ever saw her.

Frederic sat on the futon, bunched up pillows behind his back, and reached over to the hardware to activate the tranz box. The virtual screen appeared in front of him—something only he could see at the moment, thanks to his implants—and Frederic muttered the keywords that would activate the floating AI ovoid bobbing near his bed. The AI chirped and Frederic muttered the first password, got his menu, flicked a finger at the air to open *SpaceHole,* got the prompt screen, and . . .

And hesitated. It always made him nervous, kind of sick and

giddy, to open this program. Buster Shecht was still missing. But Buster was a crazy fuck, could be missing for lots of reasons. The reason didn't have to be the Azathoth.

Anyway, Buster Schecht wasn't half the programmer Frederic was; couldn't hack his way out of a paper bag. Could be he'd screwed something up and got some kind of brainfry—maybe the yellowflash feedback effect in an implant? It wasn't unheard of. Frederic was not going to screw up.

He licked his lips and spoke the three entry words—words that Buster had found online, in the Necronomicon file.

The "screen" flickered in his mind's eye, pixel bits spinning like water going down a drain in the center . . . and then in the very center of the virtual screen they interacted, as cellular automata do, and they formed a spreading organization—something ugly, jagged, but hinting darkly at life.

The whirling finished, and the image sucked away into the SpaceHole—and the Realm of Azathoth unfurled to fill the screen.

That's what Buster had called it . . . *Azathoth.* Claimed the thing living in Azathoth itself taught him the name. If it had, that must mean it was, in fact, the result of a program some brilliant game design engineer had worked up, the gamer having put that in somewhere, and not—as Frederic theorized—the result of a series of meta-program worms linking up in cyberspace, almost like the way the early forms of life had linked up to make more complex organisms, in that giant bowl of hot primordial soup the sea had been.

Of course, there was Buster's explanation—or what he claimed to believe, that last time he'd been here in the skuzz den. Probably just playing Frederic for lulz:

"Dude, I'm going to tell you this and you're gonna think I'm snagging, but man, this is for real: the fractal set I worked up outta the Rucker formula, it opened a door into a real place, man. Check with Jacques Vallee: information is a form of energy. In fact, every-

thing's a form of information. And, deep down, information is the form of everything. So we can create real objective stuff with pure information long as it's the right information . . . And I'm telling you, Azathoth is a for-real place."

"You do know I stopped smoking dope, right?" Frederic had said. *"You think you're gonna get me all freaked and shit, but it's flat not happening man . . ."*

Frederic shook his head, remembering. What he was seeing couldn't be a real place. This place couldn't *really* exist . . . except in the mind of some lunatic. It was just a cellular automata model, tessellation automata, iterative arrays.

Automata cellulare, his dad would say.

They were fractal patterns generating templates of life forms in a three-dimensionally modeled artificial environment, purely digital, and he knew from looking at great special effects all his life how animation could seem crazy-real.

And of course he was seeing it in a virtual screen, the floating AI's work projected to his chip, his chip projecting to his mind, his mind projecting to his mind's eye, so that he saw a three-dimensional place, and the things in it, hanging in space just up above . . .

There was no clear-cut edge, unlike other virtual projections. It was squamous, wrigglingly ragged along the edges of the "tank" of image that floated over him. It just plain seemed *alive.* Amazing animation work, really, given the source of it: a couple of deep-web eccentrics, Buster figured, had worked it up, made it out of some bits and pieces of online gaming environments, movie clips copied and altered, someone's personal animation program, all mixed together.

That was the only acceptable explanation for what he was seeing: a *place* that was an *entity;* an entity that was a *place.* It was as if he were looking with X-ray eyes into something's body, but he was also looking into a world, an entire landscape. Those numerous writhing protracted pyramids of ichorous green were organs of perception, maybe; but at the same time they were a kind of forest and somehow he knew that if he were to go there (horrible thought), the growths would tower menacingly over him; yet for sure that thicket was some kind of living cilia, that jade and purulent sky was a high enclosure of living tissue. At the same time he was certain that if he were to reach it himself, to ascend to it, he would penetrate *into* it, and it would go on and on and on, unending. And surely that iridescent, spiky compound tetrahedron in the foreground, slowly whirling, fulminating with bloody fury, was an angry thought crystallizing in a trapped mind.

He could almost . . . *almost* . . . hear it thinking. It thought in minatory buzzing sounds; its words became its form . . . its mind defined its world . . .

Frederic shivered. *C'est fou.* He was having some kind of weird psychological reaction to the program. And this was only the first mode; overdrive mode was faster, captivatingly visual, something you had to use big will power to look away from.

He stared into the mêlée of brutal abstract shapes, the slow-motion maelstrom of Azathoth, wondering about Buster . . .

And *Buster appeared* there, at that exactly moment, within Azathoth. Buster's chunky, acne-spackled, bearded face materialized in the center of the translucent compound tetrahedron. Buster's mouth moved; after a moment Frederic heard the words, materializing in his mind.

"Frederic, bro, I'm stuck, digesting in Azathoth, no hope for me, doesn't matter, ready to disintegrate, only way out, but your brother, nearby . . ."

Frederic's stomach lurched. "Shut up about Jackie, Buster!" he blurted.

Then he snorted at himself. Buster wasn't really there. His mind had probably superimposed the image, made up some story about Buster, put it in the program. Supposedly the AI wasn't supposed to take anything from your mind but a literal interpretation of your words, subvocalized, and occasional motional directions, and certain very defined projections . . . but for a while ecog chippers had suspected that there was an unpredictable involuntary telepathic level to the connectivity.

Here it was—this *fantôme,* this digital ghost, was proof of espering chips. He'd have to tell DG and the torrent skaters about it.

The iridescent crystal entrapping "Buster" mutated into a solid icosahedron—and went opaque.

Buster vanished.

Had Buster been—digested?

Cut it out, you're getting sucked into the fantasy. This program is some kinda lulz hoax and somewhere some programmer's laughing his fucking ass off right now.

Didn't matter. It'd do for what he had in mind—it'd do for Filrod.

He had planned to insert Jackie into the images; to toss in the candid footage he had of Filrod jerking off over tranny porn, which he'd gotten when he'd hacked Filrod's webcam system, whirl it all together in this sick place, let it iterate, copy and paste it into every variant of YouTube there was. Make Filrod pay for what he'd done.

The plan was to get Filrod stuck in this place long enough to really make him feel it—because when you went into overdrive mode on this program, that's what happened. It was hypnotic, was Azathoth, inexplicably hard to look away from, and you could mix in any image you projected so it looked as if you were in hell surrounded by . . . whatever the programmer inserted. If he wanted to put images of the new Republican president's inauguration into it, you'd see the prez and his backers splashed all over the Azathoth landscape. And you could feel weirdly trapped there . . . Images of Filrod's shame, Filrod's guilt, could be wrapped around him in overdrive mode . . .

But now—he might have a more direct mode of attack on Filrod.

Filrod himself. He had an ecog chip, after all . . .

He glanced at his watch—and right then, as if on cue, the doorbell rang upstairs.

*

Filrod was a broad-shouldered college student with widely spaced front teeth, a dull, blunt face, and faux-hawked brown hair. Frederic had heard that Filrod was barely passing his classes; the jock was not exactly stupid but never far enough from his interchatter channels to focus on anything. He was a wide receiver on the football team and wore the school jersey with his number, 8, on it.

Behind the eight-ball, you asshole, Frederic thought, as Filrod hunkered on the futon beside him.

"You wanna hit some syntha?" Filrod said, when he came in, waving the e-pipe.

"Nah, I gave it up, you go ahead," Frederic said distractedly as he tinkered with the hardware by the futon, trying to get the best signal.

Filrod sucked on the e-pipe, blinking at the floating AIs, and asked as he blew out a stream of chemical-laden water vapor. His eyes glazed as the drug hit him. "Don't those things use up a lotta power, floating around?"

"They're made of super-light materials, man, and they tend to get less interference from the drives if I keep 'em floating . . . Do have to change batteries pretty often." Frederic finished tinkering and waved smoke out of his face. "Enough with that shit, I don't want your second-hand smoke, dude."

"Whatever." Filrod switched the pipe off, tucked it away in a pants pocket. "So can you get me the stuff I need to see or not?"

"Yeah, *if* you transfer the money to my account." The money he never actually expected to get. This wasn't about money.

"You show me the stuff, I transfer, right here."

Frederic shrugged. "'Kay, fair enough." He prepared the virtual screen and gave Filrod the frequency so he could see it too.

Then he decided to prep Filrod himself a bit more. Set him up good. "Okay, you sent me the password, the ISP, all that—file names. You sure you sent me *everything?*"

"Everything! My mom's will's in there, man. I need to see it, I gotta know. She's pretty sick. But the mean ol' cow lingers on and on." He shook his head sadly. "I think I'm gonna get kicked outta school—won't have my school money, nothin' to live on. I need to know if money's coming."

Frederic looked at him. Something in Filrod's voice, a certain tightness, said *cover story.*

Christ! Was Filrod thinking of killing his moms, easing her off into the ether, since she was sick anyway? Was he going to if he had enough inheritance coming to justify the risk of a murder?

Wouldn't be surprising . . .

"Okay, Filrod, so . . . this isn't going to look like a conventional penetration program. This'll look—different. It's three-dimensional, it's cyberspace stuff, it's very . . . hard info-animation." He'd made up that last term to keep Filrod confused.

It worked. "Hard info . . . whatever. I just need to see her will and testament stuff, and I know this fucking attorney has it on e-file."

"Sure, we'll get there. But see this technique is more . . . stealth. You know? Don't want 'em to know we did this, right?"

"Right, that's for fucking-A sure. Don't want nobody to know."

"Then—lock in. Stare right into that circle you see forming there. It's called SpaceHole. Look right into it, keep your eyes on it, and we'll see what we find."

"That thing? It doesn't look like any kind of—"

"Trust me, dude, this is what you need to see."

Filrod blinked and stared into the SpaceHol, and Frederic sent a message to the AI, moving into Mode One of Azathoth.

"What the *fuck!*" Filrod blurted, staring into the change-world, the shifting landscape that was a mind—that was an entity, Azathoth; that was a program, really—and what would be Fil-rod's hell, if Frederic had anything to say about it.

Frederic sent the second signal, to overdrive Azathoth into full manifestation—and looked away from the floating three-dimensional screen as he did so.

Filrod gasped.

Frederic smiled grimly—then uploaded the first vid, of Filrod pleasuring himself as he gaped at some serious porn.

Filrod made a choking sound.

"Turn that shit off!" he managed, his voice hoarse, almost in-audible.

"Why, man?" Frederic asked calmly, looking at him. "It was you who found that video of my brother posing all sexy for an under-twenty gay dating service. My brother wasn't ready to come out to my folks yet—we got some old-fashioned grandpar-ents he was worried about—and he was going to a private school because Dad was trying to get churchy. My *père* was raised Roman Catholic—and there's been big pushback from the religious types about gay marriage last few years and the school is like brainwash-ing these kids against gays and . . . well, my brother Jacques, little Jackie, he was full-on *gay*. I knew it, but we didn't really talk about it much, and he didn't tell anybody else, he wanted to do it all private until he could face the bullshit as an adult living on his own. But then you hacked him, Filrod, because he was talk-ing to your girlfriend and *man* did you misread that shit, until you found out he wasn't hitting on your girl, you saw the dating service video he'd made for Gay Youth Meet-Up. And you told everyone, showed the jocks at his school, and they beat him up and he lost feeling in some nerves in his arm, and his left hand wasn't working, and then the priest saw the dating video, when you guys put it up online, and brought him into his office and gave him the hellfire talk and made him *thoroughly* miserable."

"I didn't know that was going to—"

Frederic shook his head and pressed on. "And *then* you post-

ed some lies about him stalking some teenager, that Danny Zo-
ski, which was *totally* not true, and so then people said Jackie
was a pedophile—he was all about real adult men, not *kids*—and
then people stopped talking to him and he took some drugs over
it that left him depressed and then they were going to kick him
outta the school and . . . lemme see, I leave anything out? Oh,
yeah. He killed himself. *He fucking hung himself.*"

"I—" Filrod made an *uck* sound.

Frederic could see Filrod was trying to look away from the
hypnotic drain of Azathoth . . . and Frederic was careful not to
look into it himself. "Yes, 'Filrod'?"

"I—I—"

"Spit it out, dude!"

"—didn't know he was your brother."

"Jackie didn't like the surname DuSang, 'cause it means 'of
blood' and Jackie had hemophilia, and my folks said he could go
by grandma's name once he turned eighteen. So he changed it.
Then you met him. Then he killed himself. Cause and effect:
sensitive person runs afoul of an emotional cretin and dies."

"Sorry . . ."

"Oh, because he was my brother? But it's okay to hound a
gay kid into suicide? Long as they're not related to someone you
know?"

"Um . . . no."

"Yeah, well, *fuck* you—and your *sorry*. You *boasted* about what
you did after he killed himself, I got the emails . . . see 'em there?
They're going up around you too. Read 'em, asshole. You're in
that world, in your mind now, and it's not easy to get out. *All*
that stuff is there. Now I'm going to upload some—"

Then Frederic heard Jackie's voice. And for a moment he was
struck dumb.

"Sorry to see you hurting dumb animals, Frederic." Jackie
said, gently chiding.

"What?"

The voice had come from the floating screen. And Frederic had to look.

He saw his brother's face in a wobbling globe of translucent emerald and gold, a *fantôme* floating over the Azathothian landscape.

His brother was looking right at him.

And Jackie said, "The idiot Filrod here is just a dumb animal. It's like poisoning a dog that bit you 'cause it went crazy being locked to a short chain all day. Not really the dog's fault it bit you. But I do hate Filrod, that's true. Even now. And it's hard to hate anyone where I am now."

"Where you are . . . ?"

"I'm in a kind of limbo sorta place kinda oblique to Azathoth. Where Azathoth is, that's where a lotta people get stuck. Poke their noses in the wrong place. Me, I'm in another world, and it's not bad. It's pretty effin' awesome. I'll be here a thousand years or so, the guardians tell me, and I don't mind. But see, it's like it's a through-the-looking-glass inside-out upside-down mirror place in relation to Azathoth; they're opposites, you know? Symmetrical opposites. It ain't heaven, where I am, and Azathoth ain't hell—but close enough."

Frederic gawked at the apparition of his dead brother. It sounded exactly like him; sure *looked* like him, even down to that typical humorously rueful expression.

Frederic wondered if he were being *pwned* somehow. Was this some hoax? Had Filrod outsmarted him?

But he could see Filrod himself, a replicant of his mind inhabiting Azathoth—trapped in a crystalline world of self-loathing. The miniature Filrod in the floating screen image was a kind of Filrod avatar, matching the physical one who gasped and moaned and whimpered beside Frederic.

Frederic shook his head slowly. "Jackie . . . is it really . . . ?"

"Yes, it is. I'm not in Azathoth—but I heard you messing around in it, I heard your mind . . . and I'm able to talk to you *through* it, because I'm in its opposite, and they're *connected,* in a weird way. Like, you know, those old yin-yang symbols, the white and black going around and around in one circle together. You know?"

"I guess . . ."

"So I'm able to talk to you from my world. See, dude, Azathoth is *real.* It's not a program. Azathoth is a real world. And a real creature—all at once. But you've got a kinda digital device for looking into it. You're not seeing into a program—you're seeing it *through* a program."

Frederic felt sick hearing that. Somehow it all came together in his mind with a click. *This is real.* "I'm going to get sucked into it!"

"I don't know if you are or not. I hope not, bro. Once you're there, I probably can't help you. Your body'll die and—well, let's see if I can head it off."

"Jackie, listen . . . I'm sorry I didn't help you . . . I should've *helped* you when you were so depressed. I was caught up in my own stuff . . ."

"I know. It's okay. I just . . . wanted to say . . . don't worry about me. I'm in pretty good shape now. It's not heaven where I am—I'm stuck in this place for awhile, but it's not a bad place. It's just somewhere you go if you kill yourself. Then you get held up there for a long, long time. So that part's not good. Killing yourself, you get *stuck* in the next world, and you have to work that off. So don't ever do that, Frederic. But it's not bad here, and one day I'll move on. And that's something I got an ache to do, to move on . . ." Jackie smiled. "To move on in the right way."

Frederic couldn't smile back. He felt a mounting terror seeing the hideous, encroaching reality of Azathoth widening, stretched out from the floating screen, like a beast widening its jaws to swallow him . . .

Then Jackie's image seemed to expand—and seemed to rush at him, getting between him and Azathoth, Jackie's face coming like the grille of an onrushing car bearing down on him, Jackie grinning mischievously—

And then Frederic felt the shove. He heard Jackie shout, *"Go, bro!"*

And there was a tremendous pressure, physically throwing Frederic backwards, so that he crashed into some of his hardware. That was going to hurt later.

But now all he felt was dazed as he lay on the angular pile of electronic odds and ends, sparking smoke around him, staring at the ceiling.

Frederic was distantly aware that he'd been about to fall into Azathoth . . . and now he was free, staring at the AI bobbing near the ceiling, the light on it like a green eye glaring down at him . . .

Jackie had saved him—his brother had pushed him out of the jaws of Azathoth.

But what about Filrod?

It's like poisoning a dog that bit you 'cause it went crazy being locked to a short chain all day.

Filrod howled pitifully.

Wincing from his bruises, Frederic sat up—just in time to see Filrod's soul being sucked out of his body; his naked form, translucent, turning in midair to try to claw its way back, struggling against the hungry vortex, face contorted with horror. Mouthing *Please help me!*

Then there was a nasty sucking sound . . . and Filrod's soul was gone, into the whirling SpaceHole.

In Frederic's room, Filrod's body slumped—lifeless.

Frederic looked at the Azathoth image, now in Mode One . . . saw Filrod's soul in there, mangled but recognizable, as jaws of crystal closed and crushed and chewed and chewed . . . and chewed harder.

Frederic looked away.

He called to the AI, floating overhead, to come to manual station—meaning into his hands.

It floated down to him. He grabbed it, switched off its flight power—and then threw it, as hard as he could, at the wall.

And the AI smashed into crackling pieces.

The floating 3-D screen vanished—Frederic thought he heard a cry of despair from Filrod as it went . . .

*

Frederic sat for a while, trembling. The trembling seemed to metamorphose into sobbing. And once, loudly, he shouted, "Jackie!"

He glanced over at Filrod's body. He didn't want to touch it. But he had to.

He got up, grimacing, and knelt by the ungainly body, felt the still-warm wrists for a pulse.

No. Nothing. The guy was stone dead.

That wasn't something Frederic had planned for. But it was hard to feel bad about it. What was he going to tell the police?

The truth. *Hey, the guy was smoking that synth dope, just a lot of it, then he keeled over. Bad ticker I guess.*

Frederic turned away and stood up, looking for a cell phone. Sooner he called the cops, the better.

He heard the door open—turned to see his father looking at him, puzzled, concerned. The old dude had heard his yell about Jackie.

Frederic felt as if he'd never seen his father's face clearly before.

The look on his father's face was so deep—had so many levels of pain. Like someone trapped in hell.

Frederic wiped his eyes, and got up. He wended his way through all his gear, went to his dad, and put his arms around him, and together they wept—though Frederic knew his dad didn't understand any of it.

It didn't seem to matter.

THE HOLY GRACE OF CTHULHU

"Where are you taking me?" asked the man on the gurney. The old man had a hoarse New England accent.

"You go to call upon your master," Kline told him. "Relax, Professor Seekley. You're getting what you always wanted."

Seekley was silent for a time as Kline wheeled him along the steel corridor. The portable bed provided its own movement. Kline had only to put his hands on it. But high-ech though it was, the wheels of the gurney made a squawking sound with each turn. On the back of the gurney was a small metal basket with medicaments, water, and a CallTab.

"I smell the sea," said Seekley, lifting his head a little. The old professor's voice was feeble.

"Yes, we're near the balcony overlooking R'lyeh." Kline was in his mid-thirties, strong, determined. His own voice had a sturdy determination about it. But inwardly he was cringing as he thought about what was to come.

"The dreaming city . . ." Seekley muttered.

"Yes."

"What year is it, Dr. Kline?"

"It's the year 2087."

"Truly? I have slept a long time."

"You were in a kind of suspended animation. You were condemned to it, you remember?"

"I . . . almost remember."

"You were engaged in something inappropriate at the time." Kline could now hear the sea pounding on the half-sunken battlements of R'lyeh. "You nearly woke the giant. No one wanted that but you, not then. Now—it seems the only alternative . . ."

"I'm not sure this is what I wanted."

"You wanted to summon him. Here's your chance! We woke you up so you could do it."

"I wondered at the end . . . if it was after all what I truly wanted. And then the men came and stopped me, just as he was stirring. Not that Cthulhu is truly a he . . . there is no gender, really, for one such as Cthulhu. But we devotees always used the male pronoun."

Kline noticed that Seekley pronounced the creature's name differently—Kline and his associates called the titan something like "Kuh-thool-hoo." Seekley pronounced Cthulhu something like "C'[tongue-click]-uh-hool-uh-y'oo"—inserting that barely audible tongue-click instead of a *t* sound. But it didn't matter how Seekley pronounced the titan's name so long as the old man knew his job.

They reached the end of the corridor, where the steel doors were already thrown open to reveal the purpling oceanic horizon and the darkening, cloud draped sky.

"Oh!" Seekley cried, startled, closing his eyes for a moment as Kline pushed the gurney out onto the metal balcony overlooking the ruins.

Mightily reinforced—so its designers hoped—against any force coming up against it, the building from which the balcony jutted was just a great block of chromium-plated steel rising in stark anomaly from its foundation on an ancient reef that skirted one side of the sunken city. Built thirty years earlier to study R'lyeh and its slumbering inhabitant, the structure was nearly featureless on the outside, apart from a cluster of intricate antennae—it had no windows, few visible vents. There was a tunnel-like entrance just below sea level, on the opposite side, for submarines; a helicopter landing pad occupied much of the roof, near a bristling apparatus. And there was this single observation balcony projecting out over the western edge of the city, about twenty meters above high tide.

"As you can see, a part of the sunken city has elevated since your time, all on its own, about twenty-five meters further above sea level," Kline remarked. "It's as if it were compensating for the rising waters of climate change. The creature's chamber has risen somewhat as well. He settled back into a slumber, after you disturbed him."

"How long ago now has he slept in peace?"

"Oh, many decades. But it is a fitful slumber."

Seekley nodded and added with soft reminiscence, "But you know—Cthulhu *has* risen in the memory of modern man."

"I've heard that claim. I've read the account."

In fact, after many readings the newspaper account was incised in Kline's memory: *The awful squid-head with writhing feelers came nearly up to the bowsprit of the sturdy yacht, but Johansen drove on relentlessly. There was a bursting as of an exploding bladder, a slushy nastiness as of a cloven sunfish, a stench as of a thousand opened graves . . .*

Seekley rubbed his eyes. "You say . . . you say summoning Great Cthulhu has become *necessary* now?"

"Yes." Kline pushed the gurney close to the balcony's railing. "You know, I always thought the actual encounter with the creature, in that account, could have been made up by the journalist. The writer might have been inspired by reports of the idols, the old sculptures that turned up from time to time."

"No, it was not fabricated." Professor Seekley raised himself on one elbow, grunting with the effort, to gaze down over R'lyeh. "Cthulhu returned to his slumber after that encounter. His regeneration was incomplete, you see. But in my own time, I was convinced the master was ready to arise for good and all. And so he *is*, now—he has far more strength this time. I can feel it! The stars are aligned; his energies are attuned." He looked out over the sunken city and murmured, "And the air fairly quivers with it at R'lyeh."

The abandoned ruins of the primeval city, which could be mistaken for a mere tumble of boulders from the air, were located approximately at the "southern point of inaccessibility," known as Point Nemo. The nearest land, more than a thousand kilometers away, was the chain holding Pitcairn's Island. In another direction, farther, was Easter Island—its grim, hulking statues may well have been erected as a warning to go no further in that direction, lest the mariner in time encounter R'lyeh.

Here stood its crumbling remains: massive stones, some cut with an irregularity that seemed perversely intentional, loomed from the whispering waves. The bare outlines of a city—its crooked avenues, its harbor—could be ascertained if one looked close. Few other artifacts had been found here, but an enormous underwater chamber, of surprising length and breadth, had been located. In it was an enormous, slumbering inhabitant, slumped on a gigantic throne carved from a single huge meteor.

"It's curious how you and Cthulhu were both in a kind of doze, since the day you nearly woke him," Kline remarked, glancing at his watch. It was almost time. "You were in Rio de Janeiro. He—*it*—in the wreckage of this old city . . ."

"Yes, it is curious," Seekley admitted, barely audible. He undid the buckles about his waist and, grunting with effort, sat up to gaze out over the half-sunken, broken shell of R'lyeh. "But in sleep, the master speaks to many who might someday be of use. *His* mind never sleeps, you see. Not really. And in my own sleep, these decades of coma . . . *sometimes great Cthulhu spoke to me!* He told me things I did not wish to know—so that when I woke I was no longer sure of what I wanted. I had seen, perhaps, a bit too much . . ."

The CallTab chimed. Kline took the tablet from the gurney's basket. "Answer."

Ihlala Gulahosi's face appeared on the CallTab's screen; clasping her long black hair was a red scarf picked out in gold thread. She was a dark woman with large brown-black eyes.

"Receiving," Kline said. The signal flickered, for a moment—few satellites were left intact—and he had to wait for it to stabilize.

"What's that, some sort of cell phone?" Seekley asked, looking over his shoulder. He blinked in the light from the declining sun glimmering over the top of the steel building.

"More or less," Kline said distantly.

"Who's calling?"

"A United World representative," Kline said. No time to explain the world government—a unity that had come about because of the invasion—nor Ihlala's work for its intelligence arm.

"They are closing in on your position," Ihlala said in a New Delhi accent. "There are about ten screwplanes at the moment, but they've sensed the anomalous activity and they seem be to bringing the Float Hive to bear."

"How much time do we have?"

"Their scouts will show up any moment. They'll probably wait for the near proximity of the Hive before they attack. This—this *summoning*, Kline . . . is it going to happen? Or is it not?"

"We're setting up for that. But if you're asking about success—I don't know."

"Place the communicator so I can observe, please."

Kline propped the CallTab on the nearer edge of the gurney, turning her camera toward the ruins. Then he looked at the graying professor. "Seekley, you must begin now."

"*Why?* I told you I wasn't sure I wanted to do it at all anymore. I need time to think! Why must I summon him *now?*"

"Because . . ." A movement from the sky caught his attention. Kline pointed toward it. "See that, up there?"

Seekley looked. The screw-shaped vehicle, a thing of unearthly materials and glossy iridescence, seemed to be corkscrewing its way down from a cloud, leaving a trail of swirled mist. The craft was about as big as a fighter jet, but it tapered, at its aft, to a crystalline glowing stub like the coal of a cigar.

"That," Klein went on, "is a scout for the Takers. That's what they call themselves, at least in English. They invaded Earth about seven months ago. They used a translation device to demand our surrender. Everyone on the planet heard the demand, all at once—unconditional surrender. Those who surrendered are believed to have been subjected to experiments, then ground up for protein. No one is quite sure—no one's come back—" He broke off, pointing. "Ah, there's another advance scout!" They could see another corkscrewing vessel screwing its way through the air in the distance. "The scouts usually come ahead of the Float Hive."

"Float Hive?"

"Their mother ship. The Hive does the large-scale destroying—the screwplanes scout and do the detail work of destruction. London is gone, simply destroyed. So are Beijing, San Francisco, New York, Paris, Mumbai, Bangkok, Hong Kong, Moscow, Tucson, Chicago, Rio, Melbourne, Houston, Washington, D.C.—even Las Vegas! In fact, Las Vegas was first to go—all the lights there seemed to draw their attention. And *we've* drawn their attention, Seekley."

Now seven screwplanes hovered, darted, corkscrewed along over R'lyeh—and began to drift toward the balcony. Toward Kline and Seekley . . .

Professor Seekley gaped up at the alien vessels in awe. "Are they—the Old Ones?"

"We don't know if they're related to the so-called 'Elder Ones,' Seekley. We've only managed to bring down three of those things and all three disintegrated with some kind of auto-destruct before we could examine their interior. But we know they're operated from the Float Hive. And we think that Cthulhu—your master—may in fact be able to penetrate the Float Hive. We've tried everything else. There are indications that Cthulhu's body may be partly formed of a plasma that, theoretically, could penetrate their shielding. Especially in the monster's dispersal form."

Seekley looked at him in alarm. "Monster? You would *insult* Great Cthulhu—*here?* Do you not suppose he is listening?"

"Listening? You mean to me?" That hadn't occurred to Kline. "But he's . . . deep under the, ah . . . you know, he's inside a stone chamber and—"

Seekley snorted. "How do you think I am to *contact* him, you fool? Telepathy! The chanting is only to focus the mind! He listens as he chooses!"

"Just—*do* the damned thing, Seekley! Or humanity's done for. Finished!"

Seekley looked up at the approaching alien vessels. "I'm parched. I need some water. And if there's anything in that medicine kit to give me a little strength . . ."

Kline busied himself getting the water bottle and an injector ready as Seekley got to his feet, leaning on the gurney for balance. Then he lurched toward the balcony's metal railing.

"Be careful, you fool! We don't have time for a cracked hip!" Kline said, as he brought Seekley the water.

Supporting himself with one hand on the rail, the old man drank thirstily. Then he tossed the plastic bottle aside as Kline applied the injector.

"I feel no injection," Seekley said, glancing at his arm. "No pain, no needle . . ."

"It's painless. Do you need me to hold you up?"

"No, the railing is enough. And I feel the drug now. I have some strength. Yes."

For several long moments they watched the screwplanes twist closer to the balcony—and closer yet, coming at them like flying drills.

Then a pulse of translucent red energy expanded from the coal-like tail of the nearest, ran forward along the screws, spinning as it went, and projected, a twist of living fire, down at the balcony, screaming with destructive glee as it came.

Seekley gasped—then one of the antennae on the roof behind them hummed and a shield of electromagnetic force appeared, up above, just in front of the twist of fire, dispersing it.

"You have a shield of some kind!" Seekley said.

"It won't work for long. It takes too much power—and we'll soon be overwhelmed. They'll blow us to bits! You must call your master!"

Seekley took a deep breath and began chanting. Mouth twisting unnaturally, he intoned, *"Ph'nglui mglw'nafh* Cthulhu *R'lyeh wgah'nagl fhtagn!"* . . . over and over.

Kline had heard a recording of a cult chanting that same wicked psalm. But now Seekley was incanting other words too guttural for Kline to understand. As he chanted the incantation his eyes rolled back to show only the whites, as if he were sinking into a profane ecstasy.

Abruptly the old man fell silent, head tilted, as if listening to the voiceless voice of great Cthulhu.

Another gleeful scream ripped the air above—a sizzling replied to it, as another bolt of energy chaos was deflected by the antennae. Several screwplanes fired at once and two of the antennae exploded . . .

In the distance, something loomed in the gathering dusk.

It had been given its human name based on its shape, like an old-fashioned beehive, a cone made in layers of pearly material, crackling with electrical energies as it pressed through the atmosphere. It was mountainous, an unnaturally symmetrical mountain pocked with cryptic passages; it came skimming over the sea, spinning slowly, making the watery surface wrinkle and draw away beneath it. Its base was nearly as big as R'lyeh itself, bigger; big as midtown Manhattan. It was the Float Hive, the extraterrestrial mother ship.

Crimson energies rippled out from it, whiplashing up to the screwplanes, but not attacking them—nourishing them, reinforcing their energies, so that soon they would have the power to destroy this building, the balcony, and end humanity's last hope.

Then something glided into view, on Kline's right—the nuclear submarine that had brought him here. The sight saddened rather than heartened him—he knew what the outcome would be.

The submarine launched its cruise missiles. They chuffed into the air and soared up to strike at the screwplanes. They struck their targets—and had little effect.

The screwplanes regrouped and angled to aim their corkscrewing tips down at the submarine.

All those men . . .

But they would serve their purpose. To delay the enemy just long enough.

"Kline!" Seekley shouted over the cacophony of the unleashed energies roaring around them. Crimson fire rained upon the submarine; cruise missiles hissed into the air. "Kline, I have called the master! I have reminded him that our world, which has sustained his organism for so long, deserves his loyalty. But Great Cthulhu says *no!* He declares it is *we* who must have loyalty—to him!"

"What the hell are you talking about, Seekley! Tell it to destroy that thing or it's going to be destroyed itself! The Hive will annihilate everything that could be any kind of obstacle!"

"The master doesn't care! How do you think Cthulhu came here? Now that he has regenerated, by that same means he can depart! *Unless!* You, speaking for humanity, must swear fealty to the master! You and all those you represent must swear your loyalty to Cthulhu! *All humanity must swear it!* Cthulhu will know! Once, in millennia past, humanity worshipped Great Cthulhu! *And must do so again!* The master demands our loyalty!"

Kline gaped at Seekley. What was he asking of them? "Perhaps we—we might . . ."

"Are you thinking of destroying Cthulhu after he has done the deed, Kline? He is too strong now! And will become stronger with this act! If you try to betray great Cthulhu—you will trade one great enemy for a worse one!"

The submarine exploded, its hull snapping in half, gouting a roaring fireball of white and blue flame. Men's bodies spun into the air, burning.

There was so little time to decide. Kline writhed inwardly with uncertainty.

"*Kline!*" came the tinny voice from the CallTab. "I have been transmitting all this to the United World! The delegates are unanimous! *We swear loyalty to Cthulhu!*"

"It cannot be undone!" Seekley shouted, eyes wild. "We have crossed into his world *and we are forever his!*"

Then Seekley turned to the sea and warbled his perverse hymn once more.

A roll of thunder boomed then, followed by a massive crackling of unseen lightning; an echoing crash, like a hundred avalanches at once; a smell like hair burning, of electrical discharge, of a billion gutted fish . . . and the balcony shuddered under their feet. Kline staggered, caught the balcony railing beside Seekley just in time to see the slick, cracked blocks of R'lyeh shrug out of the way, pushed aside from beneath.

The Float Hive drew nearer, glowing as it prepared to fire directly on the steel outpost.

Then a green titan emerged from the sea, rising up, tentacles waving furiously, throwing water and stone aside with equal ease.

Great Cthulhu reared up, higher and higher, many hundreds of meters high, tall as a skyscraper, exuding the smell of brine and burning electricity and bubbling acids, the odors washing over Kline in acrid waves.

Cthulhu's thin wings unfolded, and lightning, forking from the thickening clouds beyond, was seen through the emerald membranes. His gigantic body was both dragon-like and transparently gelatinous.

Seekley shrieked in mingled horror and ecstasy, falling to his knees, raising his shaking hands to his primordial lord.

Up, *up* rose Cthulhu, water streaming off his translucent

green wings. His body quivered as he bellowed a challenge to the Float Hive; his beard of tentacles jittered with his rage. The spider-like cluster of eyes on his squid-like head glistened with malevolent intelligence; his scaly skin, transparent and yet murky, rippled as he waded out of the ruined city toward the approaching alien mother ship: the mountainous cone of metal glowed ever brighter as it prepared to blast this new adversary.

"Great Cthulhuuuu!" shouted Seekley, his eyes bulging, face rigid with excitement.

Kline watched, sickened and eager, as Cthulhu stalked toward the mother ship—and suddenly flapped up into the air. The wings, looking too thin to support the giant body, seemed to stretch out, expanding to gather in more air, and they pulsed with a green energy that added its own lift.

And suddenly Cthulhu was flying.

The giant lifted up, streaming ocean water and seaweed, roaring with a sound that shook the world. His wings keened and hummed, almost invisible in their whipping activity. His tentacular "beard" writhed; gigantic talons stretched out.

The Float Hive fired. A beam of crimson energy big enough to melt a dozen aircraft carriers shot out of the mothership and into Cthulhu's mighty breast.

And the beam passed harmlessly through him.

It was as if the titanic body acted as a prism, separating out the energies of the red beam, keeping what Cthulhu wanted and conducting the rest out between his wings, to be dispersed in the sky. But yes—a wound, a green-edged hole, had formed . . . and as Kline watched, it quickly sealed up. Cthulhu had taken what he wished from the beam, let the rest pass through, and had healed himself, all in an instant.

The screwplanes fired on Cthulhu—their energies, too, were refracted.

The ancient titan flew higher . . . and then, diving down from above, Cthulhu pounced.

The primeval colossus from the stars threw himself upon the Float Hive, attacking the mother ship like some hideous parody of an eagle attacking its prey. Cthulhu clasped the alien spacecraft, arms and legs wrapped around the enormous cone. And the huge alien ship spun as if in impotent fury, gyrating Cthulhu about, perhaps trying to free itself with this desperate maneuver.

But instead of letting go, Cthulhu clasped tighter yet and—and then, abruptly . . . melted. Or so it seemed at first. The gelatinous giant seemed to melt *onto* the Float Hive, becoming hundreds of seeking tendrils, each separate, but with one mind squirming their way into the mother ship's cryptic openings, slithering into it.

Kline watched as Cthulhu sank into the giant alien craft.

And then, great Cthulhu vanished entirely.

Like an animal maddened by a wasp in its ear, the mother ship spun recklessly about, wobbling, turning faster, faster—blurring . . . until at last it detonated from within.

A great shockwave rumbled out from the blast, coming visibly toward the balcony. Kline turned to run, but the shockwave caught him and Seekley, threw them skidding across the balcony. Kline was stunned, dizzied as the shockwave flung him through the open doors, sliding into the steel corridor.

His body stopped moving, but his mind kept whirling . . . and he lost consciousness, sinking into a churning darkness.

The darkness was not comforting; indeed, it was not uninhabited.

"*Kline!*" came Seekley's croaking voice. "Kline!"

Head throbbing, Kline reluctantly opened his eyes. "What . . . has happened?"

"You must get up, Kline. There is more to do."

Groaning, Kline forced himself to his feet. His every muscle ached; his head resonated like the speaker of an amplifier shaken by feedback. But he followed Seekley out onto the balcony.

The dusk was thickening; the clouds churned. The screwplanes were all down—some of them had crashed into the stones of R'lyeh, and their remnants melted away, disintegrating.

A noxious brown-black cloud was dispersing in the distance where the battle had been fought. Grisly wreckage floated on the sea, human bodies from the submarine blended horribly with worm-like extraterrestrial corpses from the shattered mother ship.

And something else—was forming out there. Something was taking shape in the cloud.

Kline remembered the account he had read of what had happened when a steamship rammed giant Cthulhu: *For an instant the ship was befouled by an acrid and blinding green cloud, and then there was only a venomous seething astern; where—God in heaven!—the scattered plasticity of that nameless sky-spawn was nebulously recombining in its hateful original form . . .*

And so it was now: recombining, Cthulhu sloshed ponderously toward them, wading across the surging sea, up to his scaly translucent hips in the waves, tentacles waving, the green feelers reaching out toward the two men.

"Oh, no, no," Kline said. "We mustn't—"

"But we have no choice," Seekley declared grimly. "We made a deal. *We agreed!* And so it must be. The master will have nothing less."

A few moments more, and then great Cthulhu was rearing over them like a Cyclopean statue: reeking, dripping acid that hissed when it struck the stones of R'lyeh.

Seekley fell to his knees and clutched his head. "Yes, yes, I hear you, great one! I hear you, lord of all the Earth! You shall have one now!"

"Have . . . have one what?" Kline asked, his mouth paper-dry.

"A sacrifice," Seekley said. "But it will not be you—you have another way to serve him." He reached out his arms toward the looming giant. "Lord Cthulhu! Take me as your first offering! Honor me—and take me first!"

Cthulhu bent—his hideous transparent head came within a dozen meters of Kline, who staggered back in revulsion. Then the giant feelers clasped Seekley, drew him into the gargantuan maw hidden behind the tentacles.

Seekley screamed.

Kline saw the man's form, his body, sinking head downward, visible in the semitransparent body of the giant as it swallowed him.

Whimpering, Kline turned away.

Then he heard a voice in his head. It was a wordless voice, and yet, somehow, it spoke clearly enough. It demanded another price—the price of Cthulhu's holy grace.

Kline took a deep, shaky breath. He must do what he must do.

He turned back to Cthulhu and threw himself to his knees. "Oh, Great Cthulhu! You have destroyed our enemies! We will serve you! I myself will bring you offerings! We will offer up many to you, Lord Cthulhu! Many!" Kline salaamed to Cthulhu and cried out, "We give you our loyalty, great Cthulhu! Forever!"

And Kline found that he could pronounce the master's name now, just exactly as Seekley had.

BROKEN ON THE WHEEL OF TIME

The Journal of Glyneth Berling
Boston, Massachusetts

July 29, 1878

Perhaps it is the heat, but Ben seems most particularly quarrelsome. My husband is ever alert to quarrel, but today he seems like a fox quivering to pounce on a hen. I find that I must tiptoe about him, and that is no mere figure of speech—the floorboards creak more in the heat, and he snarls at me if I walk near his workshop. Yet the pantry is close to the workshop, and he expects me to make use of the pantry in order to prepare his luncheon. It is as well he forbids "nosy housekeepers"; I would not subject a housekeeper to Ben's choler.

He has only raised his hand to me once, and swore he wouldn't do it again—for I said I would leave him if he struck me again. But if he discovers this journal I expect he will be tempted to strike me with it; a leather volume in Ben's rough hand would make a painful slap indeed.

August 1, 1878

At last it is Sunday, the day I'm free to take the train to the countryside and be about my observations in the fields and thickets. But as I was packing a lunch, my darling husband bid me stay to home should he "need anything." His work today is most urgent, he said; he cannot be troubled to step out of the workshop to fetch a lemonade.

Ben has not much respect for naturalists, particularly lady

naturalists, and fairly jeered one morning when he saw me weeping on learning that my correspondent Genevieve Jones had died. She was another Audubon, in a sense; a student and painter of birds, and deserving of anyone's esteem. But when has Ben exhibited respect to any woman?

When he was courting me Ben seemed content to hear me comment at length on the intricate formation of bird's nests, the astonishing industry of ants and bees; he was willing to accompany me as I spoke to ship's officers at the harbor, asking after the migratory habits of the whale and the dolphin. But within a month of our wedding he fell first into a fit of melancholy, and then became steeped in his arcana. I thought it something I had done, or failed to do. Certainly I have never stinted affection or denied him marital intimacy. But I encountered his half-brother Harold, who seem concerned to ask me if all was well. I admitted that my husband's dark moods had me blaming myself. But, taking me aside, Harold allowed that Ben had a fixation on death that he was never able to put aside; he sighed that "Benjamin has always been thus." And indeed in recent years, before the marriage, Ben's fits of angry melancholy have worsened. Had I but known, there would have been no understanding between us!

I thought he had altered since our wedding; but it seems I now see his character undisguised.

I am sometimes sorry that his father left him a stipend, and a bit more; he might be a better man to get out and struggle for a living. This last winter, his fixation on these dank and cryptic volumes has only deepened his faults; his attending to the nattering of alchemists who lost themselves in phantasms before the true coming of Science only accelerated his deterioration, as cracks in a statue widen with the intrusion of ice.

He has forgotten to shave. If a man must have a beard then let him trim it; but Ben will have none of this. His linen is unclean; he will rarely avail himself of the garments I scrub and hang for him. His odor is as sour as his disposition.

Looking back on this journal, I become aware of my own sourness—which certainly has not improved my disposition. Surely a wife should have something kinder to say of her husband.

Perhaps I will attempt, once more, to talk to him about this growing distance between us. I could chance it over supper, if I can persuade him to take the meal with me. Too often he bids me leave the food on the table just inside the workshop door. Nor will he suffer me to enter further than that table—which is sadly in need of cleaning. He will not allow me to clean it, of course.

August 3, 1878

The worst of the heat has abated, as the sea breeze arrives at last. Ben's bad temper, however, has not abated. He talks to himself in his workshop, sometimes reads aloud in a foreign language, and curses when the experiment goes awry. Then he damns me when I ask if I can help.

Loneliness seems to cry out when my footsteps make the boards creak.

A year, seven months, and two weeks of marriage, and I feel like a woman who is married to a sailor long lost at sea. Yet my husband is no more than a dozen steps away.

If only Ben would allow me a pet; but he is quite firmly against it. Animals, he declares, are simply more distractions. He rarely comes to bed, and when he arrives, stinking of obscure chemicals, he falls into a troubled sleep; he seems to have nightmares with a strange regularity, nearly always just after the clock strikes one in the morning.

A little dog to sleep at my feet, to sit on my lap as I read, would be a great comfort to me. But Ben particularly mistrusts dogs. He says they hold a prejudice against him.

Perhaps I might persuade him to let me have a parakeet.

August 7, 1878

A strange change has come over Ben. I should be glorying in it, since the change has wrought a softening of his temperament, but I'm almost frightened by the transformation. I must give a full account.

I was taking my morning porridge in the kitchen, thinking that I had heard him give a plaintive cry at one hour after midnight and wondering if I should have gone to him then. But in the past, whenever I have looked in on him, no matter the provocation, he shouted vile abuse at me, and I was forced to turn away.

This morning I was quite startled to see him appear in the kitchen door, staring at me. He had not changed his clothes in several days; his overalls were blotted by chemicals that seemed a most peculiar shade of blue; here and there were spots of what looked like drips of metal, copper perhaps. He still wore his gloves, equally blotted and in some places burned through by acids; his black hair was unruly; his untended beard, for the most part hiding his lips, showed sharply against his pale skin. His gray eyes had scarlet rims, and in them was a look of shocked disorientation. He seemed a man of fifty rather than the man of thirty-two I knew him to be.

"I am sorry," he croaked at me. "Quite sorry, ma'am, to intrude on you. I found myself here . . . and I just plain don't know how I got here."

Had he had some kind of blow to the head? He seemed not to know me. "Oh, Ben . . . sit down, rest!" I took him by the arm and drew him to a chair at the kitchen table. I tugged off his gloves, and took one of his hands in mine. "Ben, have you injured yourself?"

"What did you call me? Ben?"

"Perhaps you should lie down, my dear. I'll bring you some breakfast and then you can take a nap."

Ben blinked and blinked again, quite dazedly staring around him. "He tricked me. He completely—"

"Who tricked you, Ben?" I asked. Truly he sounded like a raving madman.

Should I be afraid of him? That is—should I be mortally afraid?

He rubbed his eyes, shaking his head as if at a loss to explain. "I'm so tired." He looked around, sniffing. "There's a bad smell . . ."

"Oh—that's you, dear."

He looked down at himself. "Can I . . . bathe?"

I almost clapped my hands together. "Certainly you may!"

It wasn't until he was in the big iron bathtub and I was pouring hot water in to keep it warm—the tap water, even in August, being a bit brisk—that he asked, "What year is this?"

I cut short a gasp at the question. Then and there I decided I must get him to a doctor at the earliest possibility.

As I finished pouring the water, watching him from the corners of my eyes, I said, "As you are very well aware, Ben, it is the year 1878."

"That figures," he muttered.

I had never heard him use such an expression. "Does it? Certainly it should. You acted earlier as if you were . . . as if you didn't know where you were. Or who I was."

He looked up at me, blinking. "You would be Mrs. Berling."

I smiled at him. "I would be indeed, yes."

I shaved him as he sat in the tub and clipped his hair—I kept waiting for him to object, but he accepted the barbering with good grace—and then I helped him into a towel, and he dried himself as I went to make his breakfast.

However, I found him deeply asleep in the bedroom a few minutes later, and consumed the eggs myself so that they would not go to waste.

August 8, 1878

I should have followed the doctor's advice, I'm sure, and taken Ben to the brain specialist in Charlestown, but he had seemed to be improving so. Indeed, his company is congenial, his manners improved, and, quite handsome in the light linen suit he only wore once before, he has taken me on a goodly walk down the avenue.

Yet his behavior has been odd. He insists on sleeping on the settee in the drawing room. I feel a certain tenderness from him for all that. He now dines with me every evening and holds my hand when we take an after-dinner walk. Both the walk and the hand-holding are nearly unprecedented.

He does spend a good deal of time in the workshop, but when I venture to look in on him he does not send me out as of old. He asked me if I could name certain contraptions on the worktable—devices he himself has built. Of course, I had no knowledge of them.

Yet Ben seems reluctant to talk about the night that he collapsed—that is the expression he uses about the event—nor will he say much of the morning he presented himself to me at the breakfast table. He always comes up with a polite stratagem for putting off the discussion.

On a morning walk we saw a small child playing with a little terrier. He astonished me by petting the dog, and when I said I'd always wanted one, he said, "Why not get one, then? Surely there's a shelter, or some such, around here?"

The same morning, as we observed bees in the garden, he said, musing to himself, "I wonder if anyone knows about the waggle dance at this time, besides the bees themselves."

I looked at him in open puzzlement. "The waggle dance, Ben, did you say?"

"Yes, it's thought they communicate to one another in the hive with motions, waggling and back and forth dancing movements, about how to find . . ." Then he winced and shook his head. "Never mind. Not till 1972." Or so it seemed—perhaps he said 1872. But that would make no sense either.

"I was unaware you had an interest in bees. I supposed you were entirely concerned with electromagnetic waves, galvanic energy and—what did Mr. Edison call it? Aetheric waves."

He looked as if he were once more going to deny his own identity, but then he compressed his lips and shrugged. "We'll talk about it soon, Glyneth. I'm going to need your help. We'll speak of it after dinner."

Then he changed the subject and got me talking of bats, and of course it's a favorite subject. I rattled on, especially as—wonder of wonders!—he was carefully attending to my every word.

I must go down and make preparations for dinner.

"What I am going to tell you will be difficult to believe," said Ben as we sat on the front porch after dinner.

Regarding my disbelief, as it happened he was not overstating the case.

It was warm and humid out, but dark enough so that mosquitoes were no longer sniping at us. We sat on the wicker chairs, Ben with his hands folded in his lap. This was yet another change in him, as he had always been a restless man, tapping his fingers on the arm of every chair he sat in.

When he didn't go on immediately, I added, "I will do my best to believe!" I gave him my brightest smile, trying to encourage him.

But in fact I was afraid of what he might tell me.

He looked up and down the row of houses, as if to assure himself that no one was close by. "Okay," he said, with a great sigh. "My name is—" He looked at me. "You think I'm Benjamin Berling. But I must tell you, I'm not. My name is in fact Trevor Peaslee. Oh, I know Benjamin Berling, though I never quite met him face to face. I got to know him fairly well just before I changed bodies with him. Our minds swapped places, you see."

I smiled bravely. But, clearly, this sweeter Ben had quite taken leave of his senses. Once more I wondered if I should be afraid of him; but I found I could not be. He is so consistent in his character, so affable and kindly, I could not bring myself to fear him. There seems no falsehood in him now. This new character resonates as true as a well-tuned piano.

His own smile was rueful. "I don't expect you to believe me, not yet, Glyneth. Well, look. Today is August 8, 1878, yes? Where I live, usually, in my time, is in fact Arkham, Massachusetts—but it happens that I was raised in Wallingford, Connecticut, and as a teenager in school I was asked to write about an event in local history. I chose a certain pretty famous tornado, which killed a number of people, and which destroyed quite a bit of property. I picked that event because my own house was built as a result of that tornado. That was part of our family heritage. I looked it all up. The tornado happened—will happen—on August 9, 1878. Tomorrow."

I must have gaped at him.

But he leaned toward me and went on insistently. "It will happen tomorrow, and thirty-four people will die, seventy-three will be injured, and many houses will be flattened. It will be the worst tornado in New England history until 1953."

He said all this calmly and collectedly. It was his casual use of 'until 1953' that prompted my outburst. "Oh, really!" I could not help but laugh a little. "You prognosticate not only tomorrow—but the year 1953!"

He gave out an ironic grunt at that. "I could prognosticate more for you. Two world wars, for example. You could not conceive . . . A man walking on the moon in 1969! But for me it's not prognostication. It's history. I was born in 1976 and came here in 2015, a hundred and seventeen years from now, so it's all part of the past to me."

"Ben . . ." I put a hand on his, and was pleased when he

turned his hand to clasp mine. "Tomorrow we'll see the doctor and get the name of a specialist. Before we met—did you ever have scarlet fever, dear? When I think of it there's much of your life I don't know about. It's all quite sketchy."

Ben frowned. "Scarlet fever? Oh, I see! 'Brain fever'! You figure my brain was injured by disease and I'm having a relapse." He sighed, but he only clasped my hand more tenderly. "You're an intelligent, good-hearted woman, Glyneth. Instead of making fun of me or running away, you try to diagnose me. You're trying to help. I don't know how that son of a bitch managed to marry a woman like—" He noticed my shocked expression. "Sorry!" He took a deep breath. "Look, I mentioned that tornado for reason. Exactly because it's happening tomorrow. Thirty-four people will die! You can certainly try to warn Wallingford if you want. I can't bring myself to do it—I'm afraid of what might happen if I changed any stream of time I don't absolutely have to change. And if either of us tries to warn them, what'll they do anyway? They'll only sneer at us."

It occurred to me that this tornado business might be an opportunity to wake Ben from his delusion. "Ben—we shall look to see if this tornado happens. Telegraphs will alert the Boston papers within minutes of such a disaster, I'm sure. But if it doesn't happen . . . will you then admit that you might have an illness?"

He gave me a long, somber look. "Yes. I will."

He is once more sleeping on the sofa, though I all but implored him to come to bed that he might sleep in comfort.

And I sit up late, writing this account, trying to settle my mind. I have high hopes that tomorrow he will awaken to his true condition, and we shall set out to find the proper doctor.

August 9, 1878

The morning paper held nothing of a tornado in Connecticut, but most of the paper had been set in type the night before, of course. And so I waited till an evening edition of the *Boston Globe* might turn up. A catastrophe would spark a special edition, certainly. Once the evening paper came along with no mention of it, I could persuade Ben he must seek help.

After an early supper, Ben and I walked down to the druggist where an evening paper might be had. The shop had already closed, but there was a group of men clustered on the sidewalk waving their cigars and interrupting with questions as one of them read from the evening *Boston Globe,* relating the awful facts of the tornado that had killed numerous people in Wallingford, Connecticut. The number of the dead was uncertain, but it was thought to be at least twenty, perhaps more than thirty . . .

My heart was clamoring like a fire bell as we turned away from the corner and started back. After a few quiet minutes I turned to the man I had thought to be Ben and asked, "What did you say your name was?"

"It's Trevor Peaslee." He stopped and turned to me, offering his hand. I shook his hand in a dazed, mechanical kind of way. "Professor Trevor Peaslee," he went on, a little apologetically. "Of Miskatonic University. I am very pleased to meet you, Mrs. Berling. In my time—you are remembered as a respected naturalist."

The Notes of Benjamin Arthur Berling,
Arkham, Massachusetts.

January 2, 2015

I am not pleased with Peaslee's body. It is heavy-set and pallid; his small green eyes seem out of place somehow. I dislike his stubby hands. The brain, however, seems efficient. He was a scientist, after all. He is one still, if he survived the transition. Eventually I shall break him on the wheel of time and take my own body back, if all goes as planned.

"Trevor Peaslee," as I must call myself now, lives alone in a small suite of rooms near the university. I find no indication of a spouse in the domicile, though there is a book of color photographs showing him with a woman, pudgier than he is, but somehow it all has the look of a relationship in the past. That is well. I want no one coming here asking questions.

My own question for myself is, should I attend his classes and attempt to teach? Just to keep up appearances . . . But also, I could almost wish for students now, so that I might teach them the distinction between the mind and the brain. It is something subtle and unsubtle at once. The brain is integral to the mind, as the ground is integral to running. But the runner is who he is . . .

I probably shall call in to the university and declare myself indisposed, if I can work these cellular telephonic devices, as they exist now. Not so different from what we anticipated—telephonic devices having been patented in 1876—but much more compact. Marvels, really. Many of Peaslee's body's physical memories remain. Quite possibly my appropriated nervous system will remember how to use the device; almost instantly I intuited the use of the domicile's incandescent lamps.

Inspecting Peaslee's mind psychically, I learned of the advances of his time; of television, of orbital mechanisms and jet planes and thinking machines. And the cellular telephonic devices in particular excite me. The compression of electro-machinery alone! I must study it under a microscope.

I feel no anxiety in recording my thoughts here. Anyone coming upon such a thing would regard it as raving or mere tale spinning. Even that remark would be so regarded.

I cannot help the feeling that I have achieved what should be reserved for gods alone. That I have achieved the transcendent, the supernal; that I am destined to succeed; that nothing can stop me if I am reasonably discreet in my dealings with men of this time.

The question becomes, how am I to take control of the electronic amplification systems I need? The Yithians are quite specific about the device. But I must have sole command of it, if I am to open the way for the League. If I can complete my barter with them, I shall have all the riches of time—and they shall decide the future of mankind, for which I care not a whit. At any rate they are practical creatures, these primeval ones, and I doubt they destroy the ruck of humanity. Corpses are of no use to anyone but buzzards. But slaves are endlessly valuable. Eliminate the problematic element of mankind—perhaps a billion or two—and the rest will fall into line.

The Journal of Glyneth Berling
Boston, Massachusetts

August 10, 1878

I have thrashed it out in my mind again and again, telling myself the man I think of as my husband must have gotten lucky in his prediction about this historically destructive tornado; or he had some advance knowledge from a meteorologist somewhere. But the details are correct. There is more he told me, in advance, than I recorded here.

Finally, it's the utter transformation of his personality—or rather, if he is to be believed, it is the replacement of his personality I must accept.

For he simply is not Benjamin Berling.

I have come to accept that he is Trevor Peaslee. And he has shown me things in the workshop that are in themselves either madness, or truth.

In Ben's workshop we activated an "electronic mirror," constructed by Ben, that records psychic experiences—in this case, the glass oval reproduced a memory. I beheld the moving image of a creature shaped like a cone with four snaking upper parts, the whole twice as tall as a human; it moves on a mucous-coated underside, the muscle contracting and expanding much as a snail moves on a single flexible foot. Its upper parts seemed serpentine, one of the "serpents" ending in what could be a head. Did not that irregular sphere topping the prehensile member have a row of eyes? I only glimpsed the creature, mostly the lower parts; I hope to write a fuller account of it in time. This, I am told, is a "Yithian, a member of the Great Race from the planet Yith." So Trevor informs me. Ben and Trevor, it seems, looked into one another's minds. And each learned something startling.

It's not difficult to think of him as Trevor, despite Ben's face and body. Shaved, clean, with a completely different demeanor—gentle and receptive—Trevor seems like an entirely different person.

He describes himself as a researcher in a discipline this era does not yet know: *exobiology*, a "mostly theoretical exploration of the nature of extraterrestrial life."

"It was this fascination," he said, "that led me to being displaced in body—and displaced in time, too."

After he said that, I insisted that we go to my desk. I would transcribe his story. . . . Someday I may provide this narrative to science, though perhaps in a discreet way. It contains claims—facts, if we are to believe Trevor—that are perhaps unsuited for much of mankind. Indeed, those who are believers in the creation tale of the Old Testament will be outraged. For Trevor speaks of Earth as more ancient than they had ever supposed. And intelligent creatures here long before there could have been an Adam . . .

We went upstairs. I sat at the desk, filled my stylographic pen, and wrote down everything he said as authentically as I could.

"In the search for extraterrestrial life, exobiologists have only guesswork," Trevor said, as he paced up and down behind me. "There are indications that some primitive life-forms might be possible on the moons of Jupiter; perhaps micro-organisms exist within the soil of Mars. But we have not located any real proof of extraterrestrial life—and endless speculation is frustrating.

"Last year—in my time flow—my grandmother left me some documents written by her great-uncle, Nathaniel Peaslee. She attached a note suggesting the documents contained something that might relate to my work.

"I didn't know what to make of it. All I knew of Nathaniel Peaslee was that he was an economics lecturer at Miskatonic—of all things!—and he'd had an extraordinary case of intermittent amnesia.

"Then, page by page, unable to put it aside, I read Uncle Nathaniel's account in his own words.

"As he tells it, his periods of amnesia were blotted with strange, alien remembrances. He thought it was hallucination, but he seemed to see a tantalizing imprint of an alien influence. He found subtle but persistent traces of a prehistoric race of intelligent beings here on this planet. He stumbled over clues that led him to search for their lost library: the vault of memories."

He sighed. "You'll have to make a great leap, now, Glyneth. I am going to ask you to believe that during his lapses into amnesia the mind of my great-uncle Nathaniel was displaced by *an extraterrestrial mind* that had traveled in time to do it."

I stopped writing for a moment and turned to stare at him.

Trevor smiled apologetically—smiled with Ben's lips. "And—that's not all. This alien mind was one of countless colonists from the planet Yith; apparently they first projected themselves *mentally* from Yith; coming psychically, they took over the bodies of mobile, plant-like creatures on Earth, modifying them—"

"Mobile plants?" I interrupted. "In what sense? Plants do spread, and move through seeding and . . ."

"No, I mean they were a sort of hybrid of plant and animal and they could—deliberately travel. They could move themselves something like the way a snail moves, and they had vehicles. They had a grand civilization—and they would become something called the Great Race. All this was hundreds of millions of years ago, long before mankind. Eventually, the Yithian civilization on Earth was mostly destroyed by another race of extraterrestrials. The remaining Yithians looked around for some other way to survive. So they sent their aetheric selves—their minds, their conscious essences—to travel in time; when they found a suitable host they ejected the original mind and used the new form to explore the ages. They had taken over many bodies—choosing those positioned to access valuable data—and in this way they'd taken over Uncle Nathaniel's body.

"Nathaniel's own mind was drawn by the Yithians back in time to their era, where it occupied one of the alien bodies. Finding himself in a hybrid of vegetable and animal, using arms better suited for an octopus than a man"—Trevor chuckled—"that was very hard to get used to. But my uncle was fascinated by the civilization of the Great Ones, and by the other time-traveling minds he met there. He held on to that thread to keep his sanity.

"When the Yithians finished with him, they returned him to his original body—which at first he found repellent. But for a time, he couldn't remember most of what he'd experienced . . . just kind of fitfully.

"Looking for answers, he made his way to a certain Australian archaeological site deep in the outback. There were hints in seriously outré old books that the records of the Yithians had been stored over millennia—and they fit with some of the fragmentary memories he had—leftovers from his lapses. Uncle Nathaniel found a site the archaeologists missed, and went there totally on his own. He found a way in . . . he was down there maybe days, scrabbling through a huge, dark, crumbling underground maze. The whole place nearly collapsed on him. But he found it. The library of the Yithians—an artifact. He was drawn to a particular book . . . a book he lost when he fled the place, one step ahead of something that whistled in the darkness."

"It—whistled?"

"Kind of a doleful whistle, the way he described it. I felt a shock, Glyneth, reading that part of his story. Because I knew about a new Miskatonic expedition to Australia. Sounded like it was to the same area." Trevor groaned softly to himself. "I sound *crazy,* I know. Telling it, hearing myself—I sound like I was out of my goddamned mind to give any of this credence. But—what if it were true? I *had to know* if there were really traces of ancient extraterrestrials there. . . . See, if I could find them I might be able to explore exobiology in an entirely new way. It might be the only chance in my whole lifetime to find proof of an alien presence.

"So—I did it. I spent most of my own money getting to the most desolate place I've ever seen. I didn't care to be ridiculed, so I ditched the expedition and went off on my own, the way my uncle did. There were hints in his manuscript as to the direction—and I got lucky, if you want to call it luck.

"I found the entrance to it, but after a short trek down into the tunnel I came to a stop on an impassible heap of gigantic stone blocks. The rest of the tunnel had collapsed since Uncle Nathaniel had been there. I couldn't go any farther down, and to tell you the truth, I was relieved. And I heard it too—that sick, off-tune whistling from cracks between the old stones. A smell of ozone and something rotten—and there was this current of damp air. . . . It was as if it were pushing at me, as if it were alive, sentient. Curious about me. And not at all friendly.

"Wish I could impress you with a story that makes me sound brave. . . . But I had to get out of there."

"I'm more impressed by honesty," I said, wondering why I felt it necessary to reassure him about my feelings.

"So I started running out, just blindly trying to get away . . . when I stumbled on something. I literally tripped over it, just fell face down. I turned my flashlight and there, almost completely buried in sand, was this large metal-bound book. I carried it out and made camp. Looked the book over—parts of it were handwritten in English. Part of it was in ideograms of some kind. And it was an illuminated manuscript. There were illustrations. It was the book my great-uncle Nathaniel had found in the buried vaults of the Yithian library. The English handwriting was the same as in the documents my grandmother had sent me. It was my uncle's handwriting. Just think of it—this thing had been there for hundreds of millions of years. Because it's a book he wrote in when he traveled back in time—but he had gone back in time to an alien body. He didn't use his hands to write it. He didn't *have* hands then. He used whatever sort of digits a Yithian has. This was the book my uncle tried to carry out of the tunnels. And lost on the way. It's like it was waiting there for me, for generations . . ."

I was again tempted to doubt Trevor's sanity. "But—how would the book have lasted this long, Trevor? It would have crumbled into dust."

"It's not written on materials we know. It's written on stuff meant to outlast the planet! But—I was afraid the Australian government would claim the book before I had time to fully study it, so I found a way to hide it in a cheap aboriginal artifact sold to tourists—a small carved log—and I took it back to Arkham.

"I went over this thing for days and days. Locked myself in my place and pored over it. Parts of it were English accounts— some of Nathaniel's experiences with the alien minds he'd met while living as a Yithian. A few passages recounted his experience of what he called psychic dislocation. Other parts were written in that unknown language. I found similar images on the web here and there—no one was quite sure what they meant."

I was puzzled by his reference to a 'web,' but I did not interrupt him.

"I kept on and on, till I was half out of my mind from exhaustion. But I still I kept on, drinking endless pots of coffee, transferring the contents of the book, page by page, by scanning and typing into a computer file. Trying to interpret it. The illustrations helped, but it was choppy . . . I was only getting bits and pieces.

"My mind whirled. I got into a state I'd never experienced before, as if some latent memory were tingling in me; as if my consciousness were tugging itself away from my body. More and more I couldn't feel myself on the chair; could scarcely sense my fingers on the keyboard. Sometimes I felt myself floating above it—and seemed to see my body below, my head slumped on the desk.

"Then I would snap back into my body and awaken from the dream—at least, I took it, then, for a mere dream. I would eat a little something and go immediately back to work.

"Your Ben found me, on the fourth night of my obsession. I probably summoned him without meaning to. All that focus on the pictures and ideograms in the book, my thoughts became visions and my visions projected into the aether—they followed courses dictated by the nature of the imagery. Visualizations of the Great Ones lead psychically to other minds seeking the Great Ones, because the Great Ones have created a continuum for their own use in the fifth dimension—the realm of pure consciousness. There they created a kind of pathway, marked at intervals with projected signposts. A discarnate mind following those symbolic signposts would find its way to the Yithians—whose disembodied consciousnesses roamed freely in the stream of time.

"But—your husband found me first.

"Glyneth, did you see the device in his workshop that resembles a helmet? This was his own invention, and it was the door that opened electro-psychic possibilities to him. I found evidence in his workshop that the device works with certain arrangements of copper coils and crystals, suggested by ancient texts."

"So all this time he was not just madly tinkering—he was on to something?"

Trevor gave out an ironic chuckle. "Yes. But that doesn't mean he's not insane. The two are not necessarily mutually exclusive . . . especially when it comes to electro-psychics. And dealing with the so-called Great Ones—"

He scowled and I put my hand on his arm. "Are you all right, Trevor?"

"I . . . yes. The whole thing is a bit overwhelming. Sometimes I just have to—"

"Lie down and rest."

This time he lay on my bed, and I lay beside him—somewhat bold of me, but I could not help it. He needed me. I put my arm around him, and he seemed to fall into a restless sleep—the sleep of mental exhaustion. But not mental freedom . . .

The Notes of Benjamin Arthur Berling,
Arkham, Massachusetts

January 9, 2015

They came to me—as I slept they came to me . . .

I felt sick when I woke; I ran to the privy and vomited. But soon after, when my head was clear, the sickness was replaced by the flush of triumph.

The Yithians have come to me in my dreams, here in this time, just as they said they would!

I feared I would not remember the dream—but just as they promised it was as memorable as waking life. Their electro-psychic presence was palpable—and still remains so. A smell as of the ground burnt by a lightning strike is in the air around me.

And they showed me why I am here; why I am on the grounds of the Miskatonic University.

The device they have directed me to is called the Superfast Laser Pump. It emits photons at a high rate of energy; a photon is a packet of submicroscopic waves, I'm told; a particle that constitutes light in the electromagnetic spectrum. The superfast laser fires a bullet of light at another photon stored in a crystal; photons collide and destroy one another, and the destruction sends information to a third photon, with which it is entangled on what is in this time called the quantum level. This communication is instantaneous and carried out by means not understood even in this advanced age. But the Yithians indicate that the disparate photons exchange information through the fifth dimension; this is a dimension that communicates with our world and the plane of quantum possibilities at once.

When a simple resonance device is added to the laboratory setting, the Superfast Laser Pump will open the way for the Yithians to come to a specific area. Washington, D.C.—two places. The Capitol building and the five-sided building they call the Pentagon.

"To take over numerous human forms at one go, in a contained location, the Yithians will need my help; they will need the application of this laser pump, after certain significant alterations in it . . .

The Journal of Glyneth Berling
Boston, Massachusetts

August 11, 1878

After breakfast, as we sat in the kitchen drinking coffee, Trevor asked me to once more shave off his beard.

"I would do it myself," he said apologetically, "but I can't stand looking in the mirror. I see someone I'm really starting to hate." He cleared his throat. "I'm truly sorry to hate your husband."

"You have my sympathy," I said. "I could scarce bear him." Feeling inexpressibly bold, I went on, "You're a much better man than he is. You'd . . . make a much better husband. For some woman."

His eyes welled up a bit at that. "Ah, but you know, the real Trevor, back home in my time, is not as good-looking as Ben. Trevor Peaslee looks more like Ben Franklin at forty than he does Ben Berling."

"I don't think I'd mind that at all," I added even more daringly. "It's a man's mind I find . . . *compelling*."

"There are . . . *things* you need to know about Ben. You see, I don't have his memories exactly, but I've seen them—many of them." He hesitated, then, as if wondering if he should tell me all he'd seen.

I ventured, "I was wondering about that—if there were traces of memory in his brain." I think I blushed. After all, Ben and I have had our periods of intimacy, though they ended some time before Trevor appeared.

"Neurologically speaking, there are what I would describe as *physical* memories." He frowned at the floor. "After spending time in the workshop, my hands and some of my brain seem to remember how to use his equipment." He smiled ruefully. "I think I could now drive a horse and buggy fairly competently, too. Couldn't have done that, in my own body. But"—the smile faded away—"most of what I've learned about him I picked up clashing with him in the fifth dimension."

"There I'm lost."

He nodded sympathetically. "Difficult to explain . . . but I'll try."

I suggest we again move to where I could write it all down. We adjourned upstairs.

This time, Trevor lay on my bed, to help him relax and think. I hasten to add that I was seated at the rolltop desk nearby, writing down what he was telling me as best I could, as he lay there, hands clasped behind his head, his eyes closed, remembering aloud.

Some of his expressions are not entirely familiar to me, but I wrote them down as I heard them.

"Okay, Glyneth. So—I told you that I was in a kind of altered state from days of scarcely any sleep, fixated on the metal-bound book I'd found in the Australian ruins. I had visions of the Yithians . . ." Trevor took a deep breath. "Then, near dawn, as I was almost nodding out at my worktable, I heard a voice calling my name. It said, *'Trevor Peaslee, you feel yourself near leaving your body. Let go of it. Come with me. I will explain the book you have found; I will tell you what it means for you . . .'*"

As I scratched this down, Trevor made a faint groan. I glanced at him and saw his face contorted. "Trevor—can you go on?"

"Yes, I'm fine. Just give me a moment. Makes me feel a little sick remembering some of it." He cleared his throat and went on.

"I heard him calling me to come with him, and the voice was a lot like the one that comes from my mouth now! Like any man, Ben imagines himself speaking in his own voice, you see. I guess I went along with his suggestion because I was suddenly floating over myself. My mind was floating over my body. I could see the back of my head—then I floated farther and saw my whole body slumped on my desk. I could see I was breathing.

"I wondered what I could see my sleeping body *with*. Did I have eyes in some sort of skull? Did I have a brain? Was it some kind of subtle body, such as the mystics talk about?

"I tried to see my aetheric form—to see whatever I was now; the spirit body, or whatever it was. I got scared—because I saw nothing there at first. I had no body at all! Then I saw a flicker, as if you were to see a reflection of the moon in rippling water. It showed me the outline of my body, unclothed, semi-transparent. Not very solid, but . . . it was there. Physically, I could just barely feel the body I was floating in. Emotionally, though, I was all astir. I was scared, and my mind was racing. I felt the excitement of discovery. . . . It was as if my body were made of thoughts and emotions and just a little bit of something else.

"That's when the room got dark. I couldn't see anything at all. But—I felt something near me. It appeared to me, little by little, like a photograph coming into focus. It was one of the creatures sketched in the book: a Yithian. It got more solid-looking, and I could see one of those rubbery limbs beckoning; a 'come with me' gesture. Then a point of light appeared beyond the Yithian; the light got bigger and started to spin. It became a whirlpool of gold and red light. I wasn't sure I wanted to follow it, but I did want to see the glowing whirlpool better—

something about that vortex seemed to say 'there are infinite worlds inside me.' And just wanting to see the vortex closer was enough to propel me toward it. The focused desire to move propels the disembodied consciousness.

"I followed the creature, and I felt the whirlpool pulling at me. Drawing me in. I didn't go *down* into the vortex, because it wasn't a thing that went down—it went *beyond*.

"I emerged into another place. I had lost sight of the Yithian. I wondered if it had lured me here to abandon me. Just some cruel impulse. But by now I was too stunned by what I was seeing, too overwhelmed to really be afraid.

"I was seeing a infinite reach of space—a *skyscape* is what I'd call it. There was no bottom or top to it. It was a skyscape made out of energy and possibilities and emptiness and colors—all coalescing in endlessly mutating orbs of light exchanging streams of energy; a skyscape of metamorphosing sphere that arose from a vast emptiness. And the emptiness was itself alive.

"Oh, the colors—most of the colors there seemed completely new. If I thought something was yellow or purple, I would change my mind in a moment. No, that's *not* purple! That's *not* yellow! But it hadn't actually changed color.

"All coordinates became visibly relative. It's as if I could see relativity itself. A glowing orb that was way distant was all of a sudden nearby; when I perceived it as nearby it was also infinitely far off. Beyond it all, the sky held stars, but they were jet-black stars against a field of pulsing violet. Anyway, it was almost violet.

"And the endless spheres—maybe they were gigantic bubbles. Like a foam that couldn't make up its mind it was a foam. *But each one was as big as a world*—as big as Jupiter, or bigger. The spheres were reflecting one another, and they would spasmodically switch places, whipping back and forth. There were sounds that went with all these movements. It sounded like language at times, but it wasn't language. Sometimes the spheres seemed to *squeal* as they turned inside out, and then they looked as if they were struggling, really *agonizing* to restore their original shape. Till suddenly they found their way back to spherical. Moments later they turned inside out again. But some of them, when they failed to restore their spherical shapes, would fall apart, as if they were spawning millions of smaller spheres. The smaller spheres would merge together in a way that seemed organized, even thoughtful, but I could tell it was just the physics of this place. Only, physics here was also thought."

He paused, and I looked at him. "Go on—I'm trying to keep up, Trevor."

"I know—I'm not making any sense. But I can tell you, this place was the fifth dimension. Oh, Glyneth—I wish I could show it to you! It seemed to be *one matrix,* yet as much space as substance, but I felt as if the space between things was alive and looking at me, and . . ." He sighed. "It's impossible to describe. Trying to grasp what I was seeing—my mind could not deal with it. I wanted to scream. I was afraid I was going to fall apart and just lose myself in all this, and that'd be the end of—of whatever I think of as me.

"Then I heard the voice—the one that had spoken to my mind when I was about to leave my body. It said, *'You cannot understand this place. Simply follow me.'*

"And that's when I saw the Yithian again—that fleshy cone, floating toward me, those boneless limbs sprouting from the top wavering around it. Light from every direction rippled across the Yithian, sometimes blotting it out so that it vanished for a moment or two. But every time I saw the creature again it was a little nearer.

"I heard the voice reverberating in my mind again. *'Come to me, my friend, I will carry you safely to my time.'*

"I looked around—the glowing vortex was nowhere to be seen. So I moved toward the Yithian. The process of approaching an object in this dimension doesn't have the perspective qualities of the human world. If you approach a thing, it doesn't seem to get bigger. You just became suddenly closer—and the thing got more definite in appearance. More innate substance to it.

"I was suddenly within reach of it, and I thought, *I'm being a fool, getting this close!*

"I peered at the creature's alien, three-eyed face atop one of its prehensile members—and suddenly it went out of focus and another face appeared. It was a human face, a bearded man. Angry eyes, and mocking. It's the face I'm stuck with now. . . .

"I cursed and tried to back away—but I wasn't clear on how to do that. And I was gripped, grabbed behind, then all around me. Ben's face really came into focus then, and I saw what was holding me; saw it as if I were watching from the cosmic mind that watches all things. I was gripped in ectoplasm stretched out from Ben Berling's disembodied head. The Yithian was gone. It had never been there. It was an illusion. There was just this man's head grown crazily big and getting even bigger. Eyes gleefully popping, his mouth kind of warping, stretching to open wider. It was as if he were shaped more by his state of mind than his anatomy.

"His mouth grew bigger and bigger. I fought with what strength I could find, but my aethereal body was weaker than his. He had experience here in this dimension.

"I tried to *think* myself away from there. I thought maybe I could just *will* myself back to my physical body in the ordinary human world . . . back to my apartment, back to my desk.

"No. I was stuck in those tendrils of—I'm calling them ectoplasm. Maybe that's what they are.

"His mouth stretched still wider and wider. Inside it was a crackling blackness. Like darkness could be electrified.

"And then I was pulled in—he swallowed my entire being, anyway all of me there was in that world; swallowed my aetheric body like the whale swallowing Jonah.

"I flailed around, trying to get out. But there was no way out—just crackling darkness everywhere, stinging me. Like I was getting mean little electric shocks all over.

"And then I heard him thinking. Just phrases, here and there. *I have him now . . . He will go into the old husk, and I shall have a new, in his time. I shall have his form. He will have the world of gaslight and coal smoke and the devil with it all!*

"I was psychically linked with him, Glyneth—it was ugly. But I couldn't get out.

"Then I saw a pictures flashing in my mind's eye, like a slide show of his life, a sort of inner narrative twisted to fit his point of view. I saw your husband's memories: his growing up with an unfeeling father who sold him to be an apprentice at nine; whippings, harsh beatings from a man who seemed to have the face of a starved wolf. Ben ran away and got himself lost in Boston, until finally he was taken as an orphan by the Berlings. He became, outwardly, whatever they wanted of him. His adopted mother died, and after that his adopted father spent the days working and the nights with a bottle of brandy. And then he read about Franklin's experiments with lightning, and the miracles of Mesmer, and he wheedled his father into getting him every book that could relate to the invisible world of pure energy. And then—he met you, Glyneth. And he thought, *This woman is not without intelligence, perhaps she can learn to be of use to my work . . .*"

Interesting, hearing that—I might indeed have been of use to him. But Ben never did trust me with his work.

Trevor sat up on the bed, poured himself a glass of water from the pitcher on the taboret, and sipped, staring into space. He had a tremulous horror in his eyes.

Finally he went on. "I saw all that in his mind—and a lot more. And at the same time, he saw into my mind. He learned about my time; he learned about our technology, our society. And when I realized that, it scared me—deeply. Because to me it's obvious the guy is damaged, Glyneth. Brilliant but damaged. He's a psychopath."

"I don't know that term, Trevor. *Psychopath.*"

"It means he's without conscience, without empathy."

I myself have suspected as much. "Trevor, how did you end up—here? In my world."

"He brought me here. I was disgorged from his inner world, but I was still all tangled in his coils, dragged along behind him. Like an animal on a rope. We traveled through another vortex— and into another kind of space. A sort of interface between the fourth and fifth dimensions. We were traveling along the surface of the stream of time—in our own little pocket of time. Like a couple of tied-together balloons, following above a stream of water, but going upstream. And—somehow I knew it was spe- cifically time relating to Earth . . ."

"What did time look like from there?" I asked. I felt awe, asking the question.

"Best I can do is . . . it was made of billions of intricate shapes forming and collapsing and forming; a seamless flow of construction and destruction. On the surface it was like a chaotic river of molten glass. I couldn't look at it long—it was something that wanted to wreck all my conceptions. When I looked away I saw the velvety violet background with the black stars in it.

"Next time I looked back I saw something emerging from a shining anomaly, on the edge surface of the river of melting glass—something that might have been an Yithian. And I had the impression the Yithian was guiding us along. Ben was com- municating with it somehow.

"The League, I thought. It was something I'd heard in his mind. A faction of Yithians.

"Ben suddenly drew me down to the stream of time—there was a vortex, turning in an opposite direction from the way the other had turned. I was thrust into the golden whirlpool . . . This time there was a going *down* about it. I felt like an infinitely heavy stone dropped into an infinitely deep well.

"Next thing I knew, I was here. In your house, Glyneth. In 1878. Waking up on the floor. And I had Ben's body." Breathing hard, still sitting on the bed, Trevor turned to look at me. "There's something we must do now."

I think my eyes must have widened. But I made no objection. Then he said, "We must go to Ben's workroom—now! Because I've started to remember more—other things I glimpsed in his mind. Things that might help us."

The Notes of Benjamin Arthur Berling
Arkham, Massachusetts

January 12, 2015

It was astoundingly easy. But I shouldn't be surprised. The Great Ones have given me guidance all along. They have timed this—an amusing expression to use in this instance. *Timed.*

The Great Ones have lost some greatness; their ancient war has reduced them. And, too, I do not communicate with their racial leadership. Admittedly it is a cadre of Yithians who support me; it is a faction grown quite apart from the other members of the race.

The plan to take over a human nation by taking over its leaders—by taking command of the United States government, and the warlords in the Pentagon, from within—was somehow offensive to the primary Yithian leadership. The League of Electro-Psychic Emphasis secreted itself away from the others. The faction made its own plans.

And the League found me as I was searching through the aether with my apparatus; they found me where few journey; where all journeyers are inevitably known to those who sense the fourth and fifth realms.

They found me—because they need me. This League of the titanic race of primeval world-masters! It requires the assistance of Benjamin Arthur Berling!

Thus they sent me to seek out the little woman in the big laboratory.

Ellen Lo. Her name was on the door with several others. Her colleagues were not to be back in town until the end of January. First vacation and then, I take it, scientific conventioneering of some kind.

This the young man working at the front desk told me. He was a graduate student, I took it; a brown-skinned fellow with long curly hair. He seemed to admire me—naturally thinking I was Trevor Peaslee, who apparently has some status here.

He admitted me, and I found this Ellen Lo alone in the laboratory just as the Great Ones said she'd be. She was a rather pretty little woman, perhaps of Chinese extraction.

"Professor Peaslee!" How brightly she smiled up at me. Or at whomever she supposed me to be.

"Ellen, how very pleasant to see you," I said.

She looked confused then. I sensed I had not used the proper colloquialisms.

But she shrugged and got up from her worktable, where she'd been frowning over one of those miniature foldable computers.

"So—you finally came to see the Superfast Laser Pump?" she asked. Fairly chirped it.

"Yes indeed." I had certain blueprints, a manual of sorts imprinted in my mind. I needed to confirm the imprints, familiarize myself before I could make modifications.

The device took up a barn-sized room with a very high ceiling; the special laser apparatus was glassy and chromium and so complex it at first had no clear shape to me. But there was a keyboard and a screen at one end, and I had learned fairly quickly how to use such control interfaces. The League's imprints soon provided the rest.

The Asian woman lectured me about her beloved apparatus, and particularly caught my attention when she showed me the units that would hold the separated photons. That "cycling crystal box" could be useful on several levels, yes; it can constrain more than light. Another witticism—how they spring from me like sparks from a dynamo now.

When I felt I was ready, I made my suggestion. "Will you not go to the roof with me? You have shown me your pride and glory. In exchange I wish to show you something of an astronomical nature—with exobiological implications."

"'Will I not'?" She laughed. "You've adopted an interesting style of self-expression today, Professor. Dabbling in the drama department?"

"Precisely, yes, that is correct," I told her, bowing slightly.

"Aha! I won't make you break character. Is there a lunar eclipse tonight?"

"Something more dramatic," I told her.

"Cool! Roof access is this way."

She led the way—how ironic! Up the elevator we went, and then up a flight of metal stairs, then out upon the roof. She looked around, frowning. "Not good visibility."

"It's over here—right this way," I said.

We stepped over to the little wall around the roof, and without hesitating I pushed her over it.

She fell gasping backwards, staring at me as she went. Perhaps four stories down, a little more? It could only have been a second and a half, but it seemed to take her so long to fall. I was able to enjoy it. Down and down she went.

She struck the ground on her back and lay still.

In haste I made my way to the laboratory, found her purse on a metal table, and located her key card. What a wonder are key cards! So much imprinted on a little magnetic strip. Credit cards, key cards, identification cards, tiny little black strips interrogating us.

Once I had her card, I rushed down to the front desk, where the graduate student was looking in a cellular telephonic device. I shouted that Ellen Lo had been raving about killing herself and then she'd run to the roof, and I was terribly worried. That's why I'd come—she'd called me and told me she was frightfully depressed . . .

The campus police came, and an ambulance. They seemed to believe my story.

I did make a mistake, however. Ellen Lo is not dead. They say she fell in a garden, in soft ground. Her body is largely intact but her brain injured. She is in a coma.

Well then! That should hold her. Later I will go to the hospital, find may way in, and choke the last of her breath from her.

I have set the Laser Pump to the convergence suggested; I have added the apparatus suggested by the Great Ones.

In the morning, at the precise instant prescribed, I will open the door for the League. They will come to this time locale; they will gather aetherically over the Superfast Laser Pump. Modified, it now has a further application. It will project the first group of Great Ones from the League to one place—for in the morning the president speaks to Congress. Other League Yithians will be sent to quite another location: that curiously temple-like building they call the Pentagon. They await just beyond the curve of the horizon. The energy will reverberate from the ionosphere. The doors will open . . .

The husks of congressmen and generals and the president will be in place to receive new occupants . . .

Amusing to consider that the minds presently occupying those bodies will not be sent back to Yithian bodies, as once was the case. No. They will be flung willy-nilly into the aether. Where aetheric predators await like sharks in a sea.

I will perforce remain in this body—and the new rulers of this nation will give me whatever I like. They will reward me with the final secrets of the higher dimensions, and the river of time. All time itself will open to me.

They warn me now . . .

He will be here soon.

The Journal of Glyneth Berling
Boston, Massachusetts

August 11, 1878

Trevor and I labored in the workshop for hours. It was a most peculiar experience. Here was someone who looked like Ben, who yet was *not* Ben, asking my help to try to investigate Ben and Ben's apparatus.

In truth, with my help Trevor was beginning to piece the writings, the charts, the diagrams and apparatus together. We instantly penetrated Ben's code—he'd written it in Latin, backwards! I fetched a mirror, and we transliterated. I was more fluent in Latin than Trevor and was able to translate what he could not. Thank God Ben was terse, and the diagrams detailed.

And now I'm in that same workshop, watching Ben—no, I mean Trevor—as he sits in a trance, a near-mesmeric state, wearing the helmet, electricity fitfully crackling about him . . . power taken from the air itself. The air contains electrical energy, and Ben used a vibrating whip-like device of his own invention that sucks electricity out of the atmosphere to power his experiments.

I wait, and still I wait.

Trevor told me it would take time to find Ben. He promised me he would come back. He even squeezed my hand as he made the promise.

"I will see what he is up to," Trevor told me. "I will come back—unless something prevents it. We will decide what to do. After all—here we are always before whatever he is doing in the year 2015. Maybe there's a way I can stop him and . . . then stay here. I think I'd like that, if you'd like me to."

"You know perfectly well I want you to stay here. To come back. You, Trevor. Anyway you can."

"Then . . . I'll come back. And we'll make a plan. But I've got to try to find my way to him. I think he helmet will make it possible."

After Trevor entered the electro-psychic trance I had a terrible fear he'd not come back to me. He was entering an unknown world. Anything could happen.

I occupied myself in gaining a greater understanding of the equipment, and the process of disembodied journeying. I think I've almost grasped it.

My mind returns to its fears. Suppose something fatal happens to Trevor in this trance?

How rapidly I've become attached to him. He is not Ben at all—and it is as if Trevor and I were born in different eras purely by malicious accident, but intended, all along, to be in the same one, together.

Oh! Trevor is awakening!

His eyes . . .

The Notes of Benjamin Arthur Berling
Arkham, Massachusetts

January 12, 2015

It is done.

I was gone, in this time, but a moment, but it seems as if a great period of time has passed—the enormous psychic struggle took so much from me . . .

I am surprised at my feelings, now, about Glyneth. At the time, it was all cold fury.

I almost regret it, looking back, I almost wish—

But that is all foolishness.

The Journal of Glyneth Berling
Arkham, Massachusetts

January 13, 2015

Ben stabbed me, quite deeply, under my sternum, with a sharp tool from his workbench. I fell onto the floor, bleeding inside. I knew I could not last long.

I had no doubt at all it was *Benjamin Berling* who stabbed me. Trevor did not occupy that body anymore.

My dear husband Benjamin stood looking down on my as I bled on the floor, the sharp implement in his hand dripping blood. He tossed it onto the bench and spoke a few words.

"Your friend came after me, Glyneth—he tried to force my soul out of his body! I suppose he then planned to use my machinery to return to you. But I was ready—I was warned he was coming. And I am stronger than he. I have put him in the crystal box, my dear, where he circles forever. There is a wheel of time in that box—and your Trevor Peaslee is now broken on the wheel of time. I saw it all in his mind as I took control of him—I saw his desire for you. I saw that you have been almost whoring to him. Hence, my wife, you will burn with the house."

Ben said no more. He went downstairs to lock doors and set the fires. I could soon smell turpentine, and then smoke. I knew he would soon return to use the apparatus as the house burned.

I tore a strip away from my undergarments and stanched my wound as well as I might.

Then I had only one course. To crawl.

I crawled to the chair and pulled myself into it. The pain was monumental; it towered over my inner world. But I forced the helmet in place and worked the controls. I established the transmission beam.

I couldn't quite make the transition through the helmet—I had not the strength left. I was trapped until Ben completed the murder.

Ben found me sitting on the chair, clamped into the helmet; I was scarcely aware and nearly bled to death. My poor bandage was soaked and blood dripped down my side on to the floor.

He laughed and called me an empty-headed female for trying to use his device. He said I could never understand such complexities.

And then he strangled me. I did not have strength to resist.

But it was the moment of death—but not quite death—that liberated me to follow the transmission beam, that allowed me to be freed from my physical husk.

I separated from my body and was elevated upon on the transmission beam; up and up I went. Not to heaven, but toward the aperture into the fifth dimension.

As I went I could see Ben below me, as if from a great and increasing distance, as he removed the helmet from my body, pushed my limp corpse onto the floor, and took my place. Soon I realized he was now receding below me. The roof of the house became opaque; I could no longer see Ben. I glimpsed the flames at the rear of the building.

Quite suddenly, I was projected fully into the fifth dimension.

I was adrift, neither above anything nor below anything, but relative to everything. I looked about me—looked without having eyes, at least not the sort of eyes I can understand.

Though somewhat prepared by Trevor, I still had to struggle to retain my sanity, seeking to find some perceptual anchor. I discovered that if I kept calm and tried to sense my aetheric form, tried to feel it with my mind, some of the confusion drained away. I managed to learn movement in this abstract world, which was just as Trevor had described it: triggered by will alone.

But *where* should I go? I had no idea how to find Trevor or his time. I might be lost here forever.

Then a shimmering anomaly appeared, near and yet far; and I saw Ben there, beginning to take shape. He was translucent; almost imperceptible. But he was there. Just enough.

I drew back, into the center of a warping cloud of possibilities. It made me tingle but did me no harm, and it seemed to hide me from sight.

Ben was not expecting me there and did not perceive me. He soared in a purposeful way across the spaces of the transfiguring spheres, and I followed. Soon he descended through a glowing vortex.

Adrift in a world of implication and geometrical transformation, I waited, uncertain. After a moment, I decided I had no choice. I followed.

I fell just as Trevor described it—like an infinitely heavy stone.

Then suddenly I was in a big room, larger than a barn. Here was much apparatus—including a near duplicate of the device in Ben's workroom.

There below me was a man in a chair, his head clamped into the helmet. I knew instantly this must be Trevor's body. It was shuddering, as Ben settled into it, like a man fitted into a suit of armor.

And where was Trevor? That is—where was . . .

As a scientist it is hard for me to say it. But after the metaphysical curiosities revealed to me, I will use the term. Where was his *soul*?

Then I remembered. *"Your friend came after me—but I was warned. I have put him in the crystal box, where he circles forever, broken in time."*

Trevor's selfhood, his consciousness, was in "a crystal box" . . . somewhere near.

I saw the object: it was almost a cube; there were transparent wires, like cables of glass, entering it, and a complexity of crystalline forms around them.

I thought I heard his voice echo to me from there.

"Glyneth. Where am I?"

I looked back at Trevor's physical body. Settled into Trevor's husk, Ben outwardly looked like Trevor—a medium-sized man, a bit plump, pale and blond, wearing the unpleasantly informal trousers, shirt, and sweater they often wear in this time.

He set out, clearly in a hurry to fulfill a mission.

I kept after him, drifting above and behind. I found I could pass through walls with a little effort. I was careful not to be too close upon his heels. I did not want him to sense me.

I watched and followed, watching as he went to find the woman.

How did I know about her? In this form, glimpses are given us; at times glimmering crevices open between a maybe and a likely, and we see along trembling and temporary corridors of possibility. Extending out from Ben, in a corridor of likelihood, I saw an image of him standing over a woman in a hospital bed. Squeezing her throat. Who was she? Perhaps she was the caretaker of the laboratory.

Could I awaken her? Could I contact her somehow? Ask her to help me?

I drifted like an aethereal bloodhound along after him, kept on course by will alone. A whole angry cosmos of dislocation and disorientation wanted to tear me away from the pursuit. But I have always been a strong woman.

The hospital. I drifted in after him, down the corridors behind him, through a door.

And I saw him bend over her, Ellen Lo: I saw it on the card near the bed. She lay there, mostly dead.

I saw him begin to do to her what he had done to me.

I saw that she was empty—she was just a husk. Her consciousness had left her. Was her body broken?

How to take the next step?

Then a bizarre and ungainly shape formed, only half there, in the shadows to one side . . .

A true Yithian. It spoke to me but not in English. It was not in language as we understand it. It spoke in concepts, in pictures. I was able to translate it into English.

Few of my folk are aligned with this man. Some of us have dignity and will not debase ourselves. This man will open the door for the League, and in due course will come death for millions in this timeflow. And slavery will come to all others.

My strength ebbs. I cannot fight this man. I have repaired the cellular linkages in this woman's brain; I was able to heal some of her body, but I am weak from the process. I could not save her from the death of her selfhood. The woman's consciousness is gone; her brain is empty . . . it is awaiting you. I can only show you the next step.

There—do you see it? The line of blue . . . Enter the blue line of force . . . and I will send it into this female of your race.

I saw a quivering, intermittent stroke of blue lightning, stretching from the Yithian to Ellen Lo.

Enter a blue stroke of lightning? Will it not destroy what remains of me?

Could I trust a conical creature, spouting rubbery limbs, one of which ended in a face?

Trust was the next step . . .

I followed the blue lightning, using my will and mental focus. My mind turned blue; mind burned with far too much energy. Then I was lying on my back . . . feeling heavy, solid, achingly alive.

In a moment I was opening my eyes. I was lying on the hospital bed, staring up at the madman who was poised close to me. He had not Ben's face, but I knew it was Ben's hands tightening on my throat.

I clutched at the table nearby. There was a thick white glass vase with sagging lilies in it.

Energized by terror, I used every bit of strength I had and crashed the vase hard into the side of his head. It shattered.

He shouted wordlessly and fell over.

I sat up and felt something tugging at me. It was a needle attached to a tube, thrust in my right arm. I pulled it free and stanched the small wound with bandages laid on the table nearby.

Then I hid the vase and called for help. "My friend's fallen— he's hurt himself!" I shouted, as the nurses entered.

They stared at me. I have never seen anyone so astonished. They had thought me brain-dead.

It took these befuddled women some time to agree to release me. They argued against it, but I insisted. They found me a change of clothes left by a patient, and they fit well enough. When they went about their paperwork, I slipped way, taking with me a ring of keys I found on a hook near the counter, and located a storeroom. There I found what I needed. Then I returned to the nurses, giving them the key ring as if I'd found it on the floor, and obtained my release.

But I did not go far.

I waited outside . . . and soon saw Ben walking stiffly out of the hospital. Ben—in Trevor's body.

What had Ben told the nurses? Had he let them accept my story, that he had felt dizzy—had fallen and hit his head, shattering the vase? It seems likely. Simplest.

His head was bandaged. Watching from the shadows as he paused on the walkway outside the hospital, I could see his mouth moving—I could read his lips. He was cursing. And he was talking to someone who wasn't there. Or perhaps they were merely unseen.

I followed him once more, this time in a physical body.

He went back to the laboratory—for it was approaching dawn, and he had work to do there.

The trek was perhaps half a mile past periodic steel posts topped by incandescent lamps. We traipsed, one well behind the other; his head probably throbbed as much as mine. I felt achy and strange; indeed, my new body was bruised by the fall. I suspected there were hairline fractures in my left shoulder bone. But with each step I felt a little more comfortable in Ellen Lo's husk.

Soon we'd reach the Miskatonic campus. Ben approached a big, stark, square building of white concrete and glass and chromium. I saw no one there at this late hour. A few lights were lit in its lobby, for appearances.

I hurried after him. Once he heard me following and turned, but I slipped behind a statue of the university's founder—what a grim-faced man the founder had been! He seemed to scowl down at me.

Ben must have shrugged the sound off, for when I looked again he was at the door.

He entered the building, using what I now understand to be a key card; the door closed slowly behind him, slowly enough that I was just able to catch it.

I waited, holding my breath, but he didn't look back. And when he had gone up the stairs, I followed—not too quickly.

The laboratory door stood open. Inside, Ben, in Trevor's body, was bent over equipment below an enormous apparatus.

I crept up behind him. He heard, started to turn—and I threw all my weight upon him. Quite startled, he went down, though he was much bigger than I.

The syringe was ready in my hand—we have syringes in my century, and we certainly have morphine. Both had been easy to find in the hospital, with the nurses so distracted.

Remembering how he had stabbed me in the belly, I jabbed the syringe hard into the back of his right shoulder, stabbing through the clothing, and depressed the plunger. He yelled a curse and tried to shake me off—snapping the needle off in his flesh. He howled. And the drug had already gone home.

Ben threw me off, and I scrambled back away from him.

He came roaring at me . . . then stumbled, beginning to stagger. He stopped, gaping at me, blinking owlishly. "Is that you in there? The damned fool of a woman who—?"

He did not finish the question.

The lethal dose took effect, and he fell limply onto his face.

I crept over to him and, my hands shaking, felt his pulse. It was irregular. Stopping. Starting . . . stuttering.

In a few moments, I knew, his heart would stop. I prayed there was enough time.

I had the other syringe, too. I waited . . . until Ben's heart stopped entirely. I sensed him sliding away from Trevor's dying body.

I laughed and said, "Goodbye, Ben!"

Then I injected Trevor's dead body with the other syringe—adrenaline.

I turned Trevor's body over and listened with my ear to his chest. Nothing. Then his back arched, his breast bone thumping my head.

And his heart began beating again . . . too late to save Ben, happily. My late husband had already spiraled away into the aether.

And still I was not done. I had a picture in my mind, an imprint from the my Yithian ally . . .

I shattered the crystalline box by swinging a metal chair. Trevor was freed . . . but unsure where to go.

The Yithian flickered into view and guided Trevor.

It sent him home—to his own body.

The Journal of Glyneth Berling
Arkham, Massachusetts

March 2, 2015

Trevor recommended this new journal as therapy; as another way to adapt.

We both needed a further visit to the hospital, after the events of that awful day. Trevor had a long needle broken off in his shoulder, and a concussion; I had painful hairline fractures and massive bruising, despite the partial healing the Yithian had given me.

How curious indeed to be in the body of a young Asian woman in the twenty-first century.

I have wondered if Ben tried to go back to his body. Trevor assures me Ben could not have gone back to his body before it burned up in the fire—he'd have conflicted with his other time-traveling aetheric self. He may have tried, but he'd have been destroyed by the attempt.

Sometimes I ponder the ugly fate of my own original husk—my body burning up along with the house. I shudder, involuntarily picturing it blackening, blistering; I try to turn my mind from the image.

I must let go of that Glyneth. I am another Glyneth now, though for a while I shall pretend to be Ellen Lo.

"Now." I have come to revere *nowness*. I hope never to trade *now* for any other timeflow again. I wish to live in whatever now time gives me.

Yes, as a naturalist I deplore this age of extinctions—the destruction of species after species of wild animal due to the blind expansion of a greedy civilization.

But still, I am happy, because I am with Trevor. He looks into my eyes and knows me for who I am. I see in his eyes the Trevor I knew in 1878, though then his mind had been imprisoned in Ben's body.

Trevor is plump, his hair thin, his eyes small and fingers stubby. That is simply Professor Trevor Peaslee. And I will always love him.

When we came back from the hospital, we took the twenty-first-century variant of Ben's electro-psychic apparatus, and the modifications to the Laser Pump, and disassembled the lot in Trevor's apartment.

As we disassembled the device, I felt something draw my attention to the window. I peered out into the night and thought to glimpse, in a kind of mist beyond the glass, the dim shape of my Yithian ally. I felt it emanating approval. It spoke to my mind, wordlessly but clearly.

No more. The League is destroyed. Our era is time-locked now. No more from us. We shall pass into infinity . . .

And then it was gone.

April 7, 2015

Today, Trevor rented a very large safety deposit box in a bank vault. There we took the essential parts to Ben's disassembled apparatus.

And there, too, we locked away the metal shod book; the ancient codex found in the Australian ruins.

"Someday, when the time is right, I will give it to archaeologists," Trevor said, as he turned the key in the lock.

"Oh, yes?" I gave him a skeptical smile. "What day would that be, Trevor? When will humanity be ready for it?"

He sighed and took my hand. "I don't know. I really do not know."

Perhaps Nathaniel Peaslee's book will never again see the light of day. And, this side of death, we are not ever likely to again journey to the hidden dimensions.

It doesn't matter. We have other worlds to explore together, Trevor and I.

ACKNOWLEDGMENTS

"When Death Wakes Me to Myself," first published in *Black Wings II*, edited by S. T. Joshi (PS Publishing, 2012).

"Those Who Come to Dagon," first published in *High Seas Cthulhu*, edited by William Jones (Elder Signs Press, 2007).

"The Rime of the Cosmic Mariner," first published in *Gothic Lovecraft*, edited by Lynne Jamneck and S. T. Joshi (Cycatrix Press, 2016).

"The Witness in Darkness," first published in *The Madness of Cthulhu, Volume 1*, edited by S. T. Joshi (Titan Books, 2014).

"How Deep the Taste of Love," first published in *Hottest Blood*, edited by Jeff Gelb and Michael Garrett (Pocket Books, 1993).

"Buried in the Sky," first published in *Weird Tales* (November 2006).

"Windows Underwater," first published in *Innsmouth Nightmares*, edited by Lois H. Gresh (PS Publishing, 2015).

"At Home with Azathoth," first published in *Searchers After Horror*, edited by S. T. Joshi (Fedogan & Bremer, 2014).

"The Holy Grace of Cthulhu," first published in *World War Cthulhu*, edited by Jonathan Oliver (Dark Regions Press, 2013).

"Broken on the Wheel of Time" was written specially for this volume.